BLITZ

WALL STREET JOURNAL & USA TODAY BESTSELLING AUTHOR
DEVNEY PERRY

BLITZ

Copyright © 2024 by Devney Perry LLC

All rights reserved.

ISBN: 978-1-957376-69-1

This is a work of fiction. Names, characters, places and incidents are the product of the author's imagination or are used fictitiously. Any resemblance to actual events, locales or persons, living or dead, is coincidental.

Editing:

Elizabeth Nover, Razor Sharp Editing

Proofreading:

Julie Deaton, Deaton Author Services

Judy Zweifel, Judy's Proofreading

Cover:

Sarah Hansen © Okay Creations

OTHER TITLES

The Edens Series

Indigo Ridge

Juniper Hill

Garnet Flats

Jasper Vale

Crimson River

Sable Peak

Christmas in Quincy - Prequel

The Edens: A Legacy Short Story

Treasure State Wildcats Series

Coach

Blitz

Clifton Forge Series

Steel King

Riven Knight

Stone Princess

Noble Prince

Fallen Jester

Tin Queen

Calamity Montana Series

The Bribe

The Bluff

The Brazen

The Bully

The Brawl

The Brood

Jamison Valley Series

The Coppersmith Farmhouse

The Clover Chapel

The Lucky Heart

The Outpost

The Bitterroot Inn

The Candle Palace

Maysen Jar Series

The Birthday List

Letters to Molly

The Dandelion Diary

Lark Cove Series

Tattered

Timid

Tragic

Tinsel

Timeless

Runaway Series

Runaway Road

Wild Highway

Quarter Miles

Forsaken Trail

Dotted Lines

Holiday Brothers Series

The Naughty, The Nice and The Nanny

Three Bells, Two Bows and One Brother's Best Friend

A Partridge and a Pregnancy

Standalones

Ivy

Rifts and Refrains

A Little Too Wild

CONTENTS

CHAPTER ONE

TOREN

oren. Toren. Toren. Three people were talking to me at once.

"Toren, this football is flat. Where's the air pump?"

"Toren, do you have any more beer?"

"Toren, please please please can I watch the fireworks from the roof?"

Never again. This was the last year I hosted a Fourth of July party. Though I'd had that same thought last year. And the year before that. And the year before that.

Yet here I was again, hosting a crowd of people crammed into my house and backyard.

Would anyone miss me if I hid in my room for the rest of the night? Probably. Someone had to answer the questions.

So I started with the first. A football.

"The pump is in the top drawer of the tool chest in the garage," I told Abel, my sixteen-year-old cousin, who held the flat football in his hands.

"'Kay." He tore off for the garage with a stream of teenagers from around the neighborhood on his heels.

1

Next question. Beer.

"Did you check the coolers in the garage?" I asked Parks, a fellow coach and friend from work. "All three were full."

"Yeah, I checked. But they're almost empty, man."

"Seriously?" I glanced around. What the hell?

The six cases of beer I'd bought should have been more than enough to last until the fireworks show was over. It was more than I'd bought last year. Except there seemed to be a lot more partygoers tonight than years past.

I scanned the faces in my yard. For every familiar person, there were two strangers. "Who are all these people?"

Parks shrugged. "I thought you knew them."

"Not everyone." I rubbed a hand over my jaw, the stubble scratching on my palm because I'd been so busy prepping for this party I hadn't bothered to shave this morning.

"I assumed you expanded the invite list," he said.

I scoffed. "I didn't want to have this party in the first place."

"What? This party is a tradition."

That was exactly what my aunt had said when I'd told her I was hesitant to host the shindig again. But she'd suggested hosting it one more year. Given the drama at work lately and the scandal that had rocked the Treasure State Wildcats athletic department this spring, she'd thought these kinds of traditions might be a good way for all of us to return to normal.

Except this party wasn't normal compared to those from the past three years. Tonight was supposed to be a barbeque for family, coworkers, close friends and a few neighbors. Where had everyone else come from?

"I'm not all that excited about the number of strange faces," I told Parks, lowering my voice. "Especially if people are drinking so much that the beer is already gone. We don't need trouble tonight."

"No joke," Parks muttered. "At least you didn't have to invite the Dipshit this year."

I chuckled. "True."

Our boss—former boss—had just landed his ass on the chopping block. Neither Parks nor I wanted to be next in line behind *the Dipshit*—none of us used our ex-boss's name now that he was gone.

Granted, he'd been hosting parties for underage football players, not adults from my local neighborhood. Still, with every new face that popped into my yard, I questioned my decision to host. The goal this year was to keep our heads down, concentrate on football and not do anything to fuck it up.

With any luck, Ford Ellis would get hired as our new head football coach and he'd help us move past the Dipshit's scandal. Ford was a close friend of mine from college, and while it was being kept under wraps, they were considering him for the position. The only reason I knew was because I'd recommended him in the first place.

"Want me to kick people out?" Parks O'Haire was a good friend. He'd do it without hesitation if I gave him the nod.

"I'm sure it'll be fine. If we kick people out, it will just cause drama. But we're not adding more alcohol. Maybe since the beer is almost gone, people will go home."

"Like me?" he teased.

I chuckled. "There's beer in the fridge in the garage. Did you check in there?"

"No. Figured it was off-limits."

"Nah. Go for it."

"Thanks." He clapped me on the shoulder, then slipped past me for the garage.

Leaving me to answer the third question. Fireworks on the roof.

I planted my hands on my hips, staring down at seven-year-old Dane as he looked up at me with pleading, gray-green eyes. They were the same shade as my own. Each of my cousins had those eyes.

So had my father and uncle, and they'd passed the shade down to their sons.

"You want to watch fireworks from the roof."

"Please please please, Tor." Dane clasped his hands together in front of his chin. The fact that he'd waited patiently while I'd talked to Parks was a sign of his desperation.

"What do you think the answer to that question is going to be?"

He shrugged. "Yes?"

I chuckled. "Did you ask your mom?"

Another shrug. That meant yes, he'd asked Faith. And she'd said absolutely not.

"Sorry, bud. You can't watch the fireworks from the roof. It's too dangerous."

"Dang it." He groaned as the smile on his face disappeared. "Then I'm never gonna get to see them. There's too many people here."

He wasn't wrong. There were too many people.

"Just go stake out your spot on the edge of the lawn. Fireworks take place in the sky. Get a good spot and you'll be fine."

"I don't like sitting on the grass. It's itchy." The glare he sent me was lethal. And adorable.

I crouched in front of him, trying not to laugh. "Tell you what. You can watch from the balcony of my room."

"Really?" The glare vanished. The smile returned.

My room was strictly off-limits, not just for this party but whenever Faith brought the boys over to visit. They had free run of the house except for my bedroom. But tonight, I'd make an exception.

"You have to invite your brothers too. Take some snacks. Get away from the grown-ups." I held out my hand for a shake. "Just promise not to spill or make a mess."

"Promise." He smacked his hand in mine, shaking it quickly before he dashed away, likely to find his brothers.

My guess was that they'd sent him to ask Faith and me about the rooftop fireworks because he was the cutest and tended to get more yeses than nos.

I stood, ready to get mobbed with more questions now that those three were answered. But everyone around me was clustered in groups, talking and laughing and drinking my beer.

People streamed in and out of the sliding glass door that separated my deck and dining room. The teenagers were tossing around a football. A group of guys was locked in a heated cornhole game.

If I wasn't going to enjoy this party, at least everyone else was having a good time.

The table I'd set up with burgers and chips and salads had been decimated hours ago. The large black garbage can beside the garage was overflowing. A few cans and discarded napkins were scattered across the lawn.

Cleanup was going to be a bitch.

5

Definitely the last year.

Were the new faces from around the neighborhood? Must be.

I'd always said this party was open to anyone who lived on the block—a mistake three years in the making. Inviting the neighbors hadn't been a big deal in years past when every other lot had been vacant. But with the number of new homes and new families living on the street, I'd have to amend the open invite.

This was a newer subdivision in Mission. When I was a kid, there'd been nothing out here but fields and farmland. Now there were craftsman homes, like mine, popping up like weeds.

My place had been one of the first built on this quiet street, hence its appeal. But over the past three years, Mission had grown. More and more people were leaving larger cities for a taste of the Montana countryside. In my neighborhood, construction had boomed.

I used to know every one of my neighbors by name. Not anymore.

Another night, I might have spent hours introducing myself. But damn, I was tired. I didn't have it in me for small talk. Next year, no party. I'd just invite Aunt Faith and the boys over for the fireworks show.

Searching the crowd, I found her on the edge of the lawn, hands on her hips with a frown on her face. When she spotted me, she walked over and sighed. "Well, I've lost track of my children. This is, uh, a lot more people than normal."

"Yeah," I muttered.

"Now I feel bad for suggesting you have the party."

"It's all good." I slung an arm around her shoulders. "Abel was playing football last I saw him."

6

"Figures." She laughed. "He's obsessed. Any sign of the others?"

"Dane was just here. He wanted to know if he could watch the fireworks from the roof."

Her nostrils flared as she snarled. "That little punk. I told him no."

"Think he thought he could get a different answer from me."

"He knows better, Toren." She pursed her lips. "You told him no, right?"

"I sent him to find Abel, Cabe and Beck so they could get down the ladder. It's not that high. They'll be fine."

Faith's mouth flattened. "Hilarious."

I chuckled. "I told him he could watch the fireworks from my balcony as long as he invited his brothers along too."

"You let them into your room? Whoa."

Maybe I'd bent the rule because deep down, I wished I could be up there with them too.

"I'll go check on them. Teach them how to pull the covers back when they start eating crackers in your bed so they get crumbs in the sheets."

"Thanks," I deadpanned, and as Faith headed for the house, I fell in step behind her.

There were a few people from work in the living room, including two of the other coaches and their wives.

Drew, one of the assistant athletic directors, had brought a date. They were seated at the island that separated the kitchen from the open space, and he was explaining every-thing he did as the AD of fan development. She kept eyeing the front door.

Millie would probably come to her rescue . . .

Wait. Where was Millie?

She was one of my oldest friends and had said she'd be coming over tonight. She always came to this party.

As Faith headed upstairs to find her kids, I dug my phone from my jeans pocket. A text from Millie was waiting.

I put on sweats and don't want to change. Will you hate me forever if I skip the party?

My fingers typed a quick *You're dead to me.*

Her reply was instant. *I can live with that. See you Monday. Have fun!*

I tucked my phone away and surveyed the house. Thankfully, other than a few abandoned cans, the mess had mostly stayed outside.

It was 8:35 according to the clock on the microwave. The long Montana summer days stretched well past nine and the fireworks wouldn't be starting for at least another hour.

Well, if everyone was going to drink my beer, then I was going to enjoy my own damn party too. I made my way to the kitchen, taking out a bottle of whiskey from the cabinet above the fridge. After pouring myself a glass on the rocks, I rejoined the crush in my yard.

I introduced myself to a few people and milled around as the sky above us slowly darkened and the warm evening air began to chill. And as the stars started to pop overhead, so did the fireworks in the distance.

Everyone in the house filtered outside, squeezing into the open spaces on the lawn as all attention turned toward the show.

There was a reason I always threw the party on the Fourth of July. I had the best view.

This neighborhood was built on a rise outside of Mission. Beyond my backyard was a sunken coulee, and without any other buildings to obstruct the view, this yard was the perfect vantage point to catch the annual fireworks show from the fairgrounds.

A resounding boom echoed from miles away before a streak of light shot into the sky, exploding into a star of red.

Conversation around me quieted as all eyes turned to the sky.

Behind me, on the balcony of my bedroom, Faith leaned on the railing beside her sons.

She wiped at the corner of her eye, unaware I was watching. She always made sure that if she cried, her kids didn't notice.

I didn't need to ask why she was sad. Uncle Evan should be here, clustered on that balcony with his family.

He'd been gone for four years. The other boys had gotten longer with their dad, but Dane had lost Evan when he was only three. He didn't remember his father much. He couldn't miss him. So I missed Evan enough for us both.

Tipping my glass to my lips, I drained the last of my whiskey and took the empty glass to the deck, setting it aside to clean up later. I was about to wade through the crowd and take an empty patch of lawn next to Parks when a swish of blond hair caught my eye.

A woman emerged from the corner of the house, her eyes trained on the sky as a smile toyed at her pretty mouth.

She was stunning. Her blond hair was cut just past her chin, the silky strands curled in loose waves that tickled her shoulders. Her features were delicate and refined, from her straight, cute nose to her heart-shaped face to those pink, soft lips. Every time a firework exploded, her bright eyes sparkled.

Holy fuck. Who was that?

My throat went dry. It was too much of an effort to tear my eyes away, so I didn't bother. I stared unabashedly as she slowed to a stop, about twenty feet away, totally unaware that I was entranced and not by the fireworks.

Maybe this party wouldn't be so bad after all. Maybe I should stop griping about the new neighbors.

She was wearing a black dress that was more of a T-shirt than an actual dress. The hem covered her ass but left inch after inch of her toned, mile-long legs on display.

I dragged my gaze down those legs, my cock swelling behind my zipper. Damn, she had great legs. When I reached her feet, I did a double take.

She was barefoot. Who came to a party in bare feet?

Five steps were all it would take to close the distance between us and find out her name, find out where she lived. But I stayed put as she tilted her face to the sky, closed her eyes and smiled.

My heart stopped. A full, dead stop.

It rocked me on my heels and I swayed, nearly tripping over my own feet. When I regained my balance, I stared at my tennis shoes, shaking my head until the dizziness was gone. What the hell?

Maybe it was the whiskey, not the woman. My gaze lifted.

Her eyes were waiting.

My head started spinning again, not as fast as it had a moment ago, but enough to make me feel unsteady. Yet I didn't dare break away from her eyes. It was too dark to tell their color. Maybe brown. Maybe blue. I hoped blue. I liked women with blue eyes.

She held my stare for a long moment, her head cocking

slightly to the side. Then her smile widened, flashing me her white teeth, before she set off across the lawn.

I followed, shifting between bodies, to keep her in sight as she weaved past people until she reached the edge of my yard.

She sat down, stretching her long legs over the grass. Then she leaned back on her elbows and watched the show, content to sit alone and smile at the sky. Only when the last of the firework tendrils floated in a white-gray haze over town did she move. She sat up straight and clapped, alone, for the show.

The crowd broke apart and I lost her as people came over, blocking her from view to say goodbye.

"Thanks for having us." Drew smacked me on the shoulder. His date was at his side, having stuck around after all. "That was the best show in years."

Was it? I didn't know.

"Thanks for coming." I shook his hand, glancing over his head to try and find the woman before she left. Unless she was already gone.

"Toren, catch!"

It was dark enough I barely spotted the football before it almost hit me in the face. But I caught Abel's throw and tucked the ball under my arm.

"Sorry." He ran over and gave me an exaggerated frown. "Thought you saw me."

No. I'd been looking for someone else. But I gave up the search when Dane raced over with a blinding smile.

"Did you see that huge firework at the end?" He made an explosion sound as his hands flew wide before he tried to steal the football.

I held it up in the air so he had to jump. "Did you make a mess upstairs?"

"Yes." He giggled. "Mom made us clean up."

"Good." I ruffled his strawberry-blond hair, the same shade as Faith's, as she walked over.

"We're taking off," she said. "If I can round up the rest of my kids. Dane, go find Beck and Cabe. Tell them they're in the car in five minutes or I'm leaving without them."

"Can we spend the night here?" he asked.

"No," Faith and I said in unison.

"Thanks for coming." I kissed her cheek. "Need some help on the farm tomorrow?"

"Don't worry about it if you're busy."

"I'm not that busy." Soon, college football season would be in full swing and then I would be busy. Now was when I had some extra time to pitch in.

She worried her lip between her teeth for a moment. Faith hated asking for help, even though she needed it. "Would you mind? For just an hour or so?"

"Not at all. I'll come out around ten."

"Thanks." She gave me a hug, then looped her arm through Abel's and headed for the house.

When she spotted Beck, she hollered his name and waved for him to follow.

I held up my hand as he jogged across the lawn.

He jerked up his chin.

It was a gesture so grown up, so adult, it made me give him a longer look. When had he gotten so tall?

As they headed for their car parked on the street, I turned back to the yard, searching for the woman again.

She was still sitting on the lawn, exactly where she'd been watching the fireworks.

A couple who lived three houses down appeared in front of me, blocking my view. "Thanks for having us, Toren."

"Thanks for coming." I shook their hands and said good night, but before I could cross the lawn for the blond, more neighbors stopped to say goodbye.

By the time I was done with a string of farewells, the spot where the woman had been sitting was empty.

Damn. I turned in a circle, but she was gone.

I blew out a long breath and retreated into the house. Parks and a few of the other single guys from work were in the kitchen.

"We were just talking about heading downtown for a beer," Parks said. "Up for it?"

"Thanks, but I think I'll just stay home." There was cleaning to be done. And if I was going to work on the farm with Faith tomorrow, I couldn't ignore it until the morning.

"You sure?" he asked.

"Yeah. Thanks for coming over."

"Thanks for the burgers and beers." He gave me a quick back-slapping hug, then headed for the entryway, everyone else waving as they left.

The house went quiet as the front door closed shut. I breathed in the silence. Never again. This was the last Fourth of July party. On a sigh, I did a quick sweep of the living room, picking up a few stray bottles and cans. Then I made my way to the yard, stepping into the cool night.

I froze the moment my shoes hit the deck.

The blond woman was in the yard. She was walking around, picking up trash.

My heart stuttered, not the dead stop from earlier, but it skipped enough that there was a twinge of pain.

She dropped the trash in her hands into the overflowing

garbage can. When she turned and spotted me on the deck, the corner of her mouth turned up.

She'd stayed. Guess she'd liked what she'd seen earlier too. *Hell yes.*

I walked down the steps and met her in the grass. "Hi."

"Hey." She pulled her lower lip between her teeth like she was trying to bite back a bigger smile.

Damn, I wanted to be the one to bite that lip.

Who was this woman?

She was tall, nearly six feet. I still stood taller, but I didn't have to crane my neck to keep those eyes.

Blue. Of course, they'd be blue. She had the most stunning ice-blue eyes. Bright, despite the dim lights from the deck.

I was a fucking goner already.

"Want to come inside?" I asked.

She arched an eyebrow.

"There's more to clean up in there," I teased.

She stared at me for a long moment, then she tipped her head to the stars and laughed. It was free and sweet with a hint of disbelief, like this was as wild for her as it was for me.

That laugh was the most beautiful thing I'd heard in my life.

It ended too soon as she shook her head, still smiling, and leveled me with those sparkling eyes.

Sparks crackled between us, like the fireworks show wasn't really over. It was the most electric, instant attraction I'd ever felt with a woman.

"Who *are* you?" I asked.

"Jennsyn Bell."

Jennsyn. A unique name for an unforgettable woman.

"Nice to meet you, Jennsyn. I'm Toren Greely."

"Toren." She spoke my name like she was sampling it on her tongue. I guess she liked its taste because she slipped past me, lifting on those bare toes.

And walked inside my house.

CHAPTER TWO

TOREN

P arks knocked on my open door and poked his head into my office. "Have you seen him yet?"

"Not yet." It was the same answer I'd given him the last four times he'd checked to see if I'd spotted Ford.

Today, Ford was starting as the head football coach for the Treasure State Wildcats. He'd texted me when he'd arrived at the fieldhouse earlier, before he'd gone into a meeting with Kurt, the athletic director. He was somewhere in the building. I just hadn't seen him yet.

Parks stepped inside, his forehead furrowing as he lowered his voice. "What do you think will happen?"

"With any luck, we'll win a lot of football games this year."

He rolled his eyes. "You know what I mean."

Yeah, I knew what he meant. After the scandal with the former head coach, Ford would likely be pressured to clean house. We were all walking on eggshells at the moment, wondering if we'd get to keep our jobs.

But I'd taken it as a good sign that we were still

employed. Other universities might not have given the new head coach time to evaluate the staff. They might have canned us all last spring with the Dipshit.

Good riddance.

None of us had had anything to do with his actions, but a scandal was a scandal. Our program's reputation was in the toilet. At the moment, all of us were holding our breaths, waiting to see how this played out.

I loved this job.

I *needed* this job. I wasn't sure what I'd do if I wasn't coaching.

"It'll be fine," I told Parks. Probably.

Even if Ford was pressured to let the existing staff go, I had faith in my friend that he'd hold strong. The man was a hell of an athlete, having been drafted from the Wildcats after college and spending years in the NFL. He'd won championships and a Super Bowl ring. He'd coached professionally.

If there was any man who'd fight for us to stay, it was Ford.

Parks nodded, dragging a hand over his jaw. The worry in his dark eyes had only gotten worse over the course of the day. He didn't have a history with Ford, and he was one of the newer coaches on the staff, having only been here for one season.

Maybe I was being naïve, but I was counting on Ford to give us a chance, to let us prove ourselves, regardless of our tenure at Treasure State.

"It was my kid, Toren," he said, his voice low. "I'll be the first one asked to pack up and leave."

"Parks, you didn't know."

"Maybe I should have known. I saw that kid every day."

Parks was the offensive coordinator and quarterback coach. The player who'd gone to the ER with alcohol poisoning and a bag of Adderall in his pocket had been an offensive tackle. There'd been some whispers through the department that Parks should have known something was happening, but those accusations were pure bullshit.

None of us had had a damn clue that the former coach was hosting underage parties at his house. If we'd known, we would have spoken up and stopped it.

But the administration was under fire and pointing fingers, searching for more people to blame. What they didn't seem to understand was that we already blamed ourselves.

I'd spent countless hours replaying the past, searching memories for signs of trouble. This conversation with Parks wasn't the first. I doubted it would be the last.

"We didn't know," I told him.

He gave me a sad smile. "But he was still my kid. My responsibility."

There was a reason Parks was a good coach. He cared for his players. He tucked them under his wing and looked out for their best interests.

I did the same.

Like Parks, I'd feel guilty for the rest of my life that I hadn't known something was wrong. Whether it made sense or not, we looked out for our players. And last spring, we'd failed them.

"I'm going to take a walk outside," he said. "Get some air. Sitting in my office waiting is killing me."

"I'll let you know when I see Ford."

"Thanks." He left with a wave.

I waited until I heard a door slam shut down the hallway

before I stood from my desk, needing to move around and shake some nerves loose.

Parks wasn't the only guy on edge. I'd been dealing with this restless energy for the past two weeks.

I wanted to blame it all on work, but the truth was, I'd been edgy ever since the party on the Fourth.

Ever since my night with Jennsyn.

J-E-N-N-S-Y-N. I'd asked her to spell it while we'd been tangled together in my bed. I hadn't been at all surprised that the spelling was unusual. Everything about that woman had been exceptional.

It was the reason I hadn't called her in two weeks even though she'd been a constant on my mind.

I was man enough to admit that she scared the fuck out of me.

That night was the best time I'd had with a woman in my entire life. If I called her, it wouldn't be casual. If I called her, it wouldn't be a fling. It had only taken one night for her to crawl beneath my skin.

What happened when we had another and another and another?

There was a very real chance I'd drown in that woman.

It was unsettling. Terrifying, actually.

And rather than man up, I'd taken the coward's path for the last two weeks. Every morning, I stared at her number written on a paper towel that I'd shoved into my kitchen's junk drawer. Every morning, I pulled out my phone and keyed in those ten digits. And every morning, I cursed myself as I wimped out.

The problem now was that it had been two weeks. Two weeks too long. If—*when*—I worked up the nerve, Jennsyn would probably think I was only calling for another hookup.

Every day that passed, the hole I was digging got deeper and deeper.

Fuck, I was an idiot.

Jennsyn had unnerved me, and now I was stuck in my own head. Added to my potential unemployment and everything happening with Faith and the boys, I was coming out of my skin.

The nervous energy sent me out of my office, walking down the clean, open hallway of the fieldhouse.

They'd remodeled the building about five years ago, building new men's and women's locker rooms. They'd added a state-of-the-art fitness facility and relocated the weight room so it was more easily accessible to student athletes. The coaches' offices were right in the mix so we weren't far removed from the players.

It was vastly different than when I'd been a student here at Treasure State, and while I loved the fitness facilities, my favorite improvement was the winding hallway loop that weaved through the building.

The path circled by conference rooms and offices. It led to Upshaw Gymnasium, where the women's volleyball team played. There were other locker rooms and practice spaces. Then came the main arena, where the basketball teams played games and the rodeo team held their annual event. From time to time, they'd use the massive space for concerts or conventions.

Normally, I walked this loop once a week, usually to clear my head. I'd done it twice already today.

Most of the jitters had worked free by the time I finished the loop. I was just rounding the last corner for my office when I spotted a familiar face.

Ford.

A grin stretched across my mouth.

The last time I'd seen him had been ages ago, when I'd gone to Seattle to catch a Seahawks game. We talked on the phone and texted from time to time, but damn, he was a sight for sore eyes.

It was right, having him in these hallways again, even if they looked different. Even if he'd changed too.

Kurt stood beside Ford, practically beaming. No doubt Kurt would take full credit for bringing Ford on board. I wasn't expecting any praise for recommending Ford for the job. If it meant I got to work for my friend, a good man, I didn't need the glory.

"Well, look who the cat dragged in," I teased, smiling wider as I walked toward them, hand extended. "Kurt, I'm surprised. I didn't think you'd actually convince Ford to leave the big city."

Ford's own smile stretched across his face as he shook my hand. "Didn't take much. He promised I got to be your boss, and I couldn't resist the chance to torture you."

"Like old times." I pulled him in for a hug, slapping him on the back. "I know you're just getting settled in, but let's meet for a beer or something soon. Be great to catch up."

Ford nodded. "You're on."

"Good to have you back on Montana soil, man." I clapped him on the shoulder, then disappeared into my office, the room beside his, and breathed a sigh of relief.

It had been a long time since I'd trusted my boss. The Dipshit never had earned it in my past three years as a coach here for TSU. And Kurt looked out for Kurt, above all else. But Ford? He'd have my back.

Maybe I would get to keep this office after all.

Ford had just arrived in Montana, moving here with his daughter, Joey. She was nine and going into fourth grade.

Joey was younger than Cabe but older than Dane. Still, maybe they'd meet at school. Or maybe Ford and Joey could come out to visit the farm once they were settled in their new home.

I made a mental note to invite them later.

Taking this job had happened fast for Ford. For all of us. He'd been interviewed and hired in a span of less than a month. Kurt had asked all of us if we had recommendations for a head coach after his candidate had fallen through. Ford's name had instantly come to mind, so I'd given him a call to ask if he'd be interested.

Now he was back in Mission, contract signed, for a fresh start with Joey in Montana.

Change was on the horizon. For Ford. For the Wildcats.

Maybe for me too.

We had a good program here, despite the Dipshit's leadership.

He hadn't been a bad coach. We'd had three winning seasons in a row. But there'd always been something about him that had bothered me, even though I'd never been able to pinpoint it. There'd been no signs of his shady behavior. He'd portrayed a dedicated coach.

Until the truth had finally surfaced, and everything he'd hidden had come to light.

Last spring, one of our red-shirt freshmen had been brought into the ER. He'd gotten drunk at the coach's house, at a party the Dipshit had thrown for players.

The weasel had lied and said the players had gone over uninvited while he'd been camping, that he'd left his door unlocked and the players had broken in. What had actually happened was that he'd been tipped off and had ditched the party before the cops had arrived.

Afterward, people had started coming forward with the truth.

The Dipshit had been hosting these parties for years. The players had kept it secret because he'd warned them that if anyone found out, they'd get cut from the team. Mostly, the freshmen and sophomores would attend because they were too young to buy booze or go downtown to the bars.

The upperclassmen we'd questioned admitted to going when they were younger but hadn't lately. They said those parties were uncomfortable, especially because Coach always asked the guys to bring pretty girls.

A junior on the golf team had admitted to sleeping with the Dipshit. She'd transferred to Eastern Washington already, but we all suspected there were others.

As a coach, the easiest way to get your ass fired was to fuck a student.

The school's general counsel had managed to keep some details out of the media, but there was only so much we could keep quiet.

Donors and alumni were livid. The department was in crisis mode, doing everything we could to drag our name out of the mud.

Millie had mentioned earlier this week that the coaches would be required to attend a handful of fundraisers preseason in an effort to smooth ruffled feathers.

Hopefully, her own feathers wouldn't be too ruffled now that Ford was working here.

Maybe I should have told her that I'd recommended him for the head coaching position—she had to know by now, right? Kurt would have told her, since she practically ran the athletic department.

I doubted that Ford knew she was an assistant AD, but he'd find out soon enough.

Those two had a history and I'd learned a long, long time ago to stay out of the middle.

Granted, I probably should have given them both a warning. But I hadn't wanted anything to spook Ford—or piss off Millie. And since I was apparently taking the coward's way out in more than one aspect of my life, I'd kept my damn mouth shut.

Ford and Millie would figure out how to work together. Or they'd kill each other trying.

I was back behind my desk when Ford walked by again, lifting a hand to wave. He was probably on his way to another meeting and would be swamped with them for a while. Better him than me. I just wanted to be on the field, coaching football.

This week, I'd been coaching kids from area high schools. Our annual summer camp had just wrapped up yesterday. Both Abel and Beck had been able to attend, so it had been a good week.

I shook my mouse, about to check the inbox I'd neglected because I'd been on the field every day, when a woman flew through my office door.

"Toren." Aspen Quinn, the women's volleyball coach, was breathing hard, like she'd been running. "Have you seen a blond walk by here?"

"Uh, no."

"Shit," she hissed, dragging a hand over her sleek, auburn ponytail.

"What's wrong?" I stood and followed her into the hallway.

"I lost my new player." She cast her eyes to the ceiling high overhead. "We were in the middle of a fieldhouse tour, and I left her in the locker room while I took a quick call from my dad. When I went back, she was gone."

"What's she look like?" I asked. "I'll help you find her."

"Tall," Aspen said. "Obviously."

Like her, all of the volleyball players were tall. Aspen stood a few inches shorter than my six four.

"She's got blond hair, cropped to about her shoulders."

Blond hair to her shoulders. Tall.

Jennsyn's face popped into my mind.

No. Not a chance. It couldn't be her. That length of hair was a popular style, and there were plenty of tall, blond women. Jennsyn was just on my mind.

"There you are." Aspen sighed, eyes trained past my shoulder. "I've been looking everywhere for you."

"Sorry, Coach."

The world swept out from beneath my feet. I swayed as my stomach dropped.

That voice. I would never, ever forget that voice.

No. *Fuck fuck fuck.* This wasn't happening. It couldn't be happening.

"Where'd you go?" Aspen asked.

"Sorry, I popped in to take a look at the weight room."

Every word was like a knife through my chest.

Oh God. Jennsyn was a student. A volleyball player.

I'd fucked a student.

My career was over. Slaughtered at the hands of a gorgeous blond.

"Well, that was my next stop on the tour anyway," Aspen said. "Before we continue, I'll introduce you two."

An introduction? I nearly laughed. Nothing about this was funny, but it was either laugh or scream.

By some miracle, I managed to stay quiet as I slowly turned to face Jennsyn.

Her eyes flared. Her smile faltered for a second before she caught herself and focused on Aspen. She kept smiling even though the color drained from her face.

Thank fuck, Aspen didn't seem to notice. "This is Toren Greely. He's one of the football coaches."

"Nice to meet you." Jennsyn extended her hand, playing the part of two perfect strangers rather than two people who'd fucked like rock stars on the Fourth of July.

The air rushed from my lungs as I shook her hand. A hint of her perfume caught my nose, citrus and summer sunshine, making me dizzy, but I masked it with a polite nod. "Welcome to Treasure State."

"Thanks." She swallowed hard, then let go of my hand, looking anywhere but at my face.

Fucked. We were both entirely fucked.

We'd spent an entire night together. Hours. How had I not figured this out? Why the hell hadn't I asked more questions?

Maybe because she hadn't acted like a student. Nothing about her was young or immature. The idea that she'd be a player hadn't crossed my mind, not once.

"We'll get out of your hair," Aspen said, then started down the hallway, Jennsyn falling into step at her side.

I waited until they were gone before I dragged a hand over my face. "Fucking hell."

A student. A student athlete. And I'd been inside her

body. She'd slept in my bed. Oh God, I was going to be sick. My stomach roiled, threatening to toss up my lunch. I walked to my office on unsteady feet, closing the door behind me with too much force. It slammed shut as I planted my hands on my desk, leaning forward to close my eyes and breathe.

A student. Jennsyn was a student. I was a coach.

The rules were concrete. Inescapably clear.

There were no interpersonal relationships between students and staff. No exceptions. No arguments. The end.

I. Was. Fucked.

My head began to throb. "Damn it," I hissed.

How did I fix this? How did I go back in time and beg my past self to ask some motherfucking questions?

Whenever I picked up a woman at a bar, I always made sure I wasn't flirting with a damn student. *What do you do? Where are you from? What year did you graduate high school?* I always, always, *always* asked those questions.

Jennsyn was beautiful. She was young but I wouldn't have guessed she was under twenty-five. And she'd arrived at my house barefoot. She had to have walked from her own place.

Granted, I still hadn't figured out which house in the neighborhood was hers, but regardless, there were no students living in my neighborhood. None.

Right? Yeah, there were new faces on the block, but no students. It was a family neighborhood and every house was for sale, not rent.

Oh God, I'd fucked up. The weight of what this meant nearly sent me to my knees.

We hadn't known. I wouldn't have touched her if I'd known she was a student. Given the shock on Jennsyn's face, she clearly hadn't known either. The night of the party, I couldn't remember talking about work. I'd never mentioned I was a coach.

We were innocent. Well, sort of. Nothing I'd done with her that night had been innocent.

Maybe if I explained that this was all a big mistake, if Ford knew the whole story, I'd be able to turn this around. Somehow, I'd be able to fix this and save my career.

Never. Not this year. Not on the heels of the Dipshit's scandal.

There would be no tolerance.

So, yeah. I was fucked.

Unless . . .

No one found out. Unless it was a secret. I wasn't the only person with something to lose. Jennsyn would lose her spot on the volleyball team too. If she was on a scholarship, she'd probably be fighting to keep this a secret too, right?

What if she'd told someone already? Something like this, the news would spread like wildfire. But maybe we'd get lucky. Maybe, like me, she hadn't told a soul.

My heart was racing, pounding so hard in my chest it hurt. I stood tall, shaking off another wave of dizziness, then swiped up my keys and phone from the desk. I stormed out of my office, grateful that I didn't pass anyone along the way to the nearest exit. When I hit the parking lot, I jogged to my truck. It was an effort not to break every speed limit on the drive from campus to home.

My hands were shaking as I parked in the garage and hustled inside for the kitchen. I ripped open the junk drawer, snagging that paper towel from the top of the stack, and punched in the number to my phone.

This time, I made the call.

It rang and rang.

"Hey, you've reached Jennsyn. Leave a message."

"Damn it." I ended the call and pinched the bridge of my nose. "Fuck it."

I called her again, listening to it ring.

Except this time, there was an echo. It was faint, like it was coming from outside.

I marched through the entryway, dropping the phone from my ear, but the ringing didn't stop. Not until I opened the front door to find Jennsyn on my porch, her phone in hand.

"So you did keep my number."

CHAPTER THREE

JENNSYN

The moment Toren shifted out of the doorway, I dove into his house to get out of sight.

This is bad. This is so, so bad.

"No shit," he muttered.

"Uh . . ." Oops. I hadn't meant to say that out loud.

My heart was racing and my head spinning. It probably wouldn't be the first thought to escape without permission and there was no chance I'd play this cool.

"Okay, so, I'm freaking out." I walked through the entryway and into the open space as I pressed my hands to my cheeks. They'd been hot and flushed since that encounter at the fieldhouse.

Toren raked a hand through his soft, brown hair as he followed me into the living room. "Let's just take this one thing at a time. Did you tell anyone that we, uh . . ."

Had sex five times in one night? "No."

"Oh, thank God." His sigh filled the entire house.

"Did you?"

He shook his head. "No."

Phew. My exhale was as loud as his.

That was good. Secrecy was our only hope. We had no other options. So why was there a twinge of irritation beneath my relief?

"You really didn't tell anyone?" I asked.

He nodded. "Really."

"Huh."

That was a good thing, right? If he'd blabbed about our night, then we'd be in deep shit. Well, deeper shit than we were already in.

I hadn't told anyone because I didn't really know anyone other than my roommates. And considering we'd been roommates for only two weeks, we weren't exactly at the share-details-about-our-hookups phase.

But Toren lived here. He had plenty of friends, gauging by the sheer volume of people he'd hosted for the party on the Fourth. He really hadn't enjoyed himself enough to mention he'd had sex five times in one night?

"Why not?" I asked.

He blinked. It was a slow blink, like he was mentally rewinding the last two seconds. "You want to know why I didn't tell anyone we had sex?"

"Yeah. That was fantastic sex. If I had anyone to tell, I totally would have spilled."

His mouth opened. Closed. Opened again.

Not the most important thing right now, Jennsyn.

"Never mind." I waved it off. "I'm getting off topic."

"You think?"

"Like I said, I'm freaking out. We had sex. You're *you* and I'm *me* and we had sex." A lot of sex.

Sex against the wall behind him because once we'd started kissing, neither of us had been able to wait until we'd made it upstairs to his bedroom. Sex on the kitchen island behind him because it had been the closest surface after the wall. Sex on the couch. Sex on the floor.

Eventually, we'd made it to his bedroom. Then we'd had sex up there too.

"I'm aware that we had sex." He pinched the bridge of his nose, then pulled out a stool at the island that separated the open-concept space. "Fuck. This is bad."

I nodded. "Yup."

"Let's just talk this out."

"Smart. Right. Good idea." I started pacing, walking back and forth in the space between the living room and kitchen. My heart was beating so fast I felt like I'd just run ten miles. Nervous energy poured from my shaking fingertips. "You can't tell anyone."

He shot me a flat look. "Obviously."

I held up a hand. "Just saying. We have to be on the same page. If anyone finds out, even if we didn't know at the time, it won't matter."

I should have asked him about his job. I should have told him why I'd moved to Mission. How was it that we'd covered so many other topics in a single night but hadn't managed to share the mundane details?

Probably because instead of talking for hours, we'd had sex. My attention snagged on his brown couch. He'd bent me over the back of that couch—the leather had been buttery soft against my breasts as Toren had fucked me from behind. A shiver raced down my spine and my core clenched.

Don't look at the couch. Ignore the couch. I lifted my hands to my temples, using them as blinders until I paced out of the living room. The kitchen was wide and spacious, except with Toren at the island, all I could think about was how he'd hoisted me onto that countertop.

I gulped and focused *anywhere* else.

The paint. It was white. I liked white paint. It was clean and bright. The wooden accents throughout the house gave it warmth and charm. Nothing about this house screamed sporty football coach's bachelor pad. I'd assumed Toren was an accountant, given the way he'd organized his bedroom closet.

"Jennsyn," Toren said, pulling out the stool beside his. "Do you want to sit down?"

Absolutely not. I held up a hand and kept moving. "Still freaking out."

The scent of Toren's cologne lingering in the air wasn't helping either. It was masculine and woodsy and clean. Intoxicating, yet subtle. Exactly the opposite of the cheap, overpowering bodywash most college guys preferred.

We'd only had one night together, but already, I felt addicted to his scent. The week after the Fourth, I'd spent countless hours hoping he'd call. Last week, I'd kicked myself for thinking we'd been anything more than a hookup.

It was a good thing he hadn't called. A great decision. Didn't bother me at all, right?

Right.

"You're a coach." The knot in my stomach doubled as I said it out loud.

"And you're a student." He dragged a hand over his handsome face. He glanced to the countertop, and like he suddenly remembered exactly what we'd done on that island, he swallowed hard.

Toren had played with my body on that granite like I was his favorite toy.

A low pulse bloomed in my core, and I stifled a groan. Seriously? What was wrong with me? This was not the time to be turned on, but there was just something about Toren, and my body's response was automatic.

His gaze was hot on my profile as I kept pacing beside the dining room table, and the longer he stared, the tighter that curl of desire coiled.

"Don't look at me," I ordered.

"You're in my house. Wearing a path in my hardwood floors. And you tell me not to look at you?"

I stopped and faced him, hands planted on my hips. "That attitude isn't going to help anyone."

He did that slow-blink thing again. One second he was staring at me like I'd lost my fucking mind—accurate. Then he threw his head back and laughed, loud and frustrated and maybe a little bit hopeless.

The hopeless part was hard to hear.

"What the fuck?" He shook his head, the laughter ebbing.

"Exactly." I threw up my hands. "What the fuck are we supposed to do?"

Annnnd I was yelling. *Awesome.* My voice echoed off the vaulted ceiling and its wooden beams.

"I'm on a scholarship. This is my senior year. I'm so, so close. I don't want to screw it all up." But maybe it was too late. Maybe that ship had sailed long before I'd even come to Montana.

This was a mistake, wasn't it? Moving to Mission. Starting at a new school. Playing on a new team for my final year. At least in Montana, I didn't have any friends around who'd gladly say *I told you so.*

"We've only got one option," Toren said. "We pretend

like it never happened. Your scholarship is on the line. My entire career hangs in the balance here. Like you said. No one can ever know."

That was our only option. Complete and utter denial. If anyone asked if I'd fucked my neighbor who happened to be a Treasure State Wildcats football coach, I'd lie through my teeth.

I'd been lying all year. Should be a snap.

"Okay." I breathed, a full, deep breath, for the first time since I'd seen Toren on campus. "We'll pretend. The party never happened."

His jaw ticked but he gave me a single nod.

"I had no idea you were a coach. I swear." The last thing I wanted was for him to think I'd done this on purpose. To sabotage his career or manipulate him into something.

"And I had no idea you were a student." There was regret in his voice. The regret that came from a good man. A coach who never, ever would have crossed that line if he'd known I was on the other side.

We should regret that night. Both of us. The part of me who liked rules and order would regret sleeping with a coach. But after everything that had happened earlier this year, the part of me who'd felt trapped and suffocated for years would never regret how he'd made me feel.

Free. Alive. Special.

He could regret it. I wouldn't blame him. But I wouldn't, not really.

"So that's it," I said, walking toward him still at the island. "That's the plan. We forget each other. We'll just go about our lives and no one will ever know."

"Please." There was a desperate edge to his voice. It hurt to hear too.

"You don't have to say please." I didn't want him to beg for my secrecy. I wouldn't tell a soul. Not because of my scholarship or spot on the team. I wouldn't tell, simply because he'd asked me not to.

"Strangers." I held out my hand. "Deal."

His hand engulfed mine, and just like it had at the field-house earlier, the moment we touched, a jolt raced from my palm to my elbow. It was like touching a flame but knowing it wouldn't burn. I slipped my hand away and tucked it behind my back while it tingled.

Toren's gray-green eyes met mine and the air between us crackled. The temperature spiked with my pulse. The kitchen, the house, the sound of a dog barking outside faded to a distant blur.

Something tugged me closer like an invisible rope. It was his eyes. They were a snare, as powerful as they'd been two weeks ago. His light green irises were flecked with gray and circled by a charcoal ring. The longer I stared, the more I felt that pull. Standing still, keeping myself in place, was like fighting a magnet.

How did we forget? How would I ever not want to drown in his eyes? How did we pretend that his perfect, wicked mouth hadn't tasted nearly every inch of my body?

How did I forget the best night of my life?

My gaze dropped to his lips, my heart tumbling. I leaned in. Or maybe he leaned in.

A shout came from outside, breaking the moment. My eyes flew to the window over his kitchen sink as two boys on bikes streaked by.

Toren slid off his stool, standing so fast I blinked and he was gone. He'd put the living room between us. He walked to the fireplace along the far wall and raked a hand through his hair again, making it stand at odd angles.

He left it longer on top, the strands floppy and smooth.

Some other woman would get to run her fingers through that hair. Lucky girl.

"You know, any other situation and I'd be pissed at you for taking two weeks to call me," I said, pushing his stool into the island with the others. "But I guess it worked out for the best."

"Yeah." His voice was hoarse, like he needed a glass of ice water. "I would have. Called you."

I barked a laugh. "Liar. Any guy who doesn't call after two weeks was never going to call."

"I mean it. I would have called."

There was sincerity in his voice. I believed him. "When?"

He shrugged. "Soon. Truthfully, you kind of freaked me out."

"Exactly what a woman wants to hear."

"In a good way." The corner of his mouth turned up in a smile. "I sort of hoped we'd bump into each other."

"Ah." I nodded. "So you were hoping fate would intervene."

His eyes raked over my body, head to toe. "Something like that."

Too bad there'd be no fate. She'd already screwed us over.

I gave him a sad smile, then headed for the entryway. "I'd better go."

He followed behind me, holding the door as I scanned the street to make sure no one was around. Then I checked the driveway to make sure my roommates hadn't gotten home.

The coast was clear.

"Wait." Toren followed my line of sight. "Where do you live?"

I pointed to the house next door. "Surprise."

"No. You don't live there."

"Um, yes, I do?"

He shook his head. "I saw an older couple move in last month."

"That must have been Stevie's parents. They bought this place for her as an investment. She was in Europe, but she had to be out of her old rental, so her parents did most of the moving."

My other roommate, Liz, had been visiting her parents in Ohio and had just gotten back last night. She and I were both renting furnished rooms. Everything I'd brought with me from California had fit into my car. Coach Quinn had arranged for me to rent out the third bedroom at Stevie's place.

Most of the other girls lived in the same condo complex closer to campus. There was a room open with a couple girls in that complex too. But the reason it was open was because another girl had been cut from the team and left Treasure State.

Coach Quinn had taken away her scholarship.

And given it to me.

At this point, I wasn't sure which would be more torture. Living beside Toren, pretending he was no one. Or dealing with the girls who were pissed that I'd taken their friend's place on the team.

"Next door." Toren cast his eyes to the ceiling, almost

like he should have known. Like he'd been racking his brain to figure out where I might live and hadn't once considered it was that close. "She lives next door."

"Yep, *she* does. Don't worry. We went two weeks without crossing paths, I doubt we'll see each other often." I did one last check of my driveway and the street, then I stepped outside and into the sunshine. "Goodbye, Toren."

He lifted a hand to wave. "Goodbye, Jennsyn."

THE PARTY
TOREN

"You don't have to clean," I told Jennsyn.

"It'll go faster with two people." She followed me into the house, her arms loaded with bottles of condiments.

Letting a woman I'd just met help me clean up the party felt wrong, but if it meant keeping her around for a little while longer, I'd take all the time I could get.

Besides, she seemed set on picking up. We'd gone inside for a few minutes, and when she'd realized the bulk of the mess was outside, she'd led the way back outside.

The yard was clean and any stray cans were in the trash. The remnants of the barbeque had mostly been tossed, leaving the staples. While she carried the ketchup and mustard and relish, I had the paper plates, plastic utensils and a small stack of napkins.

"Want a beer?" I asked, hoping she'd say yes and stick around to drink it.

Wait. Did I have any beer left?

"I'm not much of a beer drinker," she said, piling bottles on the counter in the kitchen.

41

"No? What's your favorite drink?"

"I'm not much of a drinker at all, actually. But I like red wine. Cold tequila. The occasional hard cider." She opened the fridge and did a double take. "Oh my God."

"What?" I rounded the island from where I'd dropped the plates and went to stand beside Jennsyn at the fridge, expecting to find something in there that didn't belong.

Maybe a football next to my gallon of milk. A set of keys beside the pickles. The half-eaten burger of Dane's he'd promised to eat later but had forgotten. Except it looked exactly like it had earlier today when I'd taken out the potato salad for the party. Nearly empty, but the shelves were clean and free of random objects.

Jennsyn cocked her head to the side as she studied the refrigerator's door. "Your condiments are organized by color, light to dark."

Well, fuck.

"Please tell me that was intentional," she said.

"It was intentional." I chuckled, not an ounce of shame as I started adding the bottles from the barbeque into the mix. "You know, not a soul in the world who's seen the inside of my fridge has ever noticed."

Until Jennsyn.

If I hadn't been intrigued by her before, this would have done it. And either she'd appreciate that I liked an organized fridge. Or she'd bolt for the door.

"I bet your closet looks the same." She handed me a bottle of mustard to put away.

"Maybe."

It did. My shirts were hung starting with white on the left and moving to black on the right.

If she was lucky—if I got lucky—she could see my

42

bedroom closet herself. "I like an organized fridge. Helps me keep track of what's expired and what I'm missing."

She leaned back against the counter, relaxing into the space like she intended to stay awhile. "I like it."

"If you like this, you should see the fridge in the garage."

A smile toyed on her pretty lips. "Lead the way."

CHAPTER FOUR

JENNSYN

The buzz of a lawnmower outside drifted through my bedroom's open window.

Don't look. Do. Not. Look.

It took everything I had to stay seated on the bed with the book I was reading on my lap.

The view beyond the glass was breathtaking. I knew without looking there'd be nothing but blue sky, summer sunshine and the lovely town of Mission sprawled between mountain foothills and evergreen forests.

Since I'd moved into this house, I'd spent hours at my window, staring into the distance. I'd never lived in a place this beautiful. My last bedroom view had been of my neighbor's beige siding from my condo in California.

Yet as relaxing as it was to stare out over the rugged Montana landscape, it just wasn't worth it. Not while he was outside.

I closed my eyes as the mower's buzz got louder and louder, beckoning me toward the glass for a peek. The scent of fresh-cut grass infused the air, nearly luring me off the mattress.

Don't. Look. I opened my paperback, forcing myself to concentrate on the words.

I'd been reading when the mowing had started and I'd gotten up out of curiosity to see who was outside. One glimpse of Toren and I'd forced myself away from the window.

That was eighteen minutes ago. I'd been reading the same page ever since.

How long did it take him to mow his freaking lawn?

"Ugh." I closed the paperback and tossed it aside, collapsing into my pillows to stifle a groan.

This would get easier, right? After more time, after weeks or months, I wouldn't care about the noises coming from his house. I wouldn't care if I saw his truck or if we crossed paths getting the mail.

Last night, after our *we're-going-to-pretend-the-party-never-happened* discussion and I'd left his house, he'd grilled dinner on his barbeque. The scents of smoke and burgers had wafted into my room. Every inhale had been torture.

But the mowing was arguably worse.

"Why?" I pounded my fist into the pillow beside my head, then turned and flopped on my back.

Why Toren? Why couldn't I get him out of my head? Why couldn't he have *any* other job?

Clearly moving to Montana hadn't improved my luck with men.

"I'm such an idiot."

His lawnmower might as well have been humming, "Yuuuuuup."

I shoved up to a seat and turned to the window. Before I

could stop myself, I was off the bed and padding across my room's plush carpet.

Weak. I was so, so weak.

The moment I spotted him, my heart tumbled and I sagged against the wall. "Damn it."

When I'd spotted him earlier, he'd been wearing a pair of black mesh shorts and a sleeveless blue T-shirt that molded to the hard plane of his chest. His Wildcats hat was turned backward.

Part of me had hoped Toren would have gotten cold while working in the eighty-degree weather. That he would have changed into a parka and snow pants to finish his yard-work. Anything to cover up that hard body.

Nope. God, he had fantastic arms. They were roped with muscle, strong and defined. His skin was slightly shiny with sweat.

Toren shifted to push the mower with one hand, using the other to drag up his shirt and dry his face.

"Not the abs." I closed my eyes and pressed my face into the wall.

Was he trying to torment me? I didn't need to stare to see his six-pack. It was forever burned into my brain. My tongue had licked every peak and valley of his stomach.

I should have locked myself in the bathroom.

The mower stopped and the quiet was jarring. I shoved off the wall, careful to keep out of the window's frame as I peered into his yard.

Our houses were angled around the curve of the street, which meant at the rear, they were angled toward each other. From my window, I could see the entirety of his backyard.

Toren walked to the deck and swept up a water bottle,

chugging until it was gone. Then he twisted his hat the right way and went back to the mower. He glanced toward my yard and his lips pursed. He gave a slight headshake, then focused on his task.

"Move away from the window," I muttered.

I needed out of this room. I needed away from the temptation that was *Coach* Toren Greely.

Other than a quick stop to the kitchen for breakfast, I'd been hiding in my room most of the day. It was easier that way. Things with Stevie and Liz were . . . awkward.

But at the moment, I'd take awkward with my teammates rather than drooling over a man I most definitely could not have.

So I made my way downstairs, where my roommates were in the living room, both tying the laces to their tennis shoes.

"Hey." Stevie smiled. She always smiled. Her brown hair was long, past her waist, and she'd done a tight braid that trailed along her spine.

"Hey." I gave them both a wave.

"We're going for a run," Liz said, dressed in a pair of matching olive-green shorts and sports bra. The color complemented her tan skin and chocolate eyes. "Want to come?"

"That's okay. I went first thing this morning."

"Shoot." Stevie's smile faltered, just a bit. "We go every day until practice starts if you want to start running with us."

"Okay. Maybe," I lied. I used to run with a friend. Not anymore. I wasn't in Montana to make friends or have running companions.

"We're going to the store later," Liz said. "Want to come?"

"Oh, um, I think I'm good." I gestured toward the kitchen. "I stocked up a few days ago."

"Well, if you change your mind, you can definitely tag along. Or we can pick something up for you too."

"Thanks." I appreciated how hard they were trying. Really. They seemed sweet and, so far, like good roommates. But I wasn't in a place to trust fellow teammates at the moment, not after Emily.

It wasn't fair to Stevie or Liz, that they'd suffer for her sins, but my guard was up and I had no intention of dropping it again. Lesson learned. The hard way.

This arrangement was for one year only. Then I'd graduate and . . . something.

Something would happen next year. I just wasn't sure what I wanted that something to be yet.

Liz opened the door and stepped outside, raising an arm to wave. "Hi, Coach Greely."

"Hey." Toren's voice carried from his house to ours. The lawnmower had stopped.

Well, shit. I should have stayed in my room.

"Have you met Coach Greely?" Stevie asked as she stood.

Intimately.

"Yeah, at the fieldhouse yesterday. Coach Quinn was giving me a tour and we bumped into him."

"I didn't realize he lived next door." She gave me an exaggerated frown. "Not that we throw parties or anything. Liz and I are pretty low-key. But it's still a coach next door. At least he's cool."

If cool meant smoking hot. Toren was absolute fire.

"I had a flat tire last year in the parking lot at the fieldhouse," she said. "He was coming out and saw me trying to change it and helped. He's a pretty nice guy."

"Glad he's our neighbor, then." It was another blatant lie.

"See ya." More smiling as she made her way to the door.

"Have a good run."

"Thanks."

The door closed with a click as she joined Liz outside. Their voices were muffled as they spoke to Toren, then they streaked past the front windows, jogging down the sidewalk side by side.

I counted to ten. Then twenty. Then fifty.

Was he still out there?

I tiptoed to the door, peering through the glass insert just as Toren crossed the street for the mailbox cluster.

Swoon. I melted against the door. His swagger was so freaking attractive. Long legs with an easy gait. Toren walked like he owned the world, and the sexiest part was that he had no idea. His confidence was effortless and natural in every step.

I drooled over the perfect curve of his ass as he collected his mail. When he turned to retreat to his house, I backed away from the glass before he could catch me spying, then wandered to the kitchen.

This house had a much different layout than Toren's. My bedroom was in the same place as his, but it wasn't the primary suite and I didn't have a balcony. Stevie had the biggest bedroom on the first floor. Instead of his open concept, there was an arched opening that separated our dining room and kitchen from the living room. And while his place felt like a home, ours still felt a bit empty.

Stevie's parents had brought over furniture from her old rental, but clearly, this house was much bigger and the pieces didn't quite fit. Not that I was complaining. I was simply happy that they'd had a bed, nightstand and dresser for my room so I didn't have to shop.

The furniture I'd had in California I'd sold because it had been easier than paying a mover to have it brought to Montana. No one, especially my mother, would have helped me move. Not when Treasure State was my decision and mine alone.

Someday, I'd have my own furniture again. Someday.

When I was certain Toren had gone inside his house, I slipped out the front door and crossed my driveway for the mailbox.

The concrete was hot beneath my bare feet, so I jogged a few steps, rising onto my toes when I made it to the asphalt. Then I scampered to the mailbox, taking out a few junk flyers and a magazine of Stevie's.

Nothing for me. There never was.

I turned, about to dash back for the house, and froze.

Toren stood in his driveway, jaw clenched, with his mailbox key in one hand and a letter in the other. His Adam's apple bobbed as he swallowed hard. The brim of his hat shielded his eyes, so I couldn't tell if he was irked or happy or nervous or surprised to see me.

Maybe he was like me. All of the above.

When it came to Toren, it was like experiencing every emotion at once.

The heat beneath my soles became unbearable, so I hurried back to our side of the street, jumping over the curb and sidewalk and onto the closest lawn.

His.

The grass was soft and lush beneath my toes. Toren took

pride in his house, inside and out. It was very domestic. Adult. And much more attractive than it should have been.

"Hey, Coach Greely."

Coach Greely? Eww. No.

There was no way I could call him Coach Greely. He was Toren.

Toren, the guy with striking gray-green eyes. Toren, the man with a breathtaking smile of straight, white teeth. Toren, the absolute Adonis who'd made me come five times in one night.

He swallowed hard again. Was he thinking about the five orgasms too?

"Hey, Jennsyn."

I really liked how he said my name. I liked that he'd cared enough to ask me how it was spelled. I liked his deep, smooth voice and the shiver it sent down my spine.

"Hey." I'd said that already. *Awesome.*

We stared at each other for a long moment, like neither of us was sure how to break away. But it kept me from ogling his roped arms or flat stomach or bulky thighs. I didn't let myself look at his mesh shorts and the bulge that—

Don't look. Do. Not. Look.

I didn't have to look. It was another part of his incredible anatomy that was burned into my brain. My cheeks flamed. Hopefully he'd think it was because of the heat.

Toren finally broke our stare first, glancing down the block, either to see if Stevie and Liz were gone or to look anywhere else but my direction.

I followed his gaze along the sidewalk, searching for my roommates. It was probably a good thing they were off jogging through the neighborhood. It was bad enough to suffer through this awkward silence with Toren—Coach Greely—without witnesses.

"This is yours." He held up the letter that must have been put in his box rather than mine.

We met in the middle of his front lawn, stopping so far apart that we each had to stretch to swap the envelope.

It was probably a piece of junk mail. It had a yellow forwarding sticker on the front from my address in California to Montana. "Thanks."

"Sure." Toren crossed his arms over his chest and took a backward step.

I let my toes squish on the plush grass one more time before I headed for my scorching-hot driveway. I was halfway home when I glanced over my shoulder to see if he was still outside.

Toren's gray-green eyes were waiting.

I gave him a small smile.

He spun around and disappeared into his house.

The moment I was inside, safe behind my closed door, I groaned. "Why?"

Why did he have to be a coach? Of all the places in Mission to work, why did it have to be the university? Why couldn't I stop thinking about those five orgasms?

I took the mail to the kitchen counter, leaving it to sort through later. Then I filled a glass of ice water and trudged upstairs to my bedroom, picking up my book.

By the time Stevie and Liz came home, I'd managed to read a few chapters despite my mind still wandering to the man next door.

Was it weird for Toren too? Or was I the only one bothered by this? What happened when we saw each other on campus?

Liz knocked on my open door, leaning inside. "Hey. We're heading to the store. Sure you don't want to come with?"

"No, that's okay." I held up my book. "This is getting good."

"All right. See ya."

"Bye."

I waited, my book forgotten, until I felt the vibration of the garage door opening. Then I slipped off my bed, making it halfway downstairs when I heard it close. As I slipped through the front door, Stevie's red Jeep was rolling down the block. They were out of sight by the time I made it next door.

The déjà vu was staggering as I stood on Toren's porch. But unlike yesterday, there was no ringing phone. Just a doorbell and my thundering heart as I waited for him to answer.

His expression was as hard as granite when he opened the door. His jaw was still clenched, but he'd turned his hat backward again. No man had a right to be that sexy when he was sweaty.

"This is weird," I blurted.

"You think?" he deadpanned, dragging a hand over that chiseled jaw and the stubble he hadn't shaved this morning. It scraped against his palm. Two weeks ago, when he'd kissed me for the first time, it had scraped against my skin too.

I liked his stubble. And the backward hat.

"What's up?"

"Hear me out." I slipped past him and walked inside.

"Jennsyn," he growled, but he closed the door as I padded into the living room.

"I don't want it to be weird."

"Not sure there's another option." He sighed, pulling off that hat and tossing it on the island. Then he raked his fingers through his hair.

My fingers itched to tousle it for him. "Stop that."

He froze. "Stop what?"

"Nothing," I muttered.

The man could breathe, and it would turn me on. That had to stop. Immediately. Somehow, we needed to smother this charge between us.

When he finger combed his hair, I wanted no reaction. Nothing beyond a platonic appreciation for a good-looking man. I wanted to see him dressed in plain, athletic shorts without the overwhelming urge to yank them off his narrow hips and drop to my knees. I wanted to meet him at the mailbox without a heated or awkward stare. Just a hello for a neighbor and acquaintance.

"I need to know more about you. Right now, you're the mysterious hot guy who lives next door." And delivers incredible orgasms. "It's . . . attractive. Do me a favor and ruin that for me."

He quirked an eyebrow. "So you think if you learn more about me, then I'll no longer be attractive."

"Exactly."

"Jennsyn—"

"Please." I held up a hand before he could protest. "Just humor me."

He cast his eyes to the ceiling, his hands planted on his narrow hips like he was praying for patience. When he finally met my stare again, it was with a long exhale. "Fine. What do you want to know?"

"Where did you go to college?"

"Here. I grew up in Mission. I played for the Wildcats."

I wandered to his fireplace, dragging a finger over the mantel. We didn't have a fireplace, which was a shame because I loved to read, and sitting by a crackling fire was the perfect place to read. "Were you the best player on the team?"

"No. That was Ford Ellis. He's the new head coach."

"Oh." Dang.

I'd thought for sure he'd say that he'd been the best. But I liked that he hadn't. His answer was honest. Humble. Real. It made me like him that much more.

Maybe this random question-and-answer session was a bad idea.

"What kind of music do you like?" As long as he didn't say country—

"Country."

Well, shit. I guess I should have seen that coming. We were in Montana. Not that I'd had many, but my previous boyfriends had all liked hip-hop and rap. Though Christian had been into alternative rock. Every time I'd turned on country in my car, he'd turned the volume down.

"How old are you?" I asked.

"Thirty-three."

I stopped walking. "Thirty-three? No. No you are not."

He didn't look thirty-three. He looked like he was in his late twenties.

Oh God. He was twelve years older. Twelve.

"Ancient, right?" he teased.

I swallowed hard. "I'm twenty-one."

He rubbed both hands over his face. "I, uh, figured that out yesterday."

The age gap should have been sobering. It should have

been the detail I'd been seeking to send me running out of his house. Except . . . I didn't care.

I should care. Why didn't I care?

Twelve years was a big difference. Except I was an adult. He was an adult. And I just didn't care that he was thirty-three. Not even a little bit.

This wasn't working. Why wasn't it working?

"Favorite movies?" I asked as I walked toward the TV cabinet against the wall, kneeling to open the cabinet. With any luck, he'd have a stash of porn and it would be so gross and cliché that I'd go home with a sour taste in my mouth.

"Jennsyn, don't—"

The cabinet was stuffed with DVDs, so many that a handful spilled out from the open door. Except it wasn't cheap porn.

I picked up three movies off the floor, leafing through the cases. *"Pretty in Pink. The Karate Kid. Days of Thunder."*

He grumbled something from the kitchen, but I was too busy scanning titles.

"I was expecting sports." Not movies from the eighties and nineties.

Toren crossed his arms and stared at the floor, but not before I caught the slight blush creeping into his cheeks. He looked . . . shy?

Of course it was sexy too.

I took the three movies in my hand and stood, closing the cabinet. Then I walked over and saluted him with the DVDs. "I need these for research purposes."

"What do you mean, research?"

"If I don't like the movies, then I probably won't like you."

He blinked. "Huh?"

Okay, so that wasn't exactly solid logic but I was grasping at straws. "It's worth a shot."

He opened his mouth but closed it with an audible click of his teeth.

Wait. What if I liked the movies?

Was that what he'd been going to ask? *Probably.* Ugh.

"It's still weird."

"Yeah." His hair was a disaster, sticking up at all angles.

I clutched the movies tighter to keep my fingers from brushing an errant piece from his temple. "Do you regret it? The party?"

"No," he murmured, his focus dropping to my mouth.

"Neither do I," I whispered. For both our sakes, I took a step away. "Goodbye, Toren."

He didn't move as I wandered to the front door. "Goodbye, Jennsyn."

THE PARTY
TOREN

"The floor is kind of dirty," I warned Jennsyn as I opened the door that led to the garage. "Want a pair of shoes?"

"I'm good." She stepped past me and off the single stair to the cold, concrete floor, then looked to her bare toes. "Does it bug you? Some people don't like bare feet."

"No." I walked barefoot often myself.

"I hate socks," she said as she made her way to the fridge. "But I don't like wearing shoes without socks. It's a quirk. Any chance I get, I skip both."

"Why don't you like socks?"

"They're like straitjackets for your toes." She shrugged and yanked open the door to the garage fridge.

"Sounds like you need bigger socks."

"Maybe." She laughed, bending to inspect the shelves. "Well, if you ever run out of space for your ketchup bottles, you've got plenty of room to expand out here."

"Huh?" That couldn't be right. Even if Parks had taken a few beers, this fridge had been packed.

I crossed the garage, standing at Jennsyn's side to peer

over her shoulder. A rush of cold air hit my face when I looked into the fridge—the empty fridge. Apparently my new neighbors had been thirsty.

"Bastards," I muttered. "They even drank all my Dr. Pepper."

Jennsyn pulled in her lips to hide a smile.

"It was full earlier." Color coded by rainbow. Coke to Fanta to Squirt to Mountain Dew to Bud Light. Sometimes, I'd pick out a six-pack based on can alone, just to add a different color to the shelves.

Actually. Maybe it was good that Jennsyn didn't see the garage fridge in its normal state.

"Never mind." I closed the door and faced her, hoping this wasn't the end to our night.

She turned on her bare toes, scanning the garage. The minute her gaze landed on my truck, she cocked her head to the side. "You need a car wash."

My silver Tundra was nearly a two-tone pickup at this point, considering the mud and dirt caked on the bottom half. "You're not wrong."

An adorable crease formed between her eyebrows.

"What?" I asked.

"I'm trying to puzzle out the man with a refrigerator like yours and a truck like this."

I chuckled. "And I'm trying to figure out the woman in bare feet who helps clean up a party for a guy she just met."

Jennsyn's smile was brighter than any of tonight's fireworks.

My heart stopped. Again.

Hell. This whole party might have actually been worth it. To meet her, I'd let my friends and strangers clear out my beverage stash every fucking day.

"Any other refrigerators I should know about?" she asked.

"I've got a minifridge in the basement by the pool table."

She hummed, still staring at my dirty truck. Then she lifted on her toes and walked past me. The back of her hand brushed against my knuckles as she passed me for the door, and that brief touch was like a lightning bolt. "All right. Let's see this minifridge."

"You got it."

CHAPTER FIVE

TOREN

The scents of rubber and metal and concrete greeted me as I pushed open the steel door to the weight room at the fieldhouse. The lights flickered on with the movement, illuminating the space.

Thick mats covered sections of the floor. The weight machines and silver racks gleamed under the florescent bulbs. The Wildcat logo, painted the school's official royal blue, was my only companion this morning.

It was early, not quite six. Normally, I saved my workouts for the lunch hour. I'd join the other coaches to lift around noon. But coming to the fieldhouse at dawn was apparently my new routine. Not only was the gym guaranteed to be empty and quiet, but it gave me a reason to escape my house.

Or . . . the neighbor's house.

How was it that I'd gone two entire weeks after the party without so much as seeing a glimpse of Jennsyn? Yet now that I knew where she lived, I couldn't seem to avoid her.

Yesterday, I'd been in my office, paying a few bills, when

I'd glanced up to see her walk across the street for the mail-boxes. She'd been in bare feet again, walking on her toes.

The day before that, I'd been pulling into my driveway at the same moment she'd been reversing her sleek black BMW out of her own.

The day before that, I'd gotten up early to go for a light run, planning on skipping the gym for a change, only to open the door just as she jogged by. Her long legs had eaten up the sidewalk until she'd hopped over the curb and disappeared around the block.

I'd left immediately for campus.

It had been ten days since she'd marched into my house and told me I was mysterious. Ten days since she'd asked me to ruin that mystery. Ten days since she'd stolen a few of my old movies. And in those ten days, she'd stolen every one of my wandering thoughts.

The only time I managed to put her to the back of my mind was when I was working out or working. So I'd been spending extra time in my office and this weight room, pushing my body to the extreme in the hopes that sooner rather than later, Jennsyn Bell would fade to a memory.

I pulled my earbuds from the pocket of my shorts, fitting them in tight before cranking some music. Then I put my water bottle and phone on a bench before climbing onto an elliptical to warm up.

After fifteen minutes with the resistance at full, sweat beaded at my temples as I wiped down the machine. I reached behind my head, fisting the cotton of my shirt to pull it off. The moment it was free, the door opened.

My pounding heart came to a dead stop.

Jennsyn walked into the room, white earbuds fixed firmly into her ears. Her blue eyes were locked on her phone

63

as her fingers flew across the screen. She snarled at whatever she typed. With a hard tap, she sent her message and looked up.

She came to a sliding stop when she spotted me. Her eyes widened.

Fuck. What had happened to her morning jogs?

Every athlete had a code to get into the fieldhouse after hours. We wanted this place to be used by the players and staff. To be viewed as a sanctuary of sorts. If a student wanted to work out at odd hours, this was their place. We didn't want them joining the twenty-four-hour fitness place in town or using the campus's gym that was open to all students and often crowded.

I'd always advocated for players to have access. Except as Jennsyn and I stared at each other, both unmoving, maybe that had been a mistake. Maybe *I* needed to find a twenty-four-hour fitness place. The idea of using cheap equipment made me cringe, but it might be my only choice until this tension and awkwardness could pass.

Avoiding each other was impossible. While the football and volleyball teams weren't often at the same events, we all shared this building. We all shared this weight room and these halls.

And damn it, she lived next door.

I used my shirt to wipe the sweat from my face, then plucked an earbud out as she did the same. "Hey."

"Hi. Sorry." She gave me an exaggerated frown. "I didn't realize anyone would be here."

"It's fine." I waved it off.

It wasn't fine. Nothing was fine.

She was a student. She was only twenty-one years old,

way too damn young. Except she walked into a room and every cell in my being tuned into her frequency.

Jennsyn was dressed in a pair of skin-tight black leggings that hugged the toned muscles of her thighs and calves. They left absolutely nothing to the imagination. Not that I needed to imagine a damn thing.

The memory of her naked in my bed from nearly a month ago was as fresh as if it had happened last night.

She was in a black sports bra, her stomach bare. I'd licked nearly every inch of that stomach as I'd trailed down to the sensitive flesh between her thighs.

My cock twitched. *Damn it.*

"You're not working out with the volleyball team?" I asked, clearing my throat.

"Later." She shrugged. "I like to do my own workout every morning."

Then she'd join the coaching staff and other players for at least two more weight-training and conditioning programs, plus two practices.

The end of July meant the fall sports teams were in full preseason swing. The football team was here six hours per day.

Only a few of my best players would add their own self-imposed workouts.

Jennsyn fitted her earbud back into place, then strode across the gym to the far wall. She took a jump rope off its hook, then moved to an open space and began to move.

I headed to the row of power racks, planning on an upper-body lift, focusing on my shoulders. It should have taken less than a minute to set up a standing barbell press. But every few seconds, I glanced to Jennsyn, still skipping.

Her hair was tied up in a ponytail, the end swaying as she moved. Her footwork was quick and graceful. She stayed light on her toes as her wrists whipped the rope around and around.

I couldn't seem to keep my eyes off her, but she stared straight ahead, the picture of focus.

My mouth went dry.

She was stunning when she smiled. Absolutely gorgeous. But like this? Serious and locked into the zone? The world narrowed until there was only Jennsyn and the steady tick of the rope as it whacked the floor.

A flush rose in her cheeks. Sweat glistened on her skin. If she noticed me staring, she didn't so much as blink in my direction.

Had my mysteriousness worn off? Maybe she'd learned enough about me that I'd ruined the illusion. In the past ten days, while I'd been desperate to forget her, she'd managed to do what I could not.

It stung. This entire fucking situation burned. But if she'd managed to forget the night of the party, well . . . I'd keep trying until I could say the same.

So I tore my gaze away and got to work, focusing on the burn of my muscles as I pushed them harder and harder. With every rep, every movement, I expected Jennsyn to fade into the background along with everything else in the room.

I might as well have asked the sun to stop shining.

My gaze caught on her every time she moved around the room. Until finally, after nearly an hour, she moved to the mats in the corner to stretch.

She spread her feet shoulder width apart and bent at the waist, folding her long, lean frame in half.

Before I could start drooling over her ass, I went to a pullup bar mounted on the wall. With a quick hop, I let myself hang for a moment, crossing my ankles. Then I made my way to fifty, up and down, up and down. When I dropped and turned, my arms on fire, a pair of dazzling blue eyes were waiting.

Jennsyn pulled in her lips to hide a smile.

So . . .

I wasn't the only one staring today.

Thank fuck. Yeah, it made it more complicated if we were both struggling. But if this attraction was mutual, at least I wasn't the skeezy old guy creeping on her while she was just trying to move on.

She plucked out an earbud as her gaze roamed down my naked chest. Her tongue darted out to lick her bottom lip.

Blood rushed to my cock. I groaned, dragging a hand over my face as I huffed a laugh. It shouldn't be funny. This was akin to torture. "Fuck, Jennsyn."

"Sorry." She giggled. "It's still weird."

Weird. She kept using that word.

It fit. Sort of. Painful would have been my choice.

It was goddamn painful trying to shove her out of my mind. It was painful every time I remembered she was a student. It was painful how much I wanted her anyway.

She opened her mouth to say something, but before she could speak, the door opened and two guys from the basketball team walked inside.

"Hey, Coach." One of them jerked up his chin toward me.

The other's eyes locked on Jennsyn, a grin stretching across his mouth as his gaze raked over her body, head to toe.

Shithead. "Good morning," I said, louder and sharper than necessary.

The other kid's attention whipped my way, blinking like he'd just realized I was here. "Morning, Coach."

I walked over to the bench where I'd left my phone and T-shirt earlier, drying my face again before chugging my water.

As the guys came deeper into the room, Jennsyn headed for the door, her face blank and her chin held high. The idiots watched her every step, practically drooling.

Or maybe I was the idiot, thinking I had some sort of claim on that beauty.

My routine usually included sit-ups and stretching, but I needed some fresh air, so I headed into the hallway, not letting myself search for which way Jennsyn had gone. I picked up my clothes for the day from my office, then ducked into the locker room for a shower.

A cold shower.

———

FOOTBALL WAS MY FOCUS. Football was my salvation. From the moment I'd stepped out of the locker room this morning, dressed in navy shorts and a gray Wildcats T-shirt, I concentrated on work. I refused to let myself think about Jennsyn Bell.

My workday started at a coaches meeting with Ford. Then we headed to the first practice of the day, followed by a meeting with the defense to hammer out a few new formations. Another team practice. Another team workout.

When I finally returned to my office after five, I sagged in my chair and pulled out my phone. Faith had texted.

I made banana bread today. Want a loaf?

I replied immediately. *Be there in thirty.*

Anything was better than going home, where I'd inevitably spend too much time glancing out the windows that faced Jennsyn's house. So I collected my things and flipped off the lights, stepping into the hallway as Aspen came walking my direction.

"Hey, Toren," she said.

"Hey. How's it going?"

"Good? Maybe? I'm not sure yet. Ask me again in two weeks."

I chuckled. "Uh-oh. What's going on?"

"Oh, you know how it is when you add new players."

"Yep." It took a while for the team to gel together.

She sighed. "Yeah. It's one thing to add freshmen into the mix. But a senior who happens to be a national superstar has been . . . different."

Wait. So Jennsyn wasn't meshing with the team? She lived with two of them. Were they not getting along?

"It'll be fine." Aspen forced a smile. "I'm just a little frazzled after today's practice. It was the first one with the team but didn't exactly go great."

"Anything I can do to help?" Not that I had a damn clue about volleyball. But I'd listen if Aspen needed to vent. That, and maybe I'd pick up a few tidbits about Jennsyn.

Maybe her idea of getting to know each other was valid. If she wasn't the mysterious, drop-dead gorgeous woman living next door, the appeal might wear thin.

Jennsyn was young, the same age as the seniors on the football team. There wasn't a day that went by that one or more of the guys didn't do something stupid to annoy me. Granted, Jennsyn was ten times more mature than her male counterparts, but still. It was worth a shot.

I couldn't exactly ask Aspen for details, not without

raising suspicion. Jennsyn might be new to the Wildcats, but there was no reason for a football coach to ask for details about a volleyball player. But if Aspen offered them up? I'd sure listen.

"Happy to be a sounding board," I added.

"Thanks. I might take you up on that later." She pointed to the ceiling. "I'm actually heading up to Millie's office. She's always got good advice."

"That she does." I masked my disappointment with a smile. "Have a good night."

"You too."

It was probably for the best to stay out of it. I had plenty of my own players to worry about. Yet on the drive out to the farm, I couldn't stop thinking about Jennsyn. Not about the sex, nor the attraction or keeping it a secret.

But her spot on the team.

Was it Jennsyn's talent that had shifted the dynamic of the volleyball team? Or the fact that she'd probably taken another player's spot? She didn't strike me as an arrogant player but maybe she was different on the court. Stevie and Liz seemed nice enough, but could they be struggling at home?

All thoughts of Jennsyn vanished when I parked outside Faith's white farmhouse just as she came walking out of the barn.

With a dead chicken in her hand and tears streaking down her face.

"Shit." I hopped out. "What happened?"

"That fucking dog." She stabbed a finger toward the neighbor's property in the distance. To the shitty chain-link fence that never managed to contain the mutt.

This was the third time this summer that the dog had

gotten out, run over and killed a chicken. It was a nice enough dog to people and was always friendly with the boys. But if the chickens were out of their coop, it attacked. Probably because the dog didn't get enough food.

Faith made her living off this small farm. She grew vegetables from her garden and sold them at the weekend farmers markets. She was a beekeeper and collected honey. She had goats and made soaps from their milk. Every fall she harvested her pumpkin patch and sold them in town. And all year round, she sold eggs from her chickens.

That animal was part of her livelihood.

"I'll go talk to Noreen," I said.

"I was just about to go over there," she said, sniffling as she blinked the tears away. "I'll do it."

The tears weren't entirely about the chicken, were they? Some were about a widowed mom of four who was carrying more on her shoulders than she should have to alone.

"Where are the boys?"

"Beck's at a friend's house. Abel went to see his girlfriend. Dane and Cabe are inside."

"Go hug your kids. Leave that chicken," I said, pointing to the dirt. "Go inside and take a breather. I'll deal with it."

She opened her mouth, probably to argue, but then her shoulders sagged as the dead animal dropped to the ground by her boots. "All right."

I reached into the back seat of the truck, fishing out a pair of leather gloves. Then I dealt with the chicken, getting a shovel from the barn to bury it on the edge of the property, hopefully deep enough that nothing would dig it up. After grabbing some tools, I walked to the neighbor's place, pounding a fist on the door.

It took Noreen three rounds of me knocking to answer.

She was wearing a faded, floral nightgown and had a cigarette pinched between her lips. "H-hi, Toren."

"Hey, Noreen."

She squinted at the sunlight, probably because she hadn't been outside in days. Maybe weeks. Behind her, the hallway was so full of clutter that it was a wonder she'd managed to clear a wide enough path to get to the door.

For as long as I'd known Noreen, she'd been an extreme hoarder. Years ago, she'd been more apt to come outside and head into town. These days, she was practically a recluse.

"We've got a problem with your dog again."

She gulped. "Don't take him."

"I'm not going to take him." I sighed. "But he keeps getting out of the fence and killed another one of Faith's chickens."

She took a long drag from her cigarette as her face paled. "Sorry. I tried to fix the fence last time. He's a good boy, he just . . . gets excited."

"Yeah. How about this time, I fix the fence? That okay with you?"

"Thanks." She nodded and finished her smoke.

I took my roll of wire and plyers all around her yard, fixing various holes and gaps. The property was nearly as packed as Noreen's house. Grass and weeds and thistles grew waist-high in between old junker cars and tires and boxes of discarded parts. Before he'd died, Noreen's husband had been a mechanic. This was his boneyard.

It took almost two hours to fix the fence. Noreen's idea of fixing meant shifting boxes in front of the holes. She'd blocked one opening by piling three rotting garbage bags full of trash in the way. Except the dog had already rooted through the plastic, ripping a hole in its side. And then it had wiggled its way free.

When I finally finished and returned to Faith's, she came outside with a glass of lemonade.

"Thank you," she said.

"No problem." I took a long drink. "You okay?"

"Yeah." She gave me a sad smile. "Abel and Beck just got home. Abel was supposed to clean the chicken coop tonight but his girlfriend dumped him, so I'm giving him a pass."

"Ouch. He okay?"

She shrugged, looking like she was about to cry again. "When I asked him that question, he said yes. But then he slammed his bedroom door so hard it shook the walls."

"Want me to go talk to him?"

"Maybe later. I think he needs time alone."

"All right." I jerked my chin toward the chicken coop. "You're going to clean that for him, aren't you?"

She sighed. "Yeah. I've let him slack and put it off. Now it's overdue. But I'm not going to make him do it tonight."

"I'll help."

"No, you haven't even had dinner yet." She waved me toward my truck. "Go home. You already helped with Noreen."

"Cleaning will go faster with the two of us." So I strode toward the barn before she could argue, returning Uncle Evan's tools to their rightful places, then met her in the coop.

By the time I climbed in my truck to drive home, I smelled like chicken shit, ammonia and sweat.

A hot shower was calling, but my stomach growled as I walked through the door, so I washed my hands and took out a cutting board. My knife was poised over the loaf of banana bread Faith had sent home with me when the doorbell rang.

"Now what?" I frowned and walked to answer.

Jennsyn stood on my porch, the DVDs she'd taken clutched in her hand. "Hi."

"Hey." My heart thumped too hard. I was in no mood for company. But I'd take hers, even for the minute it would take her to return those movies.

Like she had ten days ago, she came inside without an invitation. Her nose scrunched up as she stepped past me. "You stink. Why do you stink?"

"I was working on my aunt's farm tonight."

"Ah." She gave me a sideways glance. "Is this like a side hustle? Or is your dream to become a farmer and this is your exit strategy from coaching?"

"No." I chuckled. "I have zero desire to be a farmer. But my uncle died a while back, and I try to pitch in with my aunt whenever I've got time."

"Oh." Jennsyn's eyes softened. "I'm sorry about your uncle."

"Me too."

She wandered deeper into the house, carrying the movies to the TV cabinet.

Was it a good thing or bad that she felt so comfortable in my home? Bad. Probably. Except why did it feel . . . normal?

"I've never been on a farm," she said, sitting on the floor and crossing her legs.

I opened my mouth, about to offer to take her to Faith's one of these days, but remembered myself and stopped short.

This had to end. It should have already ended.

My stomach growled again, so I went back to the cutting board and sliced a piece of bread. "Want some banana bread?"

"No, thanks. I already had dinner." She leaned forward

and slid the movies she'd borrowed into place, then she browsed the other titles, piling a few in her lap. "This one is still in the plastic."

She held up *Top Gun*.

"I've got it digitally," I said, taking a bite and chewing.

"The fact that you have physical DVDs is actually kind of—"

"Ancient?" Maybe if I kept reminding us both of the age difference, it would help me remember she was a student.

She flashed me a smile. "I was going to say endearing but if you'd rather say ancient, that works too."

I grinned and took another bite. Either it was the food or being home after a long day or Jennsyn's presence, maybe a little bit of all three, but for the first time in hours, I breathed. A full, calming breath.

"I don't even have a player for these," she said, picking two more before she closed the cabinet. "I had to rent them."

"Then why are you taking my DVDs?"

She shrugged and stood. "These are actually horrible movies. You know that, right?"

"Does that mean your research is working, and I'm no longer mysterious?"

"No." She frowned, the humor on her face fading as she stared at me for a long moment. Then she sighed and walked toward the island, her bare feet nearly silent on my hardwood floors.

She owned shoes. She'd been in a nice pair of Nikes this morning. But apparently shoes were optional when she was at home.

"I wouldn't have picked you as a guy who liked cheesy movies." There was a hint of curiosity in her voice, like she was trying to puzzle it out.

It was actually sort of simple if she knew the reason. But tonight, I wasn't going to explain.

My day had been long enough already.

"Are the shows on Teen Network not cheesy?" I asked.

She laughed and rolled her eyes. "Ha. Ha. Very funny."

I laughed too and ate another bite of bread.

"I couldn't stop staring at you while you were working out today," she whispered.

Really? I'd only caught her staring once. Maybe she should give me some pointers at being discreet.

Her gaze traveled to my arms, lingering for a moment as a pink flush crept into her cheeks. Then she dropped her gaze to the floor, hugging those movies closer to her chest.

When she finally looked up, she was wearing that same solid, hard expression she'd had this morning in the gym. "You stink."

"I know."

She took a step away. "Goodbye, Toren."

"Goodbye, Jennsyn."

The moment the door closed behind her, I went upstairs. And did my best not to think of her while I took another cold shower.

CHAPTER SIX

JENNSYN

C oach Quinn's office smelled like cinnamon, cloves and pears. It was the best-smelling room in this fieldhouse, and the last place I wanted to be sitting.

If this spring had taught me anything, it was that nothing good came from being called into the head coach's office.

She gave me a smile from her side of the desk, her hands gently clasped in her lap. "How's it going, Jennsyn?"

"Fine."

"Is everything going well living with Stevie and Liz?"

"Yep. They're great."

I didn't actually know them well enough to say that with confidence, but they were clean and courteous and neither seemed to mind that I spent most hours at home in my room, keeping to myself.

"That's good." There was a strain to her smile, like this already wasn't going how she'd expected, and I'd been here for less than five minutes. "Are you enjoying practices?"

I nodded. "Yes."

There'd been some minor squabbles over the past week. I

was new on the team and not exactly the type to be pushed around. There was no doubt that I was the best. If the other girls thought I'd sit on the bench while they pouted over losing their friend and former teammate, they were wrong.

I was going to play and play hard. I didn't know how to take it easy on the court, whether that was in practice or a game. I gave it my all, every day. One of the girls, Megan, had told me to chill on our first day of practice.

I'd told her to get off the court if she wasn't going to work.

We'd only had full team practices with our coaches for a week. Before that, they'd outlined practice and training regimens for us but hadn't actually been able to coach us until we were within two weeks of the volleyball preseason. It was just one of those rules everyone had to abide by.

Unless you played football. The NCAA gave them much more leeway, and the football coaches had been working with their players for weeks.

"And training?" she asked. "It's probably easier than you're used to, but you're feeling okay?" There was a way she asked the questions, like she was searching for something.

This meeting would go a lot quicker if she just cut to the chase.

"Training has been great. You've got excellent facilities." Yes, the program was easier than what I was used to, but with the all-access code to get into the building, I'd been supplementing her requirements.

"Good. That's good." She sighed, her shoulders falling. "Why are you here, Jennsyn?"

"Um, because you asked me to come in after practice."

"No, not my office. Here." She pointed to the floor. "Treasure State. Why are you here?"

"Oh." The chase.

Coach Quinn was the first person to ask me that since I'd moved to Montana over a month ago. My roommates hadn't pried, not that I'd given them much of an opening to talk to me about anything personal. None of the other girls on the team had asked why I'd transferred. And beyond them, the only other person I knew in Mission was Toren.

Maybe he would have asked if he weren't a coach and we could actually spend time together.

It had been a week since I'd gone over to his house to swap movies. My plan had been to return the three I'd borrowed and leave, but when he'd opened the door, he'd looked so tired and worn, I hadn't been able to leave until I was sure he was all right. So I'd caved to the temptation of his warm, inviting home and slipped inside.

Now I had more movies to return.

Maybe after that, our goodbyes would actually stick.

"I'm just here to play volleyball," I told Coach Quinn. For one year.

A year of playing college volleyball on my terms. A year to see if I actually even enjoyed the game.

Just one year.

Then I'd have my degree and . . . something.

Something would happen when this year was over. I just wasn't exactly sure what that something was quite yet.

My plans were like juggling pins. Every plan I'd made— every plan that had been made for me—had been tossed in the air the minute I'd walked into the compliance office and asked to be entered into the transfer portal. Now I just had to decide which plan to catch while the others fell to the floor.

"Can I be honest about something?" Coach asked, waiting for my nod. "When I got your email in May after you'd entered the portal saying that you were interested in playing here, I thought it was a mistake. I didn't actually believe it was happening until our initial call. I didn't ask you then why you wanted to leave Stanford for Treasure State. But I should have. I'll admit, I was more interested in getting you on the team than asking questions."

"It's okay." I'd been interested in getting on her team too.

"Why'd you leave Stanford?" she asked. "You were the star of a major team. You played on the U18, U19 and U20 national teams. I imagine you'll have plenty of offers to play internationally after you graduate. So what are you doing here?"

Why had I put my future professional volleyball career in jeopardy to move to a smaller conference and school? That was the real question.

That was my mother's question too.

"It's complicated," I said.

Coach Quinn blinked and waited, like she expected me to keep talking. But I didn't have anything else to say.

She'd gotten me a full scholarship, and though it had meant a junior on the team had been cut, that was just the way these things worked. Every girl on the team knew their spot was contingent on performance.

In the scheme of things, I'd been an inexpensive upgrade. At Stanford, I'd had a monthly allowance. Thousands of dollars had been deposited into my bank account each month as a stipend to cover food and rent. Plus all of my tuition and fees had been covered.

To come to Treasure State, I'd taken a hit financially. My stipend was smaller, which was part of the reason I'd agreed to live with Stevie and Liz when I really just wanted a place of my own. But at the moment, it was cheaper to split rent.

It was only for a year.

I'd play my heart out for the Wildcats this year, but otherwise, my motivations for leaving Stanford were my own.

"Okay." Coach Quinn sighed, realizing she'd slammed into a brick wall. "On another note, I got a call from your mother today."

My entire body went rigid. It shouldn't have been a shock. Mom had always been in tune with my coaches. But for the past month, I'd thought maybe, just maybe, she'd finally backed off. She'd finally respected a boundary.

Nope. She might have avoided the topic of volleyball during our weekly calls, but apparently a month was all the reprieve I'd been given.

"It was, uh . . ." Coach drew in a long breath, sagging in her chair as she exhaled. "Well, that was maybe the strangest call I've had in my years working here. I've had some parents who get passionate about their child's career, and usually I tell them that if I wanted to deal with parents, I would be coaching high school, not college. I don't talk to parents. But your mom . . ."

Was a volleyball legend. And a woman who didn't take no for an answer.

"I watched her play when I was younger," Coach said. "When she was on the Olympic team. It was a bit surreal talking to Katy Bell."

Great. Was this going to be a lovefest about my mother? I'd gladly skip hearing about Mom's accolades and accomplishments. If I wanted that laundry list, all I had to do was ask her.

"She's very, um . . . bold, isn't she?"

I nodded. "Bold is one word to describe her." Domineering. Obsessive. Those were others.

"Well, I guess it's true what they say. Never meet your heroes. She wasn't very happy when I told her I didn't need advice on how to coach my team."

That was not at all what I'd expected her to say. Good for Coach Quinn. The corner of my mouth turned up. "No, I bet she wasn't."

Mom thought that her star status as a volleyball legend gave her the authority to interject herself with my coaches. Most let her without hesitation.

The fact that Coach Quinn hadn't caved was impressive. She'd done what plenty of men in her shoes hadn't done in all my years on the court.

Coach Quinn was younger than any coach I'd had before, probably in her midthirties. Part of the reason I'd come to Treasure State was because she was a woman. Too many men ruled women's volleyball. I'd only ever had male coaches, and this year, I'd wanted a change.

Maybe I'd wanted to see how a female handled the head coach role. Maybe to feel out if it was a job I could see myself doing someday.

"I apologize," I told her. "For my mother."

She waved it off. "It's fine."

"No, it isn't. It won't happen again."

Coach stared at me for a long moment, like maybe her shutting down Mom would earn her my secrets.

It wouldn't.

She crashed up against that brick wall again, and this time, didn't bother to push further. "Thanks for coming down. If you need anything at all, my door is almost always open."

"Thank you." I stood and collected my gym bag from the floor. Then I left her office, pulling my phone from a pocket the minute I hit the hallway.

Most of the offices I passed were dark, the coaches having already left for the day. I made sure to put plenty of distance between myself and Coach Quinn's office before I ducked inside the next dark room, hit my mother's name and eased the door closed.

"Oh, good," she answered. "I just got off the phone with—"

"Mother," I snapped, my voice too loud. It filled the space, bouncing off the plain gray walls. "You called Coach Quinn."

"So?"

"That was your first and last call to her."

Mom sighed. "Jennsyn—"

"Stop. Please." My voice, still too loud, shook. "Why can't you stop?"

"Because you have all of this talent. You have what other girls would *kill* for. Maybe you're okay throwing that all away for some wilderness adventure at a no-name school in Montana, but I'm not going to let you ruin your life. Someday, you'll realize this was a mistake. I'm just trying to triage the damage."

It wasn't the first time I'd heard this lecture. The words changed slightly with each variation, but the message was loud and clear.

I'd fucked my entire life by coming to Montana.

Now she was forced to pick up the pieces even though I'd never asked for her help.

Maybe it would have meant something if I believed it was truly for me. But Mom's motivations were selfish. All the years she'd spent honing my skills, the years she'd spent asking for favors and pulling strings, couldn't be wasted.

Mom liked to pretend this was for my own good. But it was for her. It was always for her.

"Do not call her again." I hung up without another word, then made sure the phone was on silent before shoving it into my bag with my sweaty shoes and clothes from practice.

Why couldn't she let me live my life? Would she ever stop meddling? I was twenty-one years old, and she acted the same as when I'd been in seventh grade. When she'd started introducing me to coaches and pitching me for collegiate programs.

Seventh grade. I'd been twelve.

Was it my fault for not pushing back sooner? Maybe it wasn't fair that I expected her to stop pushing. I'd gone along with her plans, enjoyed them and reveled in them and supported them, for so long, that she probably had whiplash from me slamming on the brakes.

Sooner rather than later, she had to catch up.

Sooner rather than later, she'd have to back off.

I gave myself a moment to breathe before walking to the door and yanking it open. I nearly collided with a wall of muscle.

Toren.

My heart skipped. "Um, hi."

He stood, arms crossed, just beyond the threshold.

"What are you doing?" I asked, glancing past him into the hall. Was he following me? What if someone saw us?

"What are *you* doing?" He gave a pointed look to the placard beside the door.

I leaned past the frame, seeing his name in navy letters on a silver plate. "Oh. Sorry."

With a quick check side to side, making sure we were alone, he planted a hand on my stomach, pressing me backward as he came inside, closing the door behind us. "Is there a reason why you're in my office?"

"I needed to make a phone call. I didn't realize it was your office."

He cast a pointed glance to a bookshelf against the wall. On the top, there was a framed photo of him from what had to be his college days.

Toren's hair was sweaty and sticking up at odd angles. He was in a Wildcats uniform, holding his helmet at his side. He looked young and happy, his smile bright. Had I actually paid attention to the room, that photo would have totally snared my attention.

"I swear, this wasn't some elaborate scheme to sneak into your office. I just needed a quiet place to call my mother."

"These doors aren't exactly soundproof." He hooked a thumb over his shoulder. "Everything all right?"

"Great," I lied.

Toren's lips pursed but he didn't push for an explanation.

At the moment, he was the only person in my life who didn't expect anything from me. Maybe that was why I'd taken more of his movies, knowing full well I'd have to bring them back. I just wanted a few minutes of his company.

Because when we were together, I could breathe.

He was wearing a pair of gray shorts and a white Treasure State T-shirt that strained across his broad chest. He had on a blue hat, the brim shielding his light eyes. He smelled like fresh air and sunshine. A hint of his cologne caught my nose, masculine and clean.

I drew it in, feeling the knot in my chest loosen.

"Everything isn't great, actually." The words came out without my permission on an exhale. When was the last time I'd admitted that to someone? I regretted it immediately.

"Want to talk it through?"

I almost said yes. Almost.

"No." I shook my head, glancing around his office before I broke and changed my mind.

The bookshelf was sparse but not empty. One shelf had that photo of him in uniform. Another had two trophies, awards he'd won as a coach. The third shelf had a Wildcat helmet, the same style as the one he'd worn in the picture.

"No books," I whispered.

No surprise.

His desk was a mess of papers and binders.

Never before had I seen a refrigerator as orderly as Toren's. His house seemed to always be clean. But his truck was filthy and his desk in disarray.

I liked that he was both organized and chaotic. That he had quirks like any normal man.

As I inspected the bare walls, his gaze was on my profile. That gaze was as potent as any touch.

It reminded me of the party on the Fourth. I'd been curious about the noise next door, so I'd gone over to see what was happening for myself. The moment Toren had spotted me, I'd felt his stare.

"Jennsyn." That deep, smooth voice rolled down my spine like a caress.

There was a lot about Toren that had caught my attention at his party. His tall, broad frame. His chiseled jaw and breathtaking face. His dazzling eyes. But it was his voice that had sealed the deal. His voice was the reason I'd broken all of my own rules and spent the night in his bed.

"What?" I faced him, my breath hitching at the intensity in those eyes. It was too much to hold, so I dropped my own gaze to his mouth.

I should have kissed him the morning after the party. Instead of leaving my number, I should have left him with a kiss.

The air between us turned heavy, like an invisible fog of tension and desire.

Toren's throat bobbed.

The sound of a door closing doused the heat in my veins like a bucket of ice water. I stepped away as Toren shifted to the side, dragging a hand over his face.

What were we doing? This wasn't our neighborhood. This wasn't an exchange of misdelivered mail or trading of old DVDs.

I'd come into his office, uninvited. He'd closed the door. If anyone caught us in here, we'd be screwed.

"I'm sorry." I shouldn't have come in here. I shouldn't be in here.

So I slipped past him, inching the door open as I made sure the hallway was empty.

And when I left, I did it without a goodbye.

THE PARTY
JENNSYN

"Who are these kids?" I lifted a picture frame off the corner of Toren's desk.

On the way to the basement, I'd spotted his empty bookshelves and veered into his office to snoop around.

There were four boys in the picture, and the oldest looked to be a teenager. I couldn't picture Toren as the father of a teenager—or a father of four—but maybe they were his brothers.

Three of them had his brown hair, but the fourth, the youngest, had a strawberry-blond mop that fell into his eyes.

"My cousins," he said.

"Ah. They're cute."

"That they are."

I studied the photo for another minute before returning it to the desk and standing from its edge. "Your bookshelves are depressing."

He barked a laugh from where he was leaning against the doorframe, his arms crossed over that broad chest. "They're a little sparse."

"Sparse?" I walked to a shelf, dragging my finger across its empty, flat surface. "They're empty."

"Not entirely." He jerked his chin to the one and only shelf that had books.

Two copies of The Count of Monte Cristo. And three novels I'd never heard of before.

Five books when he had shelves to hold five hundred.

The shelves weren't built into the walls. They weren't permanent fixtures in the office. He'd brought them in. Built them, most likely. The white columns and rows were pristine, just waiting to be filled.

What kind of man had these shelves but no books? If he hadn't already snared my interest, this was the room that would have done it.

Maybe they weren't his shelves at all. Maybe they'd belonged to an ex and he'd taken them during a split. Or maybe they'd been a housewarming gift from a generous family member.

I crossed the office, stopping in front of Toren, who leaned against the office's doorjamb, arms crossed. He didn't so much as budge, even when I inched so close I could feel the heat roll off his body.

"Why don't you have any books?" I asked.

"I haven't read many I wanted to keep."

My heart pinched. That was the saddest statement I'd heard in years.

I loved reading. It was my favorite escape.

"I'd rather them sit empty than crowd them with stories I don't really like."

So he was waiting for the right books.

Oh my God, I was in so much trouble. I'd promised

myself no more men. Not after Christian. I'd vowed to spend this year focused on myself.

For Toren, I might have to break those rules.

"I like that," I said. "A lot, actually."

"Thanks." His smile was magnificent.

It took everything in my power not to rise on my toes and kiss the corner of that smile.

The temperature in the room spiked as he stared down at me. His eyes darkened, like I wasn't the only one thinking about a kiss. But he didn't shift, not even an inch. Not for a touch. Not for a kiss.

Tension coiled around us. Sparks filled the air. We stared at each other in challenge, like we'd spend all night pushing boundaries until one of us finally cracked. There was an unspoken dare between us to see who'd make the first move.

This was the best foreplay I'd ever experienced in my life.

If he'd let me, I'd play all night long.

"So . . . where's that minifridge?"

CHAPTER SEVEN

TOREN

Go Big Blue. Go Big Blue. Go Big Blue.

The bar hosting this postgame event was loud and packed with people, but the Wildcat chant still echoed through my mind even though the first game of the season had ended hours ago.

We'd absolutely crushed the other team. It was a high I'd be riding for hours—*had* been riding for hours.

As a coach, there was a different excitement postgame. As a player, when we'd lost, I'd felt that frustration for the team and in myself if I'd played like shit. But as the coach on the sidelines, every feeling was escalated. Sharper. Harder.

When we lost, I'd feel the disappointment for days. I'd question everything, wondering where I'd gone wrong in teaching my players. Thank fuck, we'd won. I'd actually be able to sleep tonight. These victories, and the pride I felt for my players, was my favorite part about this job.

My defense had been brutal on the field, efficient and synchronized, like we were at the end of a season, not the beginning.

This was going to be a good year. I could feel it in my bones.

A lot of that feeling had to do with the man at my side. Having Ford as the head coach was like a breath of fresh air. He cared about our team, this school, the way I cared about the program.

He was here for the football, not the glory. He stayed out of the political bullshit, and even though events like these were good public relations, Ford looked like he wanted to be somewhere else.

With someone else.

"Ford." I nudged his elbow with mine.

Nothing. The man might as well have been on another planet, not in this bar in downtown Mission.

I nudged him again.

He ripped his gaze from Millie, who stood on the other side of the bar. "Huh? What did you say?"

"I don't know why you're standing here when you clearly want to be over there." I pointed to the opposite end of the room to where Millie was talking with a few people decked out in Wildcat gear. Donors probably.

She was the best damn schmoozer I'd ever met. The fact that she was only the assistant athletic director, not the person in Kurt's position, never failed to baffle me. She ran circles around Kurt and actually had the respect of the staff.

And clearly, she had Ford's attention. His gaze tracked to her again.

"What's happening there?" I asked.

"Nothing."

Liar. Something was going on with them. I hoped, for both their sakes, they were working on putting the past behind them. Maybe starting something new.

They were both my friends. They deserved the best.

They deserved each other.

There was a no-fraternization policy for employees in the same department. How were they going to navigate that mess? Just ignore the rules?

Not my problem. I'd broken the biggest rule of them all. Ford and Millie would get no judgment from me.

Not when I couldn't stop thinking about a certain student.

It had been a month since I'd found Jennsyn in my office. Since that day, I'd done everything in my power to avoid her. If there was even a chance we'd cross paths, I changed my plans. I worked out when I knew the volleyball team was in practice. At home, I only went outside to get the mail when it was pitch-black. When I reversed out of my garage, I wouldn't let myself glance next door.

We hadn't seen each other, but that didn't mean she hadn't been on my mind. The volleyball team had won their game tonight. I'd watched scoring updates for an hour.

Jennsyn wasn't at the bar tonight, but if she showed up, I'd be as attuned to her as Ford was to Millie.

"You're staring." I shifted, turning my back to the bar so Ford could look me in the face.

He was agitated tonight and kept dragging his hands through his light brown hair. If I noticed how often he looked at Millie, chances were, Kurt or someone else would notice too.

Ford sighed, glancing around the bar, probably taking in the changes from when we'd been in college.

Most of the bars in downtown Mission looked exactly as they had years ago, when we'd been playing for the Wildcats. They catered to the college students who'd party every weekend. But this bar had undergone an extensive renovation a few years ago.

Gone was the dive bar and stale scent of cigarette smoke. Now it was stylish with a rugged edge that appealed to both students and local businessmen.

In the center of the room was the bar itself. The rectangular shape allowed patrons to order from any side. Chocolate leather, tall-backed booths lined the red brick walls. The mirrored liquor shelves were framed with dark wood posts. A large garage door with black-paned windows overlooked Main. In the summers, they'd lift the door so that the late-evening air could chase away the heat from so many bodies crammed together.

Parks was over by the door, talking with a few familiar faces. The entire coaching staff was in attendance. We'd all trickled downtown after the game and our team meeting with the players. Not a soul here wasn't wearing some sort of Wildcat gear. Even the bartenders were decked out in royal blue and silver.

I wasn't the only one riding the high from today's game.

Though Ford seemed to be riding the high of something else.

I shoved that thought away, not wanting to think about Ford and Millie. They might as well be my siblings at this point.

He checked the time on his phone. "What time does this go until?"

"The email said we had to stay until eight," I answered.

Ford's groan was swallowed up by the room's noise. His gaze scanned the crowd, stopping when it found his boss.

Kurt had been glued to Ford's side since my friend had moved to Montana. Better him than me. I didn't dislike Kurt, but I didn't like him either. He was constantly on the sidelines during games, getting in the damn way.

Ford gave him a nod, then kept searching, his focus once more stopping on Millie. They were playing with fire with so many work colleagues here tonight.

"Ford." I lowered my voice so that only he could hear me above the booming background music and loud hum of conversation. "If you keep looking at her, everyone in this bar is going to know something's going on."

He sighed and rubbed a hand over his jaw. This was a man turned inside out over a woman. A woman who'd get fired if anyone found out they were in a relationship.

Millie had worked at Treasure State for years. Sure, she had the tenure. The experience. And Ford was the newest employee in the athletics department. But he was the *head football coach*. If one of them was going to lose a job, it wouldn't be Ford.

It wasn't fair, but it was reality.

I hoped like hell they knew what they were doing.

With a quick raise of my hand, I flagged down the bartender. "Two shots of tequila, please. Best you've got. He's buying."

"Do I get one of these shots?" Ford quirked an eyebrow as he pulled out his wallet.

I grinned as we waited for the shots, then picked up a glass, clinking the rim of mine to Ford's. "Congratulations, Coach."

"Same to you."

Tossing back the tequila, I savored the burn as it warmed my insides. Maybe it would help Ford to finally relax.

An older man with a shiny, bald head clapped me on the

shoulder, then held out a hand to Ford. "Great game. Can't wait to see how the season goes."

"Thanks," I said as Ford did the same.

What was this guy's name? He'd been at a fundraiser this summer that we'd had in the stadium, but I'd met so many people that night, I couldn't remember.

Not that I had to remember. The moment the bald guy moved on, another person took his place. Then another. Then another. The names and faces began to blur together as everyone clamored for Ford's attention.

And he gave it to them.

Until exactly eight o'clock.

"I'm taking off," he said, letting out a long breath. "Thanks for everything today."

"Welcome." I smacked him on the shoulder. "Monday."

"Monday." He nodded, then disappeared into the crush.

Millie's spot at the bar was empty. She was gone too.

I raised a hand, about to flag down the bartender, when a body filled the spot Ford had just vacated.

"Hey." A pretty brunette placed her elbows on the bar, leaning in close as she smiled up at me.

"Hey."

She twirled a manicured finger in the air. "Are you here for this football thing?"

Football thing. Her tone wasn't overly judgmental, but I didn't miss the subtle dig either. And considering I was wearing the same colors as everyone else in the bar, it wasn't the best way to start this conversation when the answer was obvious.

"Yep." I popped the *p*.

"Ah. I'm just in town for the weekend. Business trip." Her brown eyes roved my face before her gaze traveled down to my chest and arms. A flush crept into her cheeks as her smile widened.

All I had to do was make small talk for a few minutes, flirt over a drink, and this beautiful woman who was clearly intent on not going to her hotel alone tonight would invite me to her room for a fuck.

Another night, another time, maybe I would have taken her up on it. Except as she shifted closer, her arm nearly brushing mine, I inched away.

This wasn't the woman I wanted.

Fuck.

Jennsyn really had twisted me into a damn knot, hadn't she? I didn't want a casual hookup with a brunette, not when I wanted my hands threaded into blond hair. I wanted to lose myself in blue eyes, not brown. I wanted a woman who'd never say *football thing* like it was beneath her.

What was I even doing here? Ford was gone. I was standing alone. Time for me to go home. "Have a nice night."

The woman blinked, a crease forming between her eyebrows, but she recovered from the rejection quickly and mustered up a genuine smile. "You too."

While Kurt was looking the other direction, I slipped out the front door and strode down the block.

Main Street was loud on Saturday nights. College kids rushed past me as they hopped from one bar to the next. Couples strolled the sidewalks hand in hand. The lampposts cast a golden glow through the night, and headlights from passing traffic reflected off gleaming shop windows.

I didn't spend much time downtown these days. If I wasn't on campus for work or at the farm with Faith, then I was at home. The last time I'd come out for dinner with friends, I'd met a woman who I'd dated for about a month.

We'd had a good time at first. But she'd hated staying in. Every time I'd suggest dinner at my place and a movie on the couch, she'd stare at me like I'd grown two heads. When I'd realized that she was more interested in hanging on the arm of a Wildcats football coach and parading me around town than actually getting to know me, well . . . I'd lost her number fast.

Since then, it had just been casual hookups.

And Jennsyn.

What was going on with me? Why couldn't I shake her? Everything that had happened that night had thrown me for a loop. Every touch. Every word.

Maybe I needed a random fling to get her out of my mind. But the idea of turning around, going back to the bar and finding that brunette made my skin crawl, so I kept on walking.

I was almost at my truck, parked a few blocks from the bar, when my phone vibrated in my pocket. *Faith.*

"Hey," I answered. "What's up?"

Her sniffle made me slow. "I'm sorry for calling late."

"It's fine. I'm downtown, just leaving an event."

"Would you be up for calling Beck on your drive home? We got into a big fight tonight."

Damn. Beck was punching every button of his mother's these days. He prodded every boundary.

I reached my truck, hitting the locks with the key fob. "I'll do you one better. Be over in a few."

She sighed, sniffling again. "I'm sorry, Toren."

"Don't be. I'll see you in a few." I climbed in my truck, hit the ignition and drove to the farm.

Beck was waiting on the porch swing when I parked outside the house.

"Hey." I sat on the seat beside him and ruffled his brown curls.

Normally, his hair was straight as a pin. But this year, he'd grown it long on top and had begged Faith to let him perm the top. It looked ridiculous, but apparently, it was the style.

He didn't swat my hand away. That meant this fight had been rough.

"What happened?"

"Got in a fight with Mom." He ducked his chin, staring at his lap. The Wildcat hoodie he was wearing was one of Uncle Evan's. It draped on his frame and the sleeves fell past his fingertips. But I guess tonight, he'd needed his dad's old sweatshirt.

"What was the fight about?"

"One of my friends," he muttered.

"Ah." I crossed an ankle over my knee as silence settled. Then I waited.

Of all Faith's boys, Beck was the most like Uncle Evan. He'd always been a man who never rushed a conversation. He was deliberate about his words. My dad had been like that too. So I gently pushed the swing, waiting until Beck was ready to talk.

"Mom doesn't like Henry because Kyle's mom told her that Henry got caught watching porn," he blurted.

"Porn." I blinked. Beck was thirteen. Wasn't that too early? When was the first time I'd seen porn? "Okay."

"Everyone is at Henry's tonight and staying over, but she wouldn't let me go. It's not fair. All of my friends are there, and she's just being strict because she doesn't want me to have any fun."

I gave that a minute to breathe, then I slung an arm over

the backrest of the swing. "You really think she doesn't want you to have fun?"

He shrugged.

"Maybe she's just looking out for you."

Beck's mouth pursed into an angry line as he glowered into the darkness. "You always take her side."

"There's no sides, bud. Not when we're all on the same team."

He sagged on a loud exhale. "Henry was the one who watched it, not me. And he got in trouble. He lost his phone for two weeks."

"Have you ever watched porn?"

Silence. That meant yes.

"Don't tell your mom," I said quietly.

He was still just a kid, especially in Faith's eyes. But he was getting older, and sooner or later, he'd be making grown-up decisions.

"We need to have the sex talk."

"Toren—"

I held up my hand, cutting him off. "You probably know all of it anyway, but in case you don't, just . . . let me get it out."

Beck groaned but stayed seated, listening to me fumble through an explanation about the birds and the bees. Uncle Evan had been alive to do this with Abel. But I'd probably be the one to give the talk to Cabe and Dane too, wouldn't I?

"Questions?" I asked him when I was finished.

"Can we never do that again?"

"Definitely." I held out a fist so he could knock his knuckles to mine. "Your mom loves you. She's just trying to do what she thinks is best for you. Cut her some slack, yeah? And I'll talk to her about Henry."

"'Kay." He stood, that hoodie falling nearly to his knees as he headed for the front door. But he paused before disappearing inside. "Thanks, Tor."

"Love you, kid."

"Love you too."

The screen door slammed on its hinges as he went into the house. I breathed in the night air, waiting until Faith slipped outside.

"Porn, huh?" I asked as she sat on the swing beside me.

She shuddered. "He's too young."

"He's thirteen. There's no containing his curiosity." About sex and, well . . . life.

Faith looked on the verge of tears, but she swallowed them down. "I wish Evan was here."

"Me too." I pulled her into my side. "I just had the sex talk with Beck."

"Oh God." She buried her face in her hands, cringing and laughing at the same time. When she looked up, she relaxed her temple against my shoulder. "Thanks for doing that."

"No problem."

"Am I messing them up?" she whispered. "I don't know what I'm doing these days."

"You didn't mess me up."

"You're fairly unflappable." She gave me a sad smile. "And I had Evan."

There was no need to say how much we missed him. It was in every breath. Every heartbeat. "You've got me."

Tears glistened in her eyes as she hugged my arm. "I love you, kid."

She was the only person on earth who called me kid. "Love you too, Aunt Faith."

"Go home." She patted my leg, then stood, wiping at her eyes. "I'm going to go hug and smother my kids until they kick me out of their rooms."

With Abel, Beck and Cabe, it would happen in minutes. They were beyond the snuggling phase. But Dane wouldn't let her go. Which meant she'd probably sleep in his bed tonight.

"I'll call you tomorrow," I said, shoving to my feet and crossing the porch.

With one last wave, she went inside as I climbed into my truck. Then I drove home, parking in the garage but staying behind the wheel for a long moment.

The rush from today's game was gone. That thrill, the good mood, had vanished.

Instead I felt . . . tired. So fucking tired.

I trudged inside and upstairs, not bothering to turn on the lights as I made my way to my bedroom. I'd just toed off my shoes and socks when I glanced out the balcony windows.

The deck light was on, casting enough of a glow to illuminate the person sitting on the edge of my yard.

Jennsyn.

My heart stopped. *Damn it.* When was that going to stop?

Her long legs were stretched in front of her as she leaned back on her elbows, staring toward the lights of town and moon hanging in the heavens.

"Go to bed, Toren." *Just go to bed.*

Except I was a fucking fool. Instead of drawing the curtains closed, pretending like she wasn't out there, I padded downstairs and slipped through the sliding door, making my way across the lawn in bare feet.

No surprise, hers were bare too.

"Hey," I said, sitting beside her on the grass.

"Hey." She didn't turn away from the view as she spoke.

Starlight kissed her profile, highlighting the delicate lines of her cheeks and chin and nose.

God, she was beautiful. As dazzling as any star. As captivating as any galaxy. It was impossible not to stare.

"Are you okay?" she asked.

Did she know that my answer a moment ago would have been no? But now that I was sitting here with her . . . "All good."

"Sorry to trespass. Your view is better." She nodded toward the row of hedges that acted as a low fence at the back of the yard behind her house. "And your grass is soft."

"It's all right."

"Heard you won your game."

"Heard you won yours too."

She nodded, shifting her gaze to the sky. "Someday, when I leave Montana, I will miss the stars."

And she would leave, wouldn't she? This was just a place for her to go to school. A place to play volleyball until she started her real life.

Because she was a student.

I'd keep reminding myself of that fact, over and over and over. If I was lucky, sooner or later, it would stick.

"Where are your roommates?" My night would be effectively fucked if Stevie or Liz came outside and saw us together.

We were just sitting on my lawn. It was innocent. Except it wasn't.

"One of the other girls was having a few people over to hang out."

"You didn't want to go?"

She shook her head. "Nah."

I couldn't think of a time I'd seen Jennsyn hanging out with Stevie, Liz or any of the other girls on the team. Apparently that rift Aspen had hinted about last month hadn't healed.

"What did you do tonight?" she asked.

"Had the sex talk."

That got her attention. She finally shifted those beautiful eyes my direction. "I hope it wasn't with one of your players."

"No." I chuckled. "My cousin Beck. He's thirteen."

"And how did that go?"

"It, uh . . . went."

"What did you tell him?"

I lifted a shoulder. "The science."

"The science? Oh my God. What exactly did you say?"

My face flamed. "Now I don't want to tell you."

"Please." She clasped her hands together. "I'm begging you. Tell me about this science."

Did she realize how impossible it was for me to tell her no?

"I told him that a man's penis enters a woman's vagina, and when he ejaculates, his semen swims through the woman's body to try and impregnate an egg. And that if he didn't want to get a woman pregnant or get a disease that would make his dick fall off, he needed to always wear a condom."

Jennsyn stared at me, eyes wide, until she threw her head back and laughed. A laugh so loud and carefree and real that it made my chest ache.

It was the same way she'd laughed the night of the party. The night she'd stolen a piece of my heart.

I really needed her to give it back.

"Oh my God." She hugged her stomach as she leaned forward, like she'd laughed so hard she'd given herself a side ache.

I chuckled, that exhaustion I'd felt earlier fading away. "How would you have done it?"

"I don't know." She shook her head, a blinding smile lighting up her face. "This was the extent of my mother's sex education."

Jennsyn held up her hands, extending her index finger on her left while she made a circle with her thumb and middle finger on her right. Then she poked her finger through the hole.

"Seriously?"

She nodded, still laughing. "Seriously."

"My explanation might have been—"

"Scientific," she finished my sentence.

"But I refrained from hand gestures."

"Excellent decision."

We laughed together, the sound fading into the night. It was too dark to see the blue in her eyes, but the city lights and stars danced in her irises. Staring at her was like being stripped bare.

No lies. No pretenses. No titles. Just us.

All I had to do was lean in and my mouth would be on hers. I fisted the grass to keep myself from taking her hand.

One more night. I wanted one more night. Then I'd put her out of my mind. I'd find a way to smother this attraction, once and for all.

I leaned, coming within an inch of her lips.

Headlights flashed as a car pulled into her driveway. Her roommates.

Jennsyn leapt to her feet, backing away so fast she nearly tripped on her heels.

Fuck. I'd almost kissed her. What the hell was wrong with me?

I dragged both hands over my face. Maybe we needed another month between us. Or two. Or three.

"Goodbye, Jennsyn," I said, keeping my ass firmly planted on the lawn.

She backed another step. "Goodbye, Toren."

CHAPTER EIGHT

JENNSYN

"Maverick Houston said hi to me in the hallway today." Megan, a junior who played libero, pressed a hand over her heart.

Maverick Houston. The punter on the football team she'd been crushing on for weeks. Any time he so much as glanced in her direction, we'd all hear about it in the locker room after practice.

I combed through my wet hair, not engaging as the other girls let out *ooh*s and *aah*s. Well, almost every girl.

Any time Stevie heard Maverick's name, her lip would curl.

What was the story there? She was clearly not a Maverick fan. Why?

I didn't ask. It wasn't any of my business. Instead, I put my comb back in my locker and reached for my sweatshirt.

There was a small grass stain on the left sleeve. I'd gotten it last weekend when I'd wandered into Toren's yard to breathe and think and stare up at the stars.

I'd meant what I'd told him about his lawn and view. His

yard was superior to mine. His house had been dark, and I hadn't expected to see him on Saturday. But I'd also caught the flash of his headlights before he'd pulled into the garage, and a part of me had been curious enough to wait.

Not to see if he'd find me in the dark.

To see if he'd bring a woman home with him after a winning football game.

Eventually, another woman would be in his bed. If there hadn't been one already. Maybe when he moved on, I'd be able to let go too.

But like this grass stain, I wasn't ready to erase him. Not yet.

"Did you guys hear about Rush Ramsey?" Megan asked, lowering her voice. She always made such a production about gossip.

The other girls shifted closer to where she was standing, her body still wrapped in a towel from her shower.

I stayed on my side of the locker room because she'd talk loud enough for everyone to hear, even me.

"I heard he got a girl pregnant," she said.

"Who?" Liz's jaw dropped. "His girlfriend?"

"No, they broke up," Megan said. "I don't know who this girl is, but they were fighting in the hallway the other day, and now everyone is talking about how she's pregnant. I think it was a random hookup and . . . oops."

The locker room filled with chatter, everyone speculating about Rush, the football team's quarterback. He happened to live with Maverick, probably why Megan was so obsessed with them both.

I walked into the bathroom and the row of vanity mirrors, then took out a blow-dryer, drowning out the gossipfest as I did my hair.

No one missed me from their discussion.

And I didn't miss them either.

There were unspoken rules when it came to gossiping about other athletes. Rumors might run rampant amongst our various teams, but never to outsiders. NARPs were never let into the circle. *Non-athletic regular persons* didn't get invited to parties or events. They were never privy to the ongoings of athletes. We kept to ourselves and never gossiped to people outside a sports program.

But within these walls, in these locker rooms? Everything was fair game. And when you were seen as competition, your teammates could be ruthless.

A lesson I'd learned the hard way.

I wouldn't make the same mistakes again.

When my hair was dry, I snagged my backpack from beside my locker, and without a goodbye to the team, walked out of the room, ignoring the way the voices dropped to actual whispers before I disappeared.

The girls could talk about me all they wanted. The worst they could say was that I was a bitch or a snob.

I doubted they'd be too harsh, considering we were undefeated so far this season and my hitting percentage was going to set a school record. I played six rotations during games, never leaving the court, and we had yet to go up against a team who could block me.

I didn't give a shit about the gossip. I was here to play. Not for them. Not for Coach Quinn.

For me.

This year, I was playing for me.

My phone vibrated in my pocket as I walked down the hall of the fieldhouse. Considering how few people called me anymore, considering what day it was, I knew who it was before answering.

"Hey, Mom."

"Did you get my message?"

So much for a hello. "Yes."

"But you didn't call me back." There was probably a frown on her face. "Jennsyn, I'm trying to salvage your career."

Wait. She'd called to talk about my career? Today? "W-what?"

"Can you hear me? I said, I'm trying to salvage your career."

A career that wasn't hers to salvage. *This* conversation was why I'd ignored her latest message along with her three most recent texts.

"I've been busy with school and practice, Mom."

"You can take ten minutes out of your *busy* schedule for this," she clipped. "I just spoke to Mike Simmons."

My feet came to a stop so fast my tennis shoes squeaked on the concrete floor.

Mike Simmons was one of the most elite sports agents in the country.

If I wanted to be on a national volleyball team someday, if I wanted a shot at the Olympics, Mike was someone who could help get me there.

"He's offered to take you on as a client," Mom said.

My heart was beating too fast to reply. Except it wasn't the excited kind of a racing pulse. It felt a lot more like dread.

Wasn't this my dream? A year ago, this call would have made me smile ear to ear. But now? I couldn't really feel my face.

"He actually thinks this move to Montana could be a

good thing." Mom scoffed softly, like she doubted Mike's assessment. The president of the International Olympic Committee could tell her I'd made a good choice with the Wildcats, and she still wouldn't believe it.

"Mike thinks you'll get to showcase your talent at Treasure State," she said. "Your percentages will go through the roof. And although you're not going to have a lot of competition this year, there's less of a risk you'll get hurt."

Mike Simmons had an opinion about *me*. Mike Simmons had offered to take me as a client. Mike Simmons thought I'd made a good decision.

It didn't seem real.

Mom kept talking, but I couldn't stop his name from running circles in my mind.

Mike Simmons. Mike Simmons. Mike Simmons.

"He'd like to have a call with you soon to discuss next steps. Just as we planned, you'll need to play internationally for a while. But he's hoping to get you an offer in Italy. That will position you for your best shot long-term when you return to the States."

Italy. Another word, another possibility, that should have made me leap for joy.

This was the plan, right? Play in college. Move to Europe and get paid to play professionally for a few years. Come home and join a national team. Go to the Olympics. Win a gold medal.

Just like Mom.

"Jennsyn, are you there?"

"I'm here." My voice was hoarse. "Sorry. This is, um . . ." Good news? Bad news? "It's a lot to think about."

"What's there to think about? This is the dream."

It used to be *the dream*. Did I even have a dream? No. Not really. Not a dream that was mine and mine alone.

"I'll set up a call with Mike," Mom said.

"No," I blurted, then closed my eyes, cringing as Mom's disappointment leeched through the phone.

"No?" she seethed.

"Not yet."

The silence stretched between us, as thick and tense as it had been the day I'd called to tell her I was moving to Montana.

All of our big, important conversations were done over the phone. It was easier that way.

Mom didn't know how to stop. She didn't know how to let something go. She didn't know how to lose an argument.

It was the reason my father had left her when I was seven, and I'd hardly seen him since.

Talking to her in person was suffocating. So I'd learned to save the heavy stuff for the phone, when I could tap a button to shut her off.

"This will pass you by," she said. "I pulled a lot of strings to get to Mike."

Strings. She was always pulling strings. She made sure to remind me of that each and every time too. Except I hadn't asked her to call in those favors. She'd done that on her own.

"I'll think about it, Mom."

"Fine."

I waited, giving her a chance to say something else. Every second that passed, my heart shriveled.

Mom hadn't called to say hello. She hadn't called because she missed me. She hadn't called me today to say happy birthday.

She'd called about volleyball.

Any desire I'd had to talk to her or Mike Simmons vanished. *Poof.* Gone.

The dream? I didn't want it. Not when it came with those strings she had to pull. Not when it came with strings of her own.

I was so tired of being my mother's puppet and protégé.

Not once in the months that I'd lived in Montana had Mom asked if I was enjoying it here. She hadn't asked if I liked my classes or if I'd made new friends.

When would I stop being surprised by the fact that her entire universe revolved around volleyball and *nothing* else?

Mom hadn't cared that I'd gotten myself into Stanford on my own merit out of high school. She'd just been angry that I hadn't gone to her alma mater in Nebraska. She hadn't worried about why I'd give up a Stanford degree to get one from Treasure State instead. She hadn't asked how I was adjusting to a new team or a new home.

She hadn't even remembered my birthday.

Tears flooded my eyes. When had I stopped just being her daughter?

"I need to go." Before she could stop me, I ended the call. Then I dabbed at the corners of my eyes and swallowed down the burn in my throat.

It was just another day. Turning twenty-two wasn't exactly monumental. I didn't need gifts or parties. I'd celebrate alone tonight with a pint of my favorite ice cream.

A hand touched my shoulder, jolting me out of my head.

Stevie stood at my side with a small smile. "Sorry. I thought you heard me walk up."

"Oh, um, sorry. I was talking to my mom."

"Is everything okay?"

"Yeah, it's great," I lied. "See you at home?"

"Sure." She nodded, backing away. Then she turned, walking toward the exit that led to the parking lot as I continued down the hall, breathing through the ache in my chest.

My phone buzzed again, this time with a text from Mom.

You hung up on me before I could say happy birthday.

I scoffed. Well, at least she hadn't forgotten. That was something, right? Maybe this would teach her to lead with the important stuff first.

Not that Mom would ever think anything was more important than volleyball.

I shifted my backpack off a shoulder, shoving my phone in a pocket so I wouldn't feel it ring. Then I headed for the stairwell door.

The study center on the second floor was reserved for athletes. It was quieter than the main library on campus, and if an athlete needed a tutor, those meetings wouldn't be held publicly for the other students to witness.

It also allowed coaches to mandate required study time, though Coach Quinn hadn't enforced any of those rules for our team. She wouldn't need to on my account.

I'd aced my classes at Stanford. I'd ace them at Treasure State too.

The room was mostly empty except for two girls sitting at a table in the corner. I dropped my backpack onto a small table with only two chairs, then slipped out to the hallway to refill my water bottle.

"Hi, Jennsyn." Millie Cunningham, one of the assistant athletic directors, walked down the hall, beating me to the drinking fountain.

"Hi, Ms. Cunningham."

"Millie," she corrected, twisting the lid off her own water bottle. "Ready for the game tomorrow?"

"More than ready."

Millie had stopped by practice a few weeks ago to introduce herself. She oversaw most of the programs in the department, including volleyball. She was gorgeous, with silky brown hair and pretty hazel eyes. I didn't know her well —I wouldn't be here long enough to know her or anyone well —but she seemed kind and genuine. She seemed to love her job too.

Maybe I could have a career with a university's athletic department like Millie. I hadn't considered administration, but I added it to my list of possibilities.

"How's school going?" she asked as she finished filling her bottle.

"So far so good. I like my classes, and this is a beautiful campus."

Mission was nestled into a valley beside the Mission Mountains. Every morning, I stood at my bedroom window and let myself stare at the peaks in the distance, marveling at their beauty. The photos on the Treasure State website didn't do the scenery justice.

"I'm glad you're enjoying it," Millie said, shifting out of the way so I could take her place at the fountain. "If you ever need anything, my door's open. I'll see you at the game tomorrow night. Good luck."

"Thanks." I waved with my free hand as she turned and walked away, rounding a corner that would lead her to her office.

Except before I was finished, before she'd gone too far, a familiar deep voice stopped her.

"Hey, Millie," Toren said.

My breath caught in my throat. I hadn't seen him since last Saturday, and today, on my birthday, I wanted a glimpse of that handsome face. One look, that was all. A gift to myself.

"Hey," Millie said. "What's up?"

"Nothing. Just finished up with practice and was going for a burger. Thought I'd see if you wanted to tag along. Maybe we could talk."

Talk. That sounded serious. Talk about what?

Wait. Was there something happening with Toren and Millie?

My water bottle was full, but I made no move to twist on the lid. Instead, I stood with feet frozen, ears straining, like a child who couldn't stop herself from listening to a conversation not meant for her.

"Talk about what?" she asked him.

"Saturday."

What had happened Saturday? Last Saturday?

He didn't want to talk to her about me, right? He wouldn't have told her about us. No. No way. Something must have happened. Before or after he'd sat with me on his lawn?

"I don't think I'm ready to talk yet," she said.

"Fair enough. But I'm still buying dinner. Burgers or pizza?"

She hummed. "We did burgers last time. Let's go pizza."

Last time. Was this a date? Another date? My stomach twisted into a knot.

This was what I'd expected to happen. Eventually, he'd find someone else. It didn't make it hurt any less.

I unglued my feet and took a step away from the drinking fountain, backing away slowly as their voices faded.

Then I slipped into the study room, my head swimming as I sank down at the table and stared unblinking at its wooden surface.

Toren and Millie.

They made sense as a couple. They had to be close to the same age. Both worked in athletics. She was as beautiful as he was handsome. Their kids would probably be stunning with dark hair and pretty eyes.

That knot in my gut pulled so tight my side ached.

Why couldn't I stop wanting him? Everything would be easier if he was just that guy who lived next door, the guy who happened to work in this building. If he was just another coach.

I closed my eyes and breathed through my nose, holding the air in my lungs until it burned. Then I exhaled and unzipped my backpack, pulling out the textbook for my Principles of Business Law course.

I'd just flipped to my chapter when the door swung open and two football players shuffled inside, both wearing baggy gray sweats and royal-blue Wildcat hoodies. One jerked up his chin in a silent hello as the other pointed to a table nearby.

The door was nearly shut, but then it swung open again as Toren walked inside.

His gaze met mine, and for a brief second, he smiled, his eyes crinkling at the sides. But that faint smile was gone in a second, masked by a polite nod before he turned his attention to the football players.

Toren walked to their table, bracing his hands on the back of an empty chair as he spoke to them both, his voice low.

This summer, the day I'd gone to his house after I'd

learned he was a coach, he'd told me that he would have called. I'd believed him then.

Was it true? Or had that just been a line? I was probably just that woman he'd fucked after his Fourth of July party and forgotten about the next day.

This had to stop. Now. Before I ruined everything all over again.

When Toren was finished, he walked from the room, leaving without so much as a glance in my direction. He had to get to dinner. Pizza with Millie.

And I just wanted to go home. So I packed up my backpack and left the fieldhouse, stopping at the nearest grocery store to buy myself a cupcake.

I ate it alone in my car, finishing the last bite as my phone buzzed with a text.

happy birthday j

My chin began to quiver, but I refused to let myself cry. Not over this. Not over the last person in the world who I wanted to hear from today being the only person to wish me happy birthday. Mom's snarky text didn't really count.

My fingers flew over the screen as I typed out my reply.

fuck you

THE PARTY

TOREN

The moment Jennsyn stepped into the basement, a smile stretched her pretty mouth. "Ah. Here's the bachelor's paradise I've been searching for."

I chuckled as she walked around the open area, taking in everything from the wet bar against the far wall to the TV mounted opposite the pool table.

As her fingertips skimmed the green felt, my cock twitched, desperate for that touch on my skin. Fuck, she was gorgeous. She floated more than walked, lifting on those bare toes from time to time like gravity didn't quite have a strong enough hold. And those legs. Long. Toned. Smooth. I wanted them wrapped around my hips.

"I've never played pool before," she said, walking to the cue rack.

"I'll show you." Not a question. Not an invitation. She wasn't leaving, not yet. Not if I could delay that exit. So I took down a cue and a square of blue chalk, then grabbed the triangle to rack the balls. When I lined up to break, her gaze was locked on my ass.

Hell yes.

The balls clinked as they scattered, and even though the four ball fell into a pocket, I handed over the cue for Jennsyn to try.

"There's no chance I'll be good at this," she said.

"It takes practice."

She lined up a shot that was going to be wide by a mile. Her eyes narrowed in concentration. Her nose scrunched up at the bridge. She pulled back the stick, holding it too long, then rammed it forward, missing the cue ball entirely.

"Told ya," she huffed, her cheeks pinking as she laughed at herself.

"Mind if I help?"

"Not at all."

I shifted closer, careful not to touch her body but close enough to draw in the sweet, citrus scent and feel the warmth from her skin.

There was a sparkle in those blue eyes, like she'd been hoping I'd offer to help.

Well, I wouldn't want to disappoint.

"Line it up again," I said, my voice dropping low.

Once she was in position, I shifted to her side, my hand closing over hers.

One touch. And this game of pool was over. We'd been circling each other all night with flirting and foreplay. Time to make a move.

Jennsyn's breath hitched. Electricity raced up my arm and heat spread through my veins.

Her eyes held mine for a heartbeat before they dropped to my mouth. "Toren?"

"Yeah."

"You should kiss me now."
Great fucking idea.

CHAPTER NINE

JENNSYN

The football stadium pulsed with noise and energy. The field was a brilliant green under the cloudless blue sky. The sunshine warmed my face, and despite the chaos and excitement around me, with every breath of the clean, fall air, the tension I'd been carrying for the past two days slipped from my shoulders.

Halftime was nearly over, and all of the fans who'd left for the tailgates were filtering back into their seats, ready to watch the rest of the game.

"Everyone ready?" Coach Quinn shouted over the clamor as she walked past us lined up beneath the goal posts.

"Ready," Stevie said from beside me, her excitement palpable and that ever-present smile beaming.

"Wildcat fans." The game announcer's voice blasted through the stadium's speakers. "Turn your attention to the end zone to welcome today's special guests: your undefeated Wildcat women's volleyball team!"

Applause carried through the air as we strode toward the center of the field and the announcer prattled off our names.

I'd ended up last in line, and when it was my turn, I held up an arm and waved to each section of the stands.

"And number eight, outside hitter, Jennsyn Bell."

My team at Stanford had been celebrated differently. Volleyball was a major sport, but I'd never fooled myself into believing it was more popular than football. We'd never been featured during halftime. And yeah, this was probably just posturing. Coach Quinn wanted people to fill the Upshaw Gymnasium for our game tonight too, and the more exposure we could get, the more likely it was we'd have a stellar crowd.

But as we retreated to the sidelines, the clapping and whistling didn't stop. It felt genuine. Refreshing. Welcoming.

These people were cheering for us simply because we were Wildcats too.

For the first time since we'd shown up, my smile didn't feel forced.

We didn't linger on the turf. Before the echo of my name had faded away, we were all jogging off the field, returning to a reserved corner by the end zone.

Music thrummed through the sound system, the bass a steady beat that made fans clap along with its rhythm. All eyes were glued to the tunnel where the football players had disappeared at the half.

Three players emerged first, their silver helmets glinting in the bright sunlight. Then the rest of the team followed, streaming out in a streak of royal-blue uniforms as they rushed for the sideline.

"Thanks, ladies." Coach Quinn motioned us all closer. "Game tonight is at seven. Be at the fieldhouse by four. If you want to stay and watch the rest of the game, this space is ours. Normally, I'd rather you rest, but since we're already here, it's up to you."

Liz and Stevie shared a look, both nodding in silent agreement to stay. Megan and a group of juniors stayed when she sent them wide, pleading eyes. No doubt she wanted to gawk at Maverick Houston, who stood directly across the field, talking with his coach.

A few girls left, slipping away as they headed for a guarded exit gate. But the rest of us lingered.

The opposing team trudged out from their locker room, heads hanging like they'd already been defeated. If I were losing forty-nine to three, I'd be trudging too.

"You're staying?" Stevie did a double take when I took the space beside her.

"Why not?" I shrugged. "We're here."

"Great." She smiled wider and tucked a lock of dark hair behind her ear.

I wasn't exactly winning popularity contests or participation awards, so her surprise was warranted. Normally, I would have been the first to leave. Except there was a man on the sidelines who'd snared my attention since we'd arrived during the second quarter.

A man who I thought about far too often.

Maybe today would be my chance to put this crush away, once and for all. Would Millie congratulate him after today's game? Would he sweep her into his arms and celebrate this victory?

The idea of seeing him with another woman made my insides roil, but in my head, I knew that would be best. Somehow, someway, I needed this obsession with Toren Greely to disappear. Before it suffocated me.

Before it ruined my season.

We had back-to-back games this weekend, and last night's had been awful. Not that we'd lost. We'd won by a landslide, and I'd played my best game so far this season.

But I could feel myself coming apart. I was edgy and unfocused. My mind wandered constantly and Toren plagued my thoughts.

The last time I'd felt this way had been my sophomore year at Stanford. I'd been crushing on a guy from my marketing class and it had rattled me to the core. I'd had a string of near-perfect games and then the worst game in a decade. Followed by another. And another. Three horrible games in a row where I couldn't seem to find up from down or left from right.

The only reason I'd gotten out of the funk was because I'd asked him out and he'd told me, despite weeks and weeks of flirting, he had a girlfriend. Asshole.

I needed Toren to have a girlfriend. Anything to make this crush go the fuck away.

It would be so much easier if he didn't look so good. He was wearing a pair of gray slacks and a blue long-sleeved T-shirt that he'd shoved up his sinewed forearms. Confident and in control. Toren's headset covered one ear and his hat shielded his face from the sun. His defense was on the field and he watched with utter concentration as the play unfolded.

"I only know the basics of football," Stevie said, either to me or to Liz on her other side.

"Same here," I admitted.

She gave me a soft smile, inching just a bit closer, almost like she was dealing with a skittish wild animal she didn't want to scare away with any sudden movements.

I sucked as a roommate, but it was easier this way. We'd

never be friends. Maybe someday, I'd tell her why. Maybe not.

At the moment, I could at least chat with her while we watched this game.

Down the sidelines a few feet, Megan was whispering with another girl, both casually pointing to Maverick.

Stevie noticed too, and the moment her gaze landed on Maverick across the field, her lip curled.

"Not a Maverick fan?" I asked, instantly regretting the question.

It was a question the old me would have asked. The Jennsyn who'd gone to Stanford. The girl who had won those popularity contests and participation awards. But I wasn't that person anymore and Stevie's beef with Maverick wasn't my concern.

"Sorry. That's none of my business."

"It's okay. I've known Maverick my whole life. Everyone loves him. I've hated him since we were ten," she sneered.

I laughed. "All right. Good to know."

"It's stupid." She flicked her wrist. "We got into a fight as kids and it's festered for a decade."

"Ah."

She leaned in closer, lowering her voice as the Wildcat defense shut out the offense in three plays. "Maverick will chew up Megan and spit her out. He's stringing her along right now. I hope she realizes it soon. I tried to talk to her about it but..."

Megan seemed determined to find herself in his bed.

"It was nice of you to try," I said.

She shrugged. "We're teammates."

Once upon a time, I'd believed that *teammates* trumped everything else.

I hoped for Stevie's sake that stayed true.

The third quarter ticked away as the Wildcats offense did everything in their power not to slow down the game. Time bled off the clock with every possession, and by the fourth quarter, we'd scored yet another touchdown.

"Fifty-six to three." I winced. "Ouch."

Misery hovered over the other team's heads down the line. On the Wildcat side of the field, our players were sharing high fives and fist bumps.

A whistle shrieked through the air as the official threw a yellow flag on the turf and waved his hands in the air.

Boos filled the stadium.

"What happened?" Stevie asked.

"No idea."

Coach Ellis's arms flew out at his sides and he shook his head at the call.

Toren's jaw clenched so hard I could see it from yards away.

"Offsides." The lead official's voice rang through the speakers as he called in the penalty.

The feed on the jumbotron shifted to a scowling Coach Ellis, the camera dragging along the Wildcat staff.

The moment Toren appeared, my heart skipped.

I groaned. "Damn it."

"What was that?" Stevie asked.

"Oh, um. That was a bad call, right?" I had no freaking clue.

Football was a bit of a mystery. In another life, I would have let Toren teach me about the game. I would have curled into his side on the couch and watched hours of football, listening to him explain the rules.

Someone else would have that spot at his side. Maybe Millie. Lucky Millie. At least she was nice.

The defense held the other team on their desperate attempt to score, and as Toren's players jogged off the field, he clapped them all on the shoulder pads.

When Rush Ramsey led the offense onto the field, Megan and a couple of the other girls leaned together to whisper, probably about the same gossip they'd shared in the locker room the other day.

If the rumors about a pregnancy were true, they hadn't seemed to affect Rush's performance. He seemed unshakeable out there today, and even though we'd slaughtered the other team, he hadn't stopped pushing. There was a determination about his play, like he was using football to escape.

I recognized that urgency. That drive. Rush Ramsey and I were kindred spirits.

In another life, maybe we would have been friends too.

Coach Ellis walked to Toren, both of them talking with their heads bent together. Toren nodded and walked toward a bench where two of his players were resting.

He wasn't celebrating yet either. The game wasn't over, and like Rush, he'd coach through the very last second.

He crossed his arms over his chest, his biceps straining the fabric of his shirt. He dropped to a crouch and the fabric of his shirt strained over his biceps and molded to the honed muscle of his back and shoulders. God, he was hot. A shiver rolled down my spine as my mouth went dry.

"It's entirely unfair that coaches are off-limits. Coach Greely is so freaking hot."

I jerked, the statement ripping my attention from Toren to Megan.

She and the other girls had moved closer, still talking to

each other. Not one of them was paying me any attention. No one had noticed me staring at Toren. They were too busy drooling over him themselves.

A sour taste spread across my tongue. I tucked my hands in the pockets of my pants so I wouldn't snap my fingers in front of Megan's face to get her to stop ogling Toren. But thankfully, the players on the field moved and blocked her view.

The guy in the middle of the line—the center?—snapped the ball to Rush, who took a few steps back, then launched it through the air.

My breath caught as it sailed right into an open receiver's hands. He took off running, every pair of eyes locked on him as he raced. Every pair but mine.

Like always, my gaze tracked to Toren. He stood unmoving until the stadium detonated in screams.

Touchdown.

Game over.

The smile on his face was blinding. It was so handsome it made my heart hurt. He looked so proud. So happy for his team.

Toren felt the victories soul-deep, didn't he? I bet the losses were devastating.

It ached to watch him smile and laugh as he congratulated his players. He shared a back-slapping hug with Coach Ellis, then he jogged across the field, moving my way. Except his gaze was on the other team, a hand outstretched to shake with the opposing team's coaches.

"Does anyone want to come over after the game tonight for a late dinner?" Megan asked.

Stevie and Liz shared a look, then nodded as the other girls on the team said, "Sure."

Megan's invite wasn't for me. Maybe it would have been if I hadn't taken her friend's scholarship and spot on the team, but I wouldn't have accepted anyway.

None of the girls seemed to notice when I turned and walked away.

I shuffled along with the crowd, making my way toward the exit as the football team jogged past me toward the tunnel where they'd likely have their postgame meeting before trekking to the fieldhouse to shower and change.

Toren blended into the crush, and for a moment, I lost him. Then I caught a glimpse of his gray hat and brilliant smile.

Was Millie around? Was this when he'd sweep her into a hug and give her a kiss?

I didn't want to see it, but I *needed* to see it. I needed to see him move on so I could let him go.

Except he walked alone across the field toward the end zone crammed with donors and faculty members. Maybe he felt my gaze, because one moment he was staring straight ahead, and the next he turned my way and found me in the crush.

His smile turned to a frown.

It was worse than seeing him with another woman.

Something crumpled in my chest. A hope. A dream. An impossibility. Like when I'd been a little girl and thought I could be an astronaut, and my mother had told me I was going to be a volleyball player instead.

Toren's jaw clenched, his irritation as loud as the people around me, as he dropped his eyes to the turf. He shoved his hands into the pockets of his slacks, then quickened his strides, following the team until he was out of sight.

A hand came to my chest, rubbing at the ache. What was

wrong with me? I was just a stupid little girl with a stupid little crush, and it was time to stop.

No more searching for him. No more staring. No more stealing movies.

It was time to focus on the reason I was here. I'd made enough mistakes when it came to men. Toren Greely didn't need to be another. I tuned out the noise and walked to the fieldhouse. And like I'd done hundreds of times, I got ready to play my own game.

That was all anyone wanted from me. Volleyball.

So I played. I gave them what they wanted.

And cried as I drove home alone.

CHAPTER TEN

TOREN

A garage door at Jennsyn's opened as I pulled into my driveway. Like with mine, there were three overhead doors. It was Stevie's that had opened, not Jennsyn's.

I shouldn't know which door was hers. I shouldn't know that she parked in the farthest from my house. I shouldn't know that she drove a sporty black BMW that would need snow tires this winter.

Did she know she'd need snow tires? That she'd need to get them ordered from the local tire shop soon or they'd get backed up and she'd have a hell of a time come December?

Not my business. That woman wasn't my fucking business.

Yet no matter how many times I reminded myself she wasn't mine to worry about, that her car and tires weren't my responsibilities, I couldn't get her out of my mind.

Every time I thought I was on the path to forgetting, I'd see her, my heart would stop, and I'd be dragged right back to the beginning to start all over again.

It was exactly what had happened at the game earlier.

One glimpse of her face and that steady thump in my chest had flatlined. For a brief moment, I'd almost smiled. Almost crossed the distance between us for a kiss. Then reality had come crashing down, and I'd forced myself to look away before anyone noticed.

What a mess. This had to stop. How did I make it stop?

It had been months since the party this summer, yet I couldn't seem to stop tucking away little scraps of information about her. The car she drove. Where she parked. Today, at the end of halftime as we'd been prepping to return to the field, I'd overheard the announcer at the game say her name.

She was number eight. An outside hitter.

Not that I had a damn clue what that meant.

So far, I hadn't let myself look up Jennsyn online, but I had the feeling tonight, I'd break that streak. I knew fuck all about volleyball. There was no reason for me to learn. But I wanted to know the rules. The positions. I wanted all of it.

I wanted her. Still. Months later, I wanted her.

This attachment, attraction, addiction—whatever the fuck I should call it—to Jennsyn Bell had to stop.

This crush would fade. This *had* to fade.

Maybe after she moved away. After she graduated. Enduring this torment for a year might send me over the edge, but I had no other choice.

I loved my house. I loved this neighborhood. And I wasn't going to move to escape her. I wasn't going to quit my job either.

"It'll fade," I muttered as I eased my truck into the garage, blew out a long breath and killed the engine.

Damn it, I was tired. The rush from today's victory had long since vanished. There'd been no postgame event to attend tonight, so instead, I'd celebrated with Faith and the boys at the farm.

For an hour, I'd thrown the ball to Abel so he could practice running a few routes for his high school playbook. Beck and Cabe had gotten into a fight about a video game, so I'd been the peacekeeper. Then I'd helped Dane put the finishing touches on the tent he'd made in his bedroom before grilling burgers for Aunt Faith so she could spend some extra time in her office, catching up on business for the farm.

With the season in full swing, there weren't as many chances for me to visit and see the boys. But I was tired tonight. More tired than I'd been in a while.

More tired than I could ever remember being after a winning game.

Something about this year felt strange. Something was off. I couldn't put my finger on exactly what, but it just . . . felt different.

Maybe because we were all still on edge from last spring's scandal. We were all walking on eggshells. Ford had been a godsend for the team, both the coaches and players, but everyone was still on their best behavior—Ford included.

Except when it came to Millie.

Neither of them had said anything for certain, but something was happening there. Something that went against the rules.

Knowing Ford, he'd say fuck it to the no-fraternization policy. But Millie? Millie liked the rules. And she loved her job. If they were sneaking around, if they were risking it all, well . . . good for them.

Maybe a part of me was jealous. Maybe a part of me wished I had a bit of their courage.

Not that this thing with Jennsyn could compare.

Two employees hooking up was one thing. But a coach and a student? That was another scandal waiting to explode. That was my job, my future on the line. Jennsyn's too.

She was too young for me anyway. She was destined for a hell of a lot more than Mission, Montana.

This would fade.

Until these feelings were gone, I'd just keep moving forward. So I climbed out of my truck and, with my keys in hand, headed across the darkened street for the mailbox cluster, collecting the stack inside that was likely all junk.

"Hey, Coach." Stevie waved as she walked out of their garage, standing in the driveway where the exterior lights glowed on the concrete.

"Hey," I said, keeping my eyes locked on her and not searching for Jennsyn inside. "How'd your game go tonight?"

"Another win." She smiled as Liz emerged wearing a pair of baggy sweats and a Wildcats T-shirt.

"Hi, Coach Greely. Good game today. Congrats."

"Sounds like congratulations are in order for you too," I said.

"Yeah." Liz laughed. "We slaughtered them."

"Jennsyn was on fire tonight," Stevie said. "She's usually unstoppable but she was in the zone tonight."

"That's great." A surge of pride I shouldn't feel swelled in my chest.

She was good, wasn't she? How good? I bit back the question, not letting my gaze wander into their garage. Not letting myself search for her or hope she'd be the next to come outside.

"What are you up to tonight?" I asked.

"Hanging out with some girls from the team," Liz said. "We're having a late dinner."

"Have a good time." I held up my hand with the mail, waving to them both, then ducked into my open garage.

My exhale was both disappointment and relief.

The quiet of my house was a stark contrast to the chaos I'd left behind at Faith's. Normally, I liked coming home to a silent house, breathing in the peace. Tonight, the empty rooms felt lonely.

Was that my problem? I was just lonely?

In years past on game nights, I'd normally head to a bar or restaurant with the other single coaches. We'd have a beer. Maybe head downtown. And that postgame rush usually meant I'd bring a woman home to bed. Maybe stay in hers.

Except I hadn't had a casual hookup, not since Jennsyn. And not a woman had appealed to me since.

I'd starved myself of sex. Maybe that was the reason I felt off-kilter. I needed to get laid. I needed a decent release.

During my morning showers, I fisted my cock and came with Jennsyn's face in mind, except those orgasms were each hollow and fast, nothing compared to our night together. Had I blown that night out of proportion? Had I convinced myself it was more than just a one-night stand?

"This has to stop." I tossed the mail on the kitchen counter and went to the fridge, taking out a beer. Except the first sip tasted flat and stale. This was a new six-pack.

It wasn't the beer. It was me. I took another sip as I rifled through the mail, my eyes catching on a sticky notice from the mailman.

The locked boxes at the carousel must have been full, and whenever that happened, he'd leave a note that my package was on the porch.

With my beer in hand, I made my way to the front door, flipping the deadbolt. On the mat was a plain brown cardboard box.

My stomach twisted. Not from that box, but the stack of five DVDs on top.

Jennsyn had brought back the movies she'd borrowed. She'd returned them when I wasn't home.

Good. That was good, right? One less interaction.

I took another swig of beer, then swept up the movies and the box, taking them to the kitchen. The beer had gone from stale to sour, so I left it on the counter with the package and movies before walking through the house for the sliding door, stepping out into the dark night.

The cool air filled my lungs and the pressure in my chest eased as I crossed the yard, toward the spot where Jennsyn liked to sit. The stars glittered in the black sky. It smelled like leaves and earth and pine. A crescent moon glowed above the twinkling lights of Mission.

I didn't spend enough time out here. I'd bought this house partly because of this view, except the only time I'd spent out here lately had been because of Jennsyn.

She'd left her mark in this yard. I doubted I'd ever think of this spot again as anything but hers.

She'd brought back the movies. That shouldn't have bothered me so much.

But it did. It fucking did.

I turned, about to head inside, when a light next door caught my eye. Warm light streamed from the window of an upstairs bedroom. And framed in the glass, eyes cast into my yard as she combed out her damp hair, was Jennsyn.

She didn't stop brushing when she realized I'd spotted

her. She just lifted her free hand and pressed her fingertips to the glass.

My heart skipped.

Fuck.

My hand dug into the pocket of my slacks, pulling out my phone, and before I let myself think about it too long, I dialed her number.

Not a saved contact. Not a number hidden under a fake name.

Her number, typed ten digits at a time.

Ten digits I'd memorized in July.

Jennsyn disappeared from the window and answered on the second ring. "Hey."

"You didn't go with Stevie and Liz to dinner with the team."

There was a long pause. "No."

"Why?"

"I didn't feel like it. After a game, I like to unwind."

No energy for gossip or small talk because she'd left it all on the court. Or maybe the team hadn't invited her along. Maybe the girls were jealous of her talent.

Star players sometimes kept apart from the team. Usually, it was because the guy felt like he was above his teammates. But that wasn't Jennsyn. She wasn't arrogant. She didn't brag.

Hell, if she was all about her talent, I would have learned at the party that she was playing for the Wildcats.

But she hadn't mentioned volleyball that night, not once. Which meant she really did need some space to unwind. Or they'd cut her out.

I hoped, for her sake, it wasn't the latter.

"You brought my movies back," I said.

"Yeah."

"When I was gone."

"Yeah." Her voice dropped to just above a whisper. "Is that why you called me?"

"No." I'd called because I couldn't stand staring at her but not hearing her voice. Because I'd wanted to talk to her at the game but had walked away instead.

I'd called because I'd missed her.

"I didn't get to say hi to you at the game."

She tucked a lock of hair behind her ear. "You didn't seem too happy to see me at the game."

Instead of smiling at her, I'd scowled.

"You caught me off guard." Story of my damn life when it came to this woman.

"We were on the field during halftime, Toren."

"I know."

Her frame sagged against the window's edge like she was just as tired as I was. She was too young to be that tired.

Jennsyn's house was angled so that from this spot, we could face each other. Because of the curve in the street, the neighbors on the other side were angled in the opposite direction.

I crossed the yard to the deck, taking one of the chairs and setting it on the lawn. Unless someone was standing right at my side, we had this privacy. Me, in the yard. Her, in that room.

I reclined back in the chair, just a guy outside on the phone. "Do you get along with Stevie and Liz?"

"Yeah. They're good roommates."

"Friends?"

She shrugged. "We're not really . . . friends."

"So you don't like them?"

"I like them."

I blinked, then a laugh bubbled free. "I don't understand women."

Even from a distance, I could see a sweet smile touch her lips. "I came here to play for the year. They're nice and it's been easy living with them, but I don't see us becoming good friends. I'm just here to graduate and have a year of volleyball on my terms."

Her terms. There was a lot behind that statement. "Want to talk about what those terms mean exactly?"

"Not especially."

"All right."

I'd leave that topic alone. But apparently, her terms meant staying at home tonight. Alone.

Though she wasn't really alone.

And neither was I, not anymore.

"What happens after this year?" I asked.

She lifted a shoulder. "Haven't decided yet."

"Do you want to keep playing?"

It must have been a heavy question because she leaned her head against the wall as the silence settled.

For any of my players, the answer would be an immediate yes. But maybe that was because they all knew they weren't going to get the chance.

This was the last stop for most seniors. They'd graduate and move on to find jobs and build lives. The only one who had the talent to play professionally was Rush Ramsey. Though given the quiet buzz throughout the team about the girl he'd gotten pregnant, none of us were sure where he'd go next, Rush included.

But for my defensive seniors, the guys I'd coached for

years, they had this season, then it was over. So if I asked them if they wanted more, they'd all say absolutely yes.

"Playing professionally is what I've worked my whole life for," she said. "To play for an international team would be a dream come true."

The flat, rehearsed tone made me sit up straighter. She spoke like she was talking to a reporter or an agent.

"Whose dream come true?" I asked.

Her head lifted with a jolt, and she stared at me, nibbling on her bottom lip. Then she exhaled so loud it was like a rush of wind from her house to mine. "My mom was a professional volleyball player. She went all the way to the Olympics to win gold."

"Damn." I whistled. "That's quite the achievement."

"She'd love nothing more than for me to follow in her footsteps," she said. "It's her dream come true. It used to be mine."

"What changed?"

She lifted a finger to the window, tracing a word on the glass. "Me."

There was a sadness in her voice that made me wish she were here. That we were having this conversation in my living room or kitchen, without so much space between us. But if she were here, I doubted I'd be able to keep myself away. Keep myself from hauling her into my arms, doing anything to take that sadness away. So I'd stay in the yard and she'd stay in her room.

"What's your dream?" I asked.

"I want to be happy," she whispered, like it was a secret she was scared to admit. "I'm a senior in college with zero aspirations other than to have a smile on my face more often than not. To have enough money to buy yummy food and rent cheesy movies from the eighties and nineties."

I chuckled. "Priorities."

Her smile widened and she drew something else on the window but I couldn't tell what she was writing. "Is it weird to have such low expectations?"

"I'm guessing most people have high expectations for you?"

"Sky-high."

"Set whatever expectations you want," I said. "But in my opinion, smiling more often than not doesn't seem like a low expectation."

She flattened her hand on the glass, almost like a hug. When she dropped her arm, I figured she'd end the call, but she relaxed against the window, shifting the phone to her other ear. "What about you? Did you always want to be a coach?"

"Yes. Ever since high school."

"Really?"

I nodded and pointed toward the city lights. "I grew up here. My coach is still at the high school. He's a good man. The kind I needed when I was that age. He pushed me hard so I'd be in a position to earn a scholarship. I loved playing and was pretty good. Maybe even great. But not great enough for the NFL. I always knew that Treasure State was where I'd play my last game."

When I looked back on my time as a player, I had no regrets. I'd had a blast in college, playing with a team. I was lucky enough to have made some lifelong friends, like Ford.

"Then what?" she asked.

"After graduation, I took a job in Oregon to coach for the Ducks. It was a long shot when I applied, but I got lucky.

Learned a lot. Worked my ass off. Then a few years ago, a spot opened up at Treasure State, so I jumped at the chance to move home."

Uncle Evan had died and Faith had needed help. Not that she ever would have asked me to come home, but the day I'd shown up, my truck loaded and towing a U-Haul, she'd had such relief on her face. Like she'd been seconds away from crumpling.

"With any luck, I'll coach my last game at Treasure State too." This job was it for me. I didn't need to be the head coach. I didn't need to leave for a bigger, more prestigious school. "Maybe that means my expectations are low too."

"I like your expectations," she said quietly.

A lull settled between us, a dip in the conversation that would have meant the end to most calls. But I couldn't bring myself to hang up. And she didn't move away from the window.

"Toren?" She didn't hang up, but she moved away from the glass, hiding somewhere in her room.

"Where'd you go?"

There was a plop in the background, like she'd slumped onto the edge of her bed. "I overheard you with Millie the other day. I was refilling my water bottle in the hall outside the study room."

"Ah." That was the day I'd forced two of my players who were barely making grades to focus more on school and less on football and girls. After I'd made sure they were settled, I'd taken Millie out for pizza. And for an hour, I'd let her dodge every attempt at a conversation about Ford.

"Millie's one of my oldest friends. We went to college together."

"Does she, um, know? About us?"

"No one does."

Another long sigh came across the line. "Are you two . . ."

I sort of loved that she couldn't finish the sentence. I sort of loved the note of envy in her soft voice. "No. It's never been like that."

Not between us. Millie and Ford? That was another story.

"Okay," she breathed.

"Okay."

It took another lull, another stretch of silence, but then she was back at the window, finger tracing idly on the glass. "You looked good on the sidelines today, Toren."

Toren. Not Coach. Not Coach Greely.

Toren.

She used my first name. Because to her, I'd never been a coach. And to me, she'd always be Jennsyn.

"I liked seeing you there," I admitted.

Two statements neither of us should be saying but were saying anyway.

"It's late," she said. "I should probably get some sleep."

"Yeah." I nodded. "Night."

"Good night." She ended the call but didn't leave the window.

And I didn't get out of my chair.

THE PARTY
JENNSYN

I ran my finger over Toren's bottom lip. The sheets were tangled around us, entwined with our naked legs. I was draped across his bare chest as he rested on the arm bent behind his head.

It was beyond late. Hours and hours had passed since that first kiss beside the pool table in the basement. By the time we'd finally made it upstairs, midnight had come and gone. But I wasn't going to sleep, not yet. Tonight had been one of the best of my life and I wasn't ready for it to end.

"You have the softest lips." Softer than any man's I'd ever kissed. "Do you use a special balm?"

"It's in the drawer." His gray-green eyes flicked to the nightstand.

I shifted over his chest and reached for the lamp beside the bed, flipping it on. It cast a golden glow into the room and the drawer as I pulled it open. I fished out a small, pink canister.

"Peppermint lip mask." I twisted off the lid and dipped my finger into the well, swiping a bit of balm before

147

smoothing it over my own lips and finishing with a smack. Then I put the tub away and moved over Toren, my legs spreading to straddle his hips.

And because his lips looked a little dry, I shared the balm on mine.

CHAPTER ELEVEN

JENNSYN

The Upshaw Gymnasium in the fieldhouse held eighteen hundred people. Not once this season had every seat been taken for a game.

Until tonight.

Stevie had warned me that the rivalry between the Treasure State Wildcats and the University of Montana Grizzlies was fierce.

"You weren't kidding," I told her as we walked onto the court, the crowd cheering and clapping so loudly it vibrated against my skin.

"I can't wait to win." Her smile had a lethal edge.

This was the Stevie I liked best. At home, she was sweet and kind. She still tried to coax me into activities, no matter how often I turned her down. She was clean, friendly and made chocolate-chip cookies on Sunday afternoons.

But during practice and at games, she was nearly as competitive as me. She never gave up on a game, even when we were winning by a landslide. She left everything she had on the court.

In that, we were the same.

She loved this game. She loved it more than I did.

And when we graduated, this would be the end for her. Stevie was a setter, and she'd play her last real game at Treasure State.

Like Toren.

Our phone conversation from last weekend had stayed with me all week. I'd replayed it over and over and over again.

All that he'd shared. All that I'd shared.

Maybe my last game would be at Treasure State too. Months ago, that notion would have sent me into a nervous tailspin. Who was I without volleyball?

But the way Toren had talked about football, how he'd moved on to coach, made that transition—the end—seem okay. Normal.

He was the first person in my life who'd ever made me consider another path. Another future.

Thoughts for later. This season wasn't close to over yet, and tonight, we had a game to win.

I walked onto the court, soaking in the noise from the crowd for another moment. Then I tuned it all out. Like Stevie, I was here to win.

———

SWEAT BEADED at my temples as I took a drink from my water bottle after the first set. Twenty-five to nine.

Usually our first set was the worst. If we played like we normally did, gaining momentum with each set, we'd be finished after three sets and would crush the Grizzlies.

Of those twenty-five points, twelve had been kills from

me. Stevie had been setting me up perfectly tonight, and not a single Griz player was going to block me.

Coach Quinn was writing on her whiteboard, running through a few changes to the defensive play. I half listened as she spoke, already knowing that she was going to adjust positioning so we'd be stronger on defense.

I absently scanned the crowd as I swallowed a gulp of water. There was a girl I recognized from my Entrepreneurship class. She smiled when she met my stare.

I took another drink, my gaze continuing to roam as my heart rate slowed with the rest. I stared at no one and everyone until a familiar pair of gray-green eyes made me take a second look.

Toren.

My breath hitched, my pulse galloping.

He'd come. He was at my Friday-night game.

Warmth crept into my cheeks as I forced myself to look away, to stare at Coach Quinn as she continued to talk.

Was he here to watch me? Or just to support the Wildcats? The football team had another home game tomorrow, then they'd be gone most weekends for a string of away games—I'd cross-checked our schedules. We had a series of games midweek coming up, then we'd be on the road too.

Which meant if Toren was going to come to a volleyball game, tonight was his only chance until November.

The rattle I'd been trying to ignore began to vibrate deep in my bones. It split my attention, stealing half of the concentration that should be on volleyball. It should bother me. It should irritate me that he'd come here and distracted me. But I didn't care.

Not even a bit. My heart was too busy soaring to care about the rattle.

I risked another glance, his stony expression giving nothing away. If he had come to watch me, he wouldn't let it show. He stared at the net and nothing else, his elbows on his knees.

The people beside him didn't seem to be with him, just other spectators. So he'd come alone.

For me? God, I wanted that to be a yes. I wanted him to see me win this game.

The pressure in my chest swelled so fast I couldn't breathe.

His Wildcats quarter-zip was pushed up his forearms. The fabric molded to those broad shoulders. Nearly two thousand people in this room and he made the rest go fuzzy.

I let myself look for another second, then swept my gaze back toward the cluster of students.

Maybe he was here because of the rivalry. Maybe he was here to support Coach Quinn. Regardless, he was here. And for a minute, I was going to pretend it was just for me.

"Let's go." Coach Quinn stood, extending her hand into the center of where we were all circled. Every player joined in, waiting for her to call it out. "One. Two. Three."

"Wildcats!" we cheered, hands flying in the air, then returned to the court, the short break between sets over.

My gaze flickered to Toren, giving myself another second to take in that handsome face and the stubble dusting his jaw, but I didn't dare stare for long.

A hand rose in the air, a quick wave, catching my attention.

Another familiar face jumped out from the crowd. A face I hadn't seen in over a year. Blue eyes the same shade as mine. Dirty-blond hair with gray at the temples.

Dad.

I blinked, making sure it was him. He smiled and nodded with another wave when he realized I'd spotted him.

But I didn't wave back. Because beside him in the fourth row was a petite brunette who probably wasn't much older than twenty-five. She had hot-pink nails that flew over the screen of her phone. She sat so close to Dad she was practically curled into his side.

That woman was not his wife.

Asshole.

I turned away and leveled a cool stare at the Grizzlies.

The girl across from me looked scared.

She should be scared.

My father had come to watch a game. So had Toren.

Time to give them a show.

———

"THAT WAS BRUTAL." Megan snorted as she laughed. "You were on fire tonight, Jennsyn."

"Thanks." My voice was flat and cold. Maybe I'd played like fire, but there was ice running through my veins.

The locker room was full of laughter and celebration. Every girl on the team wore a smile, except me.

"Are you okay?" Stevie asked.

"Yeah." I lifted my foot to the end of the bench where she was sitting. I pulled my shoe laces too hard, too fast, my fingers fumbling as I tied a knot. "It's the adrenaline. I just need to unwind. I'm edgy."

It wasn't entirely a lie. Except the edge was not from the game. It was from seeing Dad. From knowing that he'd be waiting for me in the parking lot. That he'd stand beside the BMW he'd bought me as a high school graduation gift years ago. The car he'd bought out of guilt in an attempt to pretend like he'd been a suitable father.

Meanwhile, the brunette he'd brought to my game would be waiting in his rental car, biding her time until he'd sweep her away to whatever hotel room they'd be fucking in tonight.

"See you at home," I said, picking up my bag from the floor.

I was usually the first to leave the locker room after a game. When we played at home, I'd be the first to cross the parking lot. When we were away, I'd be comfortably curled into a seat on the bus, headphones blaring as I pretended to sleep.

But tonight, I'd beat my own record for a postgame shower. The moment Coach had dismissed us from the meeting, I'd raced through a shower and hurried to get dressed. My hair was still wet and the band of my sports bra damp because I'd barely dried my skin.

I wanted Dad to be long gone to that hotel by the time the other girls came outside.

Shoving through the door, I stormed down the hallway that led to the exit. I rounded a corner, digging out my phone as I walked—and collided with a strong, male chest.

"Whoa." Toren gripped me by the shoulders, steadying me before I could lose my balance.

It was the first time he'd touched me since the night of the party.

And I was so frustrated that Dad had come here tonight, I couldn't even enjoy it.

"What's wrong?" he asked, voice low as he glanced over my shoulder to make sure we were alone.

"Nothing," I lied, forcing a smile as I backed away. "But I have to go."

I sidestepped him, about to hustle outside.

"Jennsyn." That deep, smooth voice stopped me before I could escape.

I turned.

"Good game."

My heart tumbled, and I was going to keep pretending he'd come tonight for me. "Thanks."

Without another word, I hurried to the exit. Then I raised my chin and schooled my expression to bored indifference as I walked to where I'd parked my car.

Dad, as expected, was leaning against the BMW's trunk, his phone pressed to his ear, probably talking to Tina.

His wife.

My stepmother.

When he spotted me coming his way, Dad stood tall, a smile stretching across his mouth. He said goodbye, then tucked his phone away, opening his arms wide. "There's my Jenny."

Jenny. I *hated* being called Jenny.

"Hi, Dad."

Two rows over, a car was running with its lights on.

He followed my gaze, then shifted to stand in the way, blocking my view.

Part of me wanted to ask who she was. But the other part, the one that hadn't seen her father in a year, knew it would just cause a fight. And tonight, I didn't have the energy.

He stepped close, pulling me into a tight hug. "You played great."

"Thanks."

His cologne was the same. Strong, but expensive. I hated that I'd missed that smell. That after disappointment after disappointment, I still missed his hugs. I still missed the way he set his chin on the top of my head.

He was one of the only people who could do that because he was so tall, at six seven.

I'd always wondered if Mom had actually loved Dad, or if she'd just married him because he was tall. They'd divorced by the time I was seven. He hadn't looked back and Mom had always seemed happier once he was gone. I couldn't remember them fighting when I was little. I couldn't remember them laughing either. I didn't know if they'd ever been in love and hadn't asked Mom since.

"I'm just in town for tonight," he said, letting me go. "Flying home tomorrow."

To his family. His real family. To his wife, Tina. And their two sons, Thomas and Mark. My half brothers were over ten years younger and hadn't been a part of my life because they lived in Georgia, and I'd grown up in Nebraska.

In the summers, when I was on school break and could have spent time at Dad's, I'd been at volleyball camps. And during the holidays, when I had vacations to visit, Tina— according to Dad—hadn't wanted me to take up a guest bedroom that her parents and sister's family had needed for their traditional family gathering.

Part of me felt bad for Tina because Dad cheated on her so often. The other part really didn't like Tina.

"Where were you traveling?" I asked.

"Seattle. Figured I could swing a layover for a game. Though it's not quite as easy to get to Montana as it was San Francisco."

Couldn't pass up his chance to needle me for switching schools, could he? Not because he cared where I went to school. But because traveling to a small town like Mission had meant more flights and stops. Less time with the girlfriend.

How many times had he told Tina he was coming to watch one of my games when he'd actually spent the weekend with his girlfriend instead?

I really didn't want to know.

"What's her name?" I asked, nodding past him to the car.

"Oh, uh . . ." He dragged a hand through his light hair, the strands graying at his temples. "That's Maggie. We work together. She's a volleyball fan. I told her I was coming to watch my star daughter and she tagged along. We'll head back to Atlanta tomorrow."

"Glad you could make it."

"Me too." His eyes softened as he looked over my face. "I missed your birthday."

"Yes, you did." My nose started to sting but I clenched my teeth, refusing to cry.

It wasn't the first time he'd missed my birthday. It wouldn't be the last.

"I'm sorry," he said, his voice thick. "I was swamped with work, and the boys have been so busy with basketball. I'm trying to coach Mark's team and—"

"What time is your flight in the morning?" I cut off his string of excuses. I'd heard them all before. "I could meet you for an early breakfast."

"Oh, darn. It's at six."

"Shoot." *Thank God.* "Good to see you, Dad. It was nice of you to come and watch."

"You played great, Jenny. It's really something to watch."

I nodded and leaned in for another quick hug, then moved for the driver's side door of the BMW, climbing in without a backward glance.

Dad was already walking away. Off to *Maggie*.

It hurt how little he cared. When would it stop? How many birthdays did he have to miss until I just didn't give a damn?

My chin quivered, but I bit my bottom lip and started the car, not glancing back as I drove out of the parking lot.

The house was empty when I walked inside. The bag with my clothes and shoes inside weighed a thousand pounds as I trudged upstairs to my bedroom, catching my reflection in the window.

Not a smile to be seen.

I was too tired to smile.

Last weekend, I'd told Toren that maybe my expectations were too low if all I wanted was to smile more often than not. At this point, maybe that was too much to hope for. Too much to dream.

The bag slipped from my shoulder, landing with a thud as I toed off my street shoes. The carpet was soft and plush beneath my feet, my steps silent as I retreated downstairs and to the sliding door that led to our backyard.

The difference between our lawn and Toren's was so noticeable, I knew the instant I crossed onto his property. Only a few homes in the neighborhood had fences, likely those with families who wanted to keep their kids contained. But most of the yards simply blended from one lawn to the next.

My toes squished in Toren's lush grass. The weight on my chest that had been there from the moment I'd spotted Dad seemed to float away into the black sky.

Why was it always easier to breathe out here? My house, my room, my belongings were fifty feet away. My bedroom was usually my sanctuary. At least, it had been before I'd moved to Montana.

Except here, the place that seemed to give me the most comfort was right here on the edge of a yard, staring out at glittering town lights, Toren's house standing guard over my shoulder.

A flare of headlights cut through the night, followed by the sound of a garage door opening. I didn't turn around to see if it was Stevie or Liz.

There was no reason for them to hurry home.

But Toren would.

Because he'd seen through the lie I'd delivered in the hall that nothing was wrong.

His sliding door opened and closed. I counted the seconds it took him to cross the yard—fourteen. Then he was at my side, his hands in his jeans pockets as he stared ahead. "Your feet are going to get cold."

My feet were already cold. "I'm okay," I lied.

"Are you?"

No. "My dad was at the game tonight."

"Ah. Tall guy? Black sweater? Not far from my seat?"

"Yeah. How did you know?"

"Your face changed when you saw him. Then you played like the game was a matter of life and death."

"I was mad." I let out a dry laugh. "I usually play well when I'm mad."

"I noticed." He took a step forward and turned to face me. "You didn't know he was coming."

"No." I shook my head. "He does this once or twice a season. He'll randomly show up at a game without so much

159

as a text to say he's coming. Usually he'll have a girlfriend along. This one's name was Maggie. I feel bad for his wife."

Toren took a step forward and turned to face me. "Your mom?"

"Not for a long time. His wife's name is Tina."

His face hardened in a frown. "He cheats on her."

There was so much in that reaction it made me want to throw my arms around his shoulders and smash my mouth to his.

Toren didn't know Tina. He didn't know the dynamic with Dad. But he'd judge the cheating.

God, he was making it hard to move on. Not that I'd really tried. But at this rate, my feelings for Toren would last long after the day I moved off the block.

"Can I tell you something?" I asked.

Toren's answer was to step closer, like he knew the only way I'd be able to speak this truth was in a whisper.

"I only see him when he comes to a game like he did tonight," I said. "What happens if I stop playing?"

It was rhetorical. I knew the answer.

Chances were, I wouldn't see my father again.

Toren gave me a sad smile. "I'm sorry."

"Me too." I swallowed the lump in my throat. "Why did you come to the game?"

He didn't answer. Instead, he arched his neck and stared up at the heavens. As he swallowed, his Adam's apple bobbed and my mouth went dry. Swallowing shouldn't be sexy, but everything Toren did snared my interest.

When he finally dropped his gaze back to mine, the air between us warmed. It seeped into my skin, spreading heat all the way to my cold toes.

"Why did you come to my game?" I asked again.

"Don't make me answer that." His voice was pained.

"Okay," I whispered.

What were we doing? Why couldn't we stop? My gaze dropped to his mouth and it took every bit of strength not to close the gap between us. Not to run my finger over those lips to see if they were as soft as I remembered.

"Toren?"

"Jennsyn?"

"Do you still use that peppermint lip mask?"

He closed his eyes, his jaw ticking as he skipped that question too and, instead, asked one of his own. "What do you want from me?"

"To forget about you." Not really. But that was the smart answer and I was a smart girl. "Why can't I?"

His eyes opened and the desperation in them had to match my own.

The party had just been one night. Just one fucking night.

Why couldn't either of us forget?

I unglued my frozen toes from the grass before I did something we'd both regret. I took one step backward, then another. "Goodbye, Toren."

He didn't move. He didn't stop me from leaving his yard. "Goodbye, Jennsyn."

CHAPTER TWELVE

TOREN

October ninth.

It was one of three days that I dreaded each year. January sixteenth. September seventh. October ninth.

Seventeen years ago today, my mother had died. A year later, Dad had been gone too.

I'd lived longer without Mom than I'd had with her. It wasn't fucking fair.

God, what I wouldn't give to be busy today. To have a grueling practice or game to serve as a distraction. Except this year, October ninth fell on a Tuesday. The quietest day of the week.

Practice was nothing more than a brief meeting. Players were expected to fit in a light workout, but otherwise, Tuesday was their day to catch up on schoolwork and give their bodies a rest.

Tuesday was the day coaches could hit emails and admin tasks. I wasn't in the mood to do much of anything except go home and watch movies on the couch, but I'd forced myself to come to the office today, knowing that if I sat at home alone, it would just be that much harder.

"Toren." Parks blew through my open door, pushing it closed before he plopped in one of the empty chairs across from my desk. "Help."

It was about a woman. Before he even opened his mouth, I knew it was about a woman. "What's up?"

"It's about this girl I've been seeing."

"Ah." Of course, it was. They'd probably met online.

"We met on Tinder."

"Okay," I drawled. And either she was blowing him off. Or he wanted to break up but still have sex.

"I think she's about to end it."

"Why do you say that?" I leaned back in my chair, grateful for once that he was horrible at relationships. Today, I'd take any distraction I could get.

"She stopped texting me."

Then she wasn't about to end it, she'd already ended it. And Parks wasn't ready to admit defeat.

Every one of us on the coaching staff was competitive, but Parks took it to the extreme in every aspect of his life. He thrived in attack mode. It worked when he was on the field, and he pushed his players hard but not too hard. He knew when to back off when it came to football and coaching.

But with women? Not so much.

"How long have you been dating?" I asked.

"Three weeks, give or take."

"As in the last three weeks?" We'd been on the road for two of the three weekends for away games. During the week, we'd been slammed with practices most evenings. Which meant this woman he'd been seeing had probably gotten

Tuesdays and not much else. "How often have you seen her?"

"I don't know." He shrugged. "We hooked up a couple times early on. I've been texting her but it's been hard to line up our schedules."

"Maybe she just wanted something casual."

"Yeah, I guess." He shook his head. "Honestly, I don't know why it's even bothering me. She made a comment on our last date about football being shallow."

Ouch. "Then I wouldn't be too upset that she's not texting you back."

He groaned. "You're right. I just . . . liked her. She was sweet."

"If she doesn't understand how grueling a season can be, if she's going to throw shade at a game we love, I think you're better off moving on."

Was that why I liked Jennsyn? Because she understood what this world was like? She understood dedication to a sport. To a team. That the demanding travel and practice schedules were a sacrifice we were all glad to make.

"Yeah," he grumbled, sagging in the chair and exhaled. "Dating sucks."

"It does." Not that I went on many dates. One-night stands, sure. Hookups, yeah. But dates?

It was rare that I'd meet a woman I wanted to give the little time I had to spare this time of year.

Until Jennsyn.

I hadn't seen her in three weeks. Nearly a month. At this point, I felt like a starved man. It should have been good to put that time and distance between us. To let her fade away. Except it wasn't fading.

She'd been on the road for her own games, and the one

weekend we'd played at home, the volleyball team had been in Colorado. I hadn't seen her coming or going from the house. I hadn't found her in my backyard.

If not for the highlight reels posted on social media, I wouldn't have even seen her face. But I'd become the volleyball team's most loyal follower. I checked my phone constantly, hoping to see a recap or clip from a game. Hoping to see her smile after a win.

They were still undefeated. She was still playing with that fire.

And fuck my life, but I'd missed it. I'd missed her.

"Guess it's back to Tinder," Parks muttered, shoving out of the chair. "But first, I get to tell two of my guys on the line that if they don't get their grades up, they're on the bench Saturday."

"Good luck."

"Thanks. Door open or closed?"

"Closed." I needed a few minutes to myself.

"See ya." He let himself out, closing the door behind him.

I shook the mouse for my computer, about to check on my own players' grades, when a knock came at the door. Before I could answer, Ford peeked his head inside.

"Hey."

"Hi." Ford came inside and closed the door, then took the seat Parks had just vacated, slumping against its back. "Got a minute?"

"Sure. What's up?"

"Guess who showed up in Mission on Saturday."

With the dread in his voice, it had to be his ex-wife. "Sienna."

"Yep." He popped the *p*.

"Damn." I cringed. "Sorry."

I'd known Sienna in college when she'd dated Ford. She'd been drama back then and, after everything he'd told me about their divorce, was still drama now. But he was stuck with her in his life, at least until their daughter, Joey, graduated high school.

"How long is she here?"

He shrugged. "No idea. For Joey's sake, hopefully more than a weekend."

Sienna hadn't seen their daughter since Ford had moved. He had full custody of Joey, and Sienna was still living in Seattle.

"You okay?" I asked.

"Not especially. Millie wants to take a pause while Sienna is in town. Whatever the fuck a pause means."

A pause. That meant there was something *to* pause. Neither of them had officially confirmed their relationship, though I'd suspected they were together for a while.

"So . . . you and Millie are official?"

"We're keeping it quiet. For obvious reasons."

"How's this going to shake out with work?" I asked.

He dragged a hand through his hair. "I don't know. But if it means I have to quit, then I'll quit."

Damn. He'd give it all up for Millie?

Working for Ford had been a dream this year. He was a strong leader and never left us guessing. Yet he didn't meddle in our shit either. He trusted us to do our jobs and we trusted he'd have our backs.

I loathed the idea of a different boss. But I'd rather my friends be happy. Besides, I liked that Ford would quit for Millie. That he knew her worth. That he'd fight to keep her, even if it cost him a career.

"You know I won't say a thing," I said.

"Was never worried you would." Ford blew out a long breath. "I don't want her to be lonely during this fucking pause or whatever. If you're free, would you mind taking her out for a cheeseburger or something one night? Make one of those bets you make with her to see who can eat more fries."

I chuckled. "You got it."

Millie and I had bet on a lot of stupid shit over the years, all in good fun. Who could run faster. Who could eat a dozen chicken wings the fastest. Who could hold their breath the longest.

We hadn't made a trivial bet in a while. Maybe tonight, in an effort to keep my mind off October ninth and to give Ford some peace of mind, I'd take Millie out for dinner. We'd see who could put away the most tacos.

"Thanks." He smacked his hands on his knees before he stood. "Want to grab lunch?"

"Actually, I think I'm going to hit the gym." I hadn't felt like getting out of bed to work out this morning, but sitting at this desk all morning had made me stiff and restless. "Rain check?"

"Of course." He left with a wave.

Before anyone else could swing by for relationship advice, I grabbed my phone and earbuds, then headed for the locker room to change.

The sound of metal clanging greeted me as I stepped into the weight room. The lunch hour was always open. Millie made sure there were windows of time every day where students and staff members in the department could work out.

The steady thump of shoes on a treadmill pounded in

the background as I fitted in my earbuds, drowning out the noise.

Usually, there were no students during the lunch hour, just faculty members. Two employees who worked upstairs with Millie had come in to lift. But on that treadmill, I caught the swish of a short, blond ponytail. The long legs. The toned shoulders and slender waist.

The air whooshed from my lungs.

Jennsyn stared ahead, the screen on her treadmill black. She ran with easy, graceful strides, arms pumping and shoulders straight.

For a moment, I almost turned around. I almost left her to do her workout while I found another way to clear my head. Except it had been three weeks.

I'd missed her face.

It was October ninth.

And today, I didn't give a fuck about the rules. I just wanted to see her smile.

So I crossed the space, nodding as I passed a guy stretching on the mats in the corner. Then I climbed on the treadmill three down from hers, not sparing her a glance as I hit the buttons and started to run.

Jennsyn's gaze flicked my direction through the mirrors on the far wall and she did a double take. Her mouth parted, like her breath had hitched, and damn it, that was almost better than a smile.

She was dressed in a pair of black leggings and a strappy white sports bra. She studied me for a moment, her eyes narrowing. Then she cocked her head to the side, like she did when she was trying to figure me out.

When she faced forward again, there was a crease

between her eyebrows. But soon she found an invisible spot in those mirrors and gave it her undivided attention.

I did the same, keeping my focus trained ahead. But she was there. She was close.

That was enough.

So I ran, one mile, then two. After three, I normally stopped to lift, except she was still running, steady and strong. I wasn't ready to walk away yet.

There was a slight sheen on her forehead and a flush to her cheeks, but otherwise, she made it seem effortless.

By mile four, my legs were getting tired. I didn't train as a distance runner, and beyond a simple warm-up, I never spent much time on the treadmills. But Jennsyn hadn't stopped, so I didn't either.

She hit a button, and for a moment, I sighed, glad to finally be done. Except it wasn't to quit. She increased the speed.

Son of a bitch. There was a ghost of a smile on her lips, like she was daring me to stop. Challenge accepted.

I punched the plus sign on my machine, picking up my pace in an attempt to match her strides until I hit five miles. My lungs were on fire and sweat dripped down my face.

Fuck. I gobbled air more than breathed. But I didn't stop. I didn't slow. Not until finally, at nearly six miles, Jennsyn slowed down to a walk, lifting her hands above her head as she breathed.

I ran for another minute, waiting until the distance marker hit six before I smacked my hand onto the stop button. Then I got the hell off this fucking treadmill, walking to the drinking fountain to gulp some water. I used the hem of my shirt to dry my face, though the sweat kept dripping.

Plucking out my earbuds, I shoved them in a pocket and

braced my hands on my knees. My chest heaved as I tried to regain my breath.

A pair of neon-orange-and-white tennis shoes appeared in my line of sight. Jennsyn's shoes.

She was closer than a student should stand to a coach. Except when I scanned the weight room, it was empty. While I'd been trying to run myself into the ground, the rest of the people had cleared out.

"Are you okay?" Jennsyn's hands were braced on her hips. She didn't sound at all winded.

"Yeah." I waved it off. "I'm not a runner."

"I'm not asking about the workout." She gave me a sad smile. "You look sad."

Well, I was sad. And the only person who'd noticed was this woman.

This woman who I wanted to haul into my arms and kiss until she couldn't breathe either.

"It's not the best day," I said.

"You should watch a cheesy movie to cheer yourself up later." That pretty mouth curved into a dazzling smile. A smile that made those six fucking miles worth every step.

"Any recommendations?"

"*Mannequin*. Or *Ferris Bueller's Day Off*."

Both were in the stack she'd returned last month.

They'd been two of my mother's favorites. Exactly what I should watch on October ninth.

Jennsyn had no idea, but that was probably the best recommendation I could have asked for.

I nodded, swallowing the lump in my throat. "Good idea."

It took everything in my power to stop it there. To not invite her over to watch a movie on my couch tonight.

Her head cocked to the side again as her gaze roved over my body, head to toe. It wasn't sensual. It was concern, like she was trying to find the source of the pain.

Her eyes settled on my chest. On my heart.

"Toren—"

The door opened and Millie walked inside, dressed in running shorts and a tank top, her hair in a long ponytail.

Jennsyn jolted, then sidestepped me for the water fountain, acting like we were just two people who needed a drink.

Millie smiled when she spotted me, though it didn't quite reach her eyes. Probably because of whatever was happening with Ford. She was probably here to run ten miles in an effort to block it out.

I crossed the room, stopping in front of her. "Hey. Want to go out for tacos tonight? Bet you ten bucks I can eat more than you."

"You're on." There was a shadow in Millie's gaze she couldn't hide even though she tried. "Thanks."

"Welcome." As she made her way to a treadmill, I risked a glance toward the water fountain.

But Jennsyn was already gone.

THE PARTY
TOREN

Jennsyn's finger drew a line across my jaw as she yawned.

My hand was snaked around her waist beneath the sheets, my own fingers tracing tiny circles on the dimples in her lower back.

A yawn stretched my mouth too. It was three o'clock in the morning, and I was so fucking tired. With every passing second, it was getting harder and harder to keep my eyes open. But damn if I wouldn't force myself to stay awake until she fell asleep.

"Someday, you should grow a beard," she whispered as her finger scraped along my stubble.

I arched my eyebrows. "A beard?"

"Yeah. I bet you'd look sexy with a beard."

"Are you saying I'm not sexy?"

She laughed. "Grow a beard, Toren."

When she said my name like that, her voice low and breathy, I'd do whatever the hell she wanted.

"We should sleep." She yawned again.

"Not yet." I rolled on top of her naked body, fitting myself between her hips. My cock throbbed as it pressed against her wet center.

She moaned as I took her mouth.

And all that yawning came to a stop.

CHAPTER THIRTEEN

JENNSYN

The library on campus was crammed with students and whispering study groups. Every table and cubby around me was occupied, and even though it was silent, I was struggling to block out movements and footsteps and shuffling papers. The girl next to me kept tapping the eraser of her pencil on her table and the *tat, tat, tat* was making me edgy. My headphones were inconveniently at the bottom of my gym bag at the fieldhouse.

I tucked a lock of hair behind my ear and leaned in closer to my textbook, rereading a paragraph for the second time just as my phone rang, its chime so loud it seemed to fill the library's entire second floor.

Shit. My fingers fumbled as I rushed to silence the call. Heat swamped my face as I glanced up, finding more than a few glares aimed my way. The main library wasn't as forgiving as the study hall for athletes in the fieldhouse.

"Sorry," I mouthed to the girl at the table beside mine as she scowled.

She rolled her eyes and kept tapping that goddamn pencil.

Mom's name was still on my phone's screen, but I let her call go to voicemail as I swept up my books and notebooks, stuffing them in my backpack. Then I slipped away from the table where I'd been sitting for the past hour and made my way toward the stairs.

By the time I jogged from the second floor to the first, my phone vibrated in my hand with a message.

Jennsyn. You need to call me back.

"Nope," I muttered, then set off across the dark campus.

Tall, bright lamps lit the campus sidewalks but it was quiet tonight. Only a few other students were out walking around. Two girls came out of a lecture hall. An older man with a satchel strung across his torso, probably a professor, emerged from the chemistry building.

My phone buzzed again, this time with a text from Mom. *Call me. Tonight.*

I'd been dodging her calls and texts for over a month. It was the longest I'd ever gone without speaking to my mother.

If I thought she actually wanted to talk to me, I would have called her back. But she was going to hound me about Mike Simmons, and since I still hadn't decided if I wanted him as my agent, there was no point in a discussion with Mom.

I wasn't in the mood to get reprimanded about my future. To hear her disappointment when I told her I had doubts. I wasn't quite ready to admit what I was still coming to terms with myself.

This was my last year of volleyball.

Maybe. Probably. I wasn't one hundred percent sure yet.

If I couldn't decide for myself, I sure as hell wasn't going to bring my mother into the mix. She'd lose her damn mind. So I'd ignored her. Entirely.

She knew I was busy. We were in the thick of the season, traveling across the West for various games. Classes were busy, and I'd just finished midterms. Practices were daily, and whenever I had a free moment, I tried to fit in additional workouts. Like last week, when I'd gone into the weight room over the lunch hour after one of my classes had been canceled and Toren had come in to run on a treadmill.

Something had been wrong with him that day. There'd been a cloud hanging over his head. I'd wanted to ask about it, but then Millie had come into the room and we'd had to pretend to be strangers. I hadn't seen him again since. With football and volleyball overlapping, his schedule was as hectic as my own.

Was he okay? I hoped he was okay.

Like he had been for months, Toren was a constant on my mind, whether we crossed paths or not. He'd stolen so much of my attention I wasn't sure what I'd do when this crush stopped. And if I quit volleyball, then what would I think about? What would I have left?

A surge of restless energy shot through my veins, so I walked faster, hoping to shake it off as I made my way to the fieldhouse. My car wasn't alone beneath the parking lot's bright lights. Wednesdays were typically busy nights on campus with club activities and regular study hours. It was usually so busy in the study hall that there were no empty seats, hence why I'd decided to skip it altogether and study in the main library after grabbing dinner from the student union once we'd finished practice.

The team was leaving tomorrow for a series of games starting in Idaho and ending in Utah. Before we left, I'd wanted to finish up an economics assignment due Monday. With it finished, now I could go home and relax. Maybe tonight I'd rewatch my favorite of Toren's movies.

Except the moment I started my car and buckled my seat belt, the phone rang again, the jingle blaring through the speakers. Mom's name popped up on the console.

"Ugh."

Apparently, over a month was as long as she was going to let me ignore her. She was just going to keep calling until I answered, wasn't she? My mother was a stubborn, stubborn woman.

I tensed, my heart climbing into my throat, and hit the button to accept. "Hi, Mom."

"Jennsyn."

Did all mothers have the ability to make the name they gave you sound like a slap in the face? Or just mine?

A thick, heavy silence filled the car as she waited for me to respond.

There was no point in making small talk or excuses, so I put the car in drive and started for home, replacing that silence with the whir of my tires on pavement.

"You're really not going to say anything," she said. Her nostrils were probably flaring. "Fine. You have a meeting with Mike Simmons on Monday. He'll be calling you at noon. Answer. That. Call."

No. It was on the tip of my tongue to say no.

But . . .

What if I didn't close the door on volleyball yet? What if I kept it open for just a little bit longer to see what happened? Until I decided for certain?

Did I want to play professionally? Maybe. It was the smart choice. After graduation, I needed a job, and playing in Europe for a while would be a great way to set myself up financially for the future.

The least I could do was get that information from Mike, right?

"Okay," I blurted before I could stop myself.

"Thank you." Mom sighed. "You're lucky he's even still willing to talk. I cannot believe you've dragged your feet on this. What is going on with you?"

"Nothing. I'm just busy."

"I have a hard time believing you're busier at a nowhere Montana university than you were at Stanford."

I gritted my teeth to keep from replying. Why had I answered this call? Why?

"I'm not buying the busy excuse," she said. "Something is going on. Is it your father?"

I blew out a long breath. "No. It's not about Dad."

"Have you talked to him lately?" Mom asked.

Years ago, I'd learned to answer that question carefully. If she wasn't satisfied with the answer, she'd call and lecture him about making an effort with his only daughter. Then Dad would call me and the *effort* he put forth made everything awkward.

Dad didn't know me. He'd never tried to get to know me. I didn't want him calling me because he felt guilty.

I wanted him to call because he missed me. Because he thought of me. If the attention he tossed my direction was because she'd forced his hand, well . . . I'd rather not speak to him at all.

We hadn't talked or texted since he'd come to Montana, and I didn't expect to hear from Dad again until the next game he decided to watch. If there was a next game.

"He came to a game," I told Mom. "He was in Seattle and stopped over on his way home."

"Ah. Was he alone?"

Another mistake I'd made years ago. I'd confided in Mom that Dad was cheating on Tina. She hadn't acted surprised. Maybe he'd cheated on Mom too. Probably.

"No," I admitted.

"So he came to your game as an excuse to get away with his latest girlfriend. Typical Warren."

"It's fine, Mom."

"It's not fine."

No, it wasn't. But it was my reality. "I'll talk to Mike on Monday," I said.

"Good. Call me afterward."

"All right."

Mom ended the call without a goodbye. Without a question about me. About how I was doing or how school was going. She hadn't even asked about the team. Though that was probably because she saw the scores posted each week. She knew we were crushing everyone we played. That, or she didn't care about my victories at Treasure State.

In her eyes, they probably didn't count, since this wasn't Stanford. Was that why she hadn't come out to watch? Because she was still mad that I'd transferred without her approval?

Last year, Mom had come to eight of my home games. Afterward, she'd take me out to dinner and coach me on everything I'd done wrong. For our away games, she'd deliver pointers on our next phone call.

This year, other than her determination to get me signed with Mike Simmons, she hadn't said a single thing about my play. And Mom hadn't once mentioned flying over from

Nebraska to catch a game. The lack of critique and attention was eerie. Liberating.

It hurt, a little. But it was mostly a relief. For the first time, I felt like I was playing outside of her reach. It had required I drop to a smaller school and smaller program. But it was like stepping out from beneath her umbrella, expecting to get rained on. Instead, sunshine warmed my face.

It was freeing to simply play and know that the only person who'd instruct me later was Coach Quinn. She'd given me a few pointers lately about timing, but her advice was different than I'd gotten from other coaches. She'd been teaching me how to draw the best out of the other girls.

It was a different way to think about the game. Rather than just my performance, my dominance, it was about how I could set the other girls up for their best too. Especially Stevie. The last few games, she'd played different. Better. Stronger. It was . . . fun.

It had been a long time since *fun* had been at the top of the list whenever I'd described volleyball.

The price I was paying for that fun was my mother's devotion.

Maybe it hurt more than a little.

The neighborhood was quiet as I turned down our sleepy street. Light spilled from windows as I rolled down the street, easing into my driveway. The only dark house on the block was Toren's.

Where was he tonight? Out to dinner? At a friend's house? On a date?

Not my business.

I pulled into the garage and headed inside. Stevie was studying at the dining room table, her earbuds in to block out the noise from the TV. Liz was sitting cross-legged on the couch, a sitcom playing in the background as she bent over the notebook splayed across her lap.

"Hey," I said as I walked into the living room.

"Hi." Liz looked up and smiled. "You got a package today. I put it on your bed."

"Thanks. Have a good night."

"Night." Liz used to give me a strange look when I'd retreat to my room before nine. But they'd gotten used to the fact that I didn't spend much time in the common areas. I used the kitchen to cook and the laundry room to wash clothes, but otherwise, I kept to myself.

So I climbed the stairs and closed myself in my bedroom, dropping my backpack on the floor before I picked up the package on my bed.

With a quick tear, I ripped open the seal of the box. Then I eased out the four DVDs inside, smiling to myself as I inspected them front and back.

Toren might love the cheesy eighties and nineties movies. But these were a few of my old favorites. *Alien, The Silence of the Lambs,* and *It.*

They were movies that had scared the living shit out of me when I was younger. Movies I'd sneak on nights when Mom was out to dinner with her friends and would leave me home alone.

The fourth movie was one I'd bought to watch on my laptop. It was one I couldn't remember Toren having, but of all the movies I'd watched, something about it had become my favorite.

The Karate Kid Part II

It was corny. It was nauseatingly sweet. And I loved it anyway.

As much as I wanted to race downstairs and jog to Toren's to put them on his doorstep, my roommates would definitely ask questions, so I set the DVDs aside and finished up another hour of studying before calling it quits. I brushed my teeth and pulled on a pair of comfortable sweats, then lay on my bed reading on my Kindle, the lights off and my door closed, listening for when Liz finally went to her own bedroom.

I waited another thirty minutes, until it was after eleven, then grabbed the movies and slipped out of my room. My bare feet were noiseless as I tiptoed downstairs, making sure none of the lights were on and Stevie had gone to bed too. I held my breath as I crept to the front door.

My pulse roared in my ears as I flipped the lock, tensing as it clicked. God, this was stupid. But the house was still and dark. The living room was empty and the only sound came from the air blowing through the vents.

I stepped outside, only breathing once the door was closed and I was jogging toward Toren's.

Dim light flickered through his living room windows, like he was watching TV. I leapt up the single step to his porch, setting the movies on his welcome mat. Then I whirled, about to make my escape home—and froze.

My heart raced, pounding against my sternum so hard it was like I'd run twenty miles, not twenty feet.

Go home. Go home, Jennsyn.

I turned back toward his door, pulling my bottom lip between my teeth. Screw it. With a quick rap of my knuckles, I knocked on his door. If he didn't answer, in ten seconds, I'd go home.

Ten Mississippi. Nine Mississippi. Eight Mississippi.

When I reached zero, the door was still closed.

My heart sank as I spun to leave, but before I could step off that concrete step, the door swept open. And then he was there, filling its frame and looking more handsome than ever.

Twelve *Mississippi*s. I'd needed to give him twelve seconds. "Hi."

"Hey." He stared for a moment, his expression solid and unreadable.

I tucked a lock of hair behind my ear, suddenly feeling very exposed beneath his porch light. Feeling like I was a stupid girl for sneaking over here like a teenager with a crush. "Sorry to bother you."

"It's fine." His gaze traveled down my body in a quick assessment. When he reached my bare feet, he frowned.

I simply shrugged, then walked to the movies, bending to pick them up off the mat. "These are for you. Your collection is lacking other genres, so I thought we'd start with my favorite."

He took them from my hand, scanning the spines before he arched an eyebrow. "Horror movies?"

"There's something magical about being terrified in your own home for two to three days after finishing a movie."

He chuckled, shaking his head. Then he shifted out of the way, nodding for me to come inside. "Get in here. Before you lose a toe to frostbite."

"It's not that cold."

"Jennsyn. Inside."

It was foolish and reckless. We needed time apart, not together. But I slipped past him and inside anyway.

"Just for a minute." I'd stay for no more than sixty seconds, then I'd go home. Except the moment I crossed the threshold into the warmth of his home, trying to give him as much space as possible, I caught a hint of his cologne in the air.

Cedar and soap and Toren.

Not a chance one minute would be enough.

I followed him through the entryway as he carried the movies to the kitchen. The TV was on in the living room with ESPN playing. But he didn't move to turn on any other lights, and in the darkness, he was temptation personified.

He was in a pair of jeans that hung low on his hips. His plain gray T-shirt stretched across his biceps and chest, molding to the muscles of his arms. His feet were bare too and his hair disheveled. He looked slightly rumpled, like maybe he'd fallen asleep on the couch.

The woman who'd get to curl up beside him on quiet Wednesday nights for the rest of her life was luckier than she'd ever know.

"Thank you." He set the movies on the counter. "What are they for?"

"You seemed sad last week when I saw you in the gym. I thought these might cheer you up."

"Horror movies cheer you up?"

"Yes." I nodded. "Actually, they do. They take me out of my head."

"Ah." He scanned the titles again, pulling out *The Karate Kid II*. "You consider this a horror movie?"

"No." I smiled. "I didn't think you had that one. After watching all of the ones I borrowed, it popped up as a recommendation, so I rented it. Figured you should have it for your collection."

"Ah." He studied it for a moment. "I don't have this one."

"Do you not like it?"

"Never seen it."

"Oh. It's good. Probably one of my favorites."

He leaned a hip against the counter of the island, crossing his arms over his chest. "Why? Is it not as corny as the others?"

"Oh, it's corny. But he fights for her. Literally."

Something about that movie had hit me so hard I'd started crying. Those tears you cry when you're just so overwhelmed with emotions they leak out as tears.

Maybe because I wasn't sure I'd ever have someone fight for me.

Toren hummed and dipped his chin. The scene changed on the TV, making the room flash brighter and giving me a better look at his face. At the stubble on his jaw. It was thicker than normal, like he hadn't shaved in days.

"You're growing a beard." It was part statement, part question, part hope.

He lifted a shoulder.

That meant yes.

He was growing a beard. For me.

Okay, maybe it was for himself. Maybe that conversation we'd had months ago had just sparked his own curiosity about a beard. But tonight, I was taking the credit. I was claiming the beard as my own.

Even though it wasn't mine.

And neither was he.

I took a step away while I still had the strength and willpower. "Have a good night."

Except before I could leave, his voice, quiet and deep and smooth, made me stop.

"October ninth is a hard day for me. It's the anniversary of my mom's death. That's why I looked sad when I saw you in the gym last week."

"Toren." I pressed a hand to my heart. "I'm so sorry."

"Me too. She died a long time ago. Running six miles beside you helped take my mind off of it. Thanks for that. I'm never running again, by the way."

I laughed. "Oh, come on. You're not a quitter."

Something flashed across his expression, almost like a challenge. A dare that had nothing to do with running.

"Jennsyn." He straightened and stood tall, his eyes holding mine as they smoldered. There was no other word for it. He looked at me so intensely, fire sparked beneath my skin.

The same fire I'd felt months ago.

My heart thumped too hard. My chest felt too tight to breathe. I was well past my one-minute time limit, but I couldn't pick up my feet. I was glued to this spot, held captive by those gray-green irises.

"I can't stop thinking about you." His voice was no more than a murmur. "You were supposed to fade away."

"So were you," I whispered.

He swallowed hard, his Adam's apple bobbing. "I need to stop thinking about you. This is rash, and there's too much on the line."

I nodded. "I know."

He was right. He was so, so right. But here I was, standing barefoot in his house because I couldn't walk away.

Toren closed the gap between us, towering over me as his gaze searched mine. An inch of crackling, electric air was all that separated us. He lifted a hand, his fingertips brushing the hair off my temple.

The moment he touched me, my entire body seemed to sigh. To relax. Like I'd been on edge for months, holding my breath, just waiting to be right back here where I could exhale.

"I can't stop thinking about you," he repeated, his voice taking on a darker edge this time. "Say goodbye, Jennsyn. Tell me goodbye. And mean it this time."

"Goodbye, Toren." There wasn't a hint of confidence in my voice. Not a bit.

Because I had no idea how to say goodbye to this man.

CHAPTER FOURTEEN

TOREN

Her breath was a whisper across my lips. Those beautiful blue eyes were locked on mine as she held perfectly still.

Waiting.

Wondering.

This woman. This fucking woman. I wanted her more than I'd ever wanted anything in my life.

Why Jennsyn? What was it about her that had me so enchanted? We hardly knew each other. We'd had one night together months ago and nothing more than a few chance encounters and conversations. Except somehow, she'd crawled under my skin.

That soft, pink mouth was just an inch away. An inch that meant putting my career on the line. My financial stability. My reputation. An inch that meant throwing all caution to the wind.

Was it worth it?

Was *she* worth it?

Yes. My heart thundered in my chest. It might as well have been spelling out *yes* with each thump.

Jennsyn was worth it. I knew it as surely as I knew my name was Toren Greely. As certainly as I was thirty-three years old. As unquestionably as I was a man made of flesh and bone.

She was worth the risk.

A growl rumbled in my chest. "Fuck it."

I crushed my mouth to hers.

A gasp escaped her throat, like she hadn't expected me to make a move. That tiny noise shot straight to my cock and sent fire coursing through my veins. My arms banded around her, hauling her close until that inch between us was vapor. I groaned against her mouth as I licked the seam of her lips.

She parted for me instantly, her entire body melting against mine.

This fucking woman. We were doomed.

I swept my tongue inside, tangling it with hers. I poured every bit of frustration, every bit of longing, into this kiss, sinking so deep I didn't even care that I was about to drown.

This was what I'd been missing since July. Her. Holy hell, I'd missed her. More than I'd even realized.

Jennsyn's arms circled my shoulders, cinching tight as she pulled closer and closer. Her tongue swirled against mine as she whimpered, her fingers diving into my hair.

Another low hum escaped my chest as I slanted my mouth over hers, devouring and exploring every corner of her mouth. Taking everything I'd wanted since the summer.

My arms tightened, holding her so tight that she'd never wiggle free. It wasn't just a kiss, it was a claiming. Damn the cost. We weren't done. Not yet. Not by a long shot.

With every nip, every stroke or slide of my tongue, every

lick, Jennsyn matched my intensity. We clung to each other, like this kiss alone could fuse us together.

One of my hands drifted down the curve of her back, sliding past her hip to that perfect, tight curve of her ass. I squeezed hard, swallowing her hiss. Then I moved lower, down a long, sexy thigh to hook my hand under her knee and haul her leg around my own.

With a tilt of my hips, I ground my arousal into her center.

Jennsyn mewled, shifting closer to grind right back.

With a quick lift, I picked her up off the floor and pivoted her to the island, setting her on the edge of the counter, never once breaking the kiss. Then I feasted on that luscious mouth, reacquainting myself with every inch as she spread her legs wide, making space for me to keep rocking against her core.

Her legs wrapped around my hips, holding me in place as I tore my lips from hers and kissed a wet trail along her jaw to her ear.

"Toren," she murmured.

God, I loved my name in her voice. "Say it again."

"Toren." Her head lolled to the side as I moved down her neck, licking her pulse before sucking it into my mouth.

Every cell in my body screamed to mark this woman. To show the world that she was mine.

But she took my face in her hands, pulling my mouth away, like she knew exactly what I'd almost done. No marks on her neck. I'd have to find another place to leave my trace.

I latched my teeth on to her earlobe, pulling it into my mouth with a bite.

Jennsyn moaned. "Yes."

"Fuck, I want you."

"Yes. Get this off." She pulled at my T-shirt, fisting the fabric at my shoulders in her hands.

I slid my fingers beneath the hem of her hoodie, finding smooth, warm skin. With a kiss at the delicate spot beneath her ear, I skimmed her ribs, moving up and up and up for her breasts. "I'm going to fuck you all night long."

"All night." She yanked harder on my shirt.

When my hands reached the band of her sports bra, I splayed them wide across her ribs, positioning my thumbs at her nipples. They were pebbled, ready for my mouth. I flicked them both, pressing hard as she arched into my touch.

I shifted my mouth to the shell of her ear, my nose dragging in the sweet, citrus scent of her hair. "I'm going to fuck you right here. I'm going to bury myself inside you and fuck you until you scream."

Her body trembled against mine, her breath coming in short pants as I kept toying with her nipples. "Yes."

"Then we're on the couch again. I want you riding my cock."

"Toren," she whimpered. "More."

"And then we'll go upstairs." Where she'd be in my bed all night long.

"Oh God." She gulped. "Set an alarm. Right now. I have to be home by four."

I kissed that spot beneath her ear again, then I ripped myself away and strode into the living room where I'd left my phone on an end table. I'd set the alarm. Then the world could burn down for all I cared as long as Jennsyn was in my bed.

Except the moment I picked up my phone, a string of missed notifications filled the screen.

Five missed calls from Faith. Four texts. The latest made my stomach drop.

Call me. Abel was in an accident.

"Oh my God." I punched her name, pressing the phone to my ear as I dragged a hand over my face. "Be okay."

Please, be okay. He had to be okay. Our family couldn't take another hit. Faith couldn't survive another blow.

As the phone rang, my head started to spin. What kind of accident? It was a Wednesday. It wasn't winter, so the roads were clear. How bad was it?

I closed my eyes, sucking in some air as my body started to sway.

A hand wrapped around my elbow, an anchor to keep me steady. When I opened my eyes, Jennsyn's were waiting.

"Hey," Faith answered, her voice wobbly. "He's okay."

The air rushed from my lungs. "What happened?"

"He rolled his car. Or his friend rolled his car. They were out driving on one of those winding country roads toward the mountains and were going too fast."

"But he's okay?"

"He's okay." She sniffled. "He's in deep shit. He was drinking. But he's okay."

My shoulders sagged. "Where are you?"

"The emergency room."

"I'm on my way." My feet started moving before I'd even ended the call, carrying me toward the hall that led to the mudroom. I shoved my phone in my pocket as I jogged. "I've got to go. My cousin was in an accident. He's in the ER."

"Is he okay?" Jennsyn asked, trailing behind me.

"Yeah. But I need to be there." I snagged a pair of tennis shoes from the tray beside the door that opened to the garage.

"Okay." She moved for the tray too, stepping her bare feet into the navy Crocs I wore around the house. Then she snagged a baseball hat from a hook, trapping her blond hair beneath the brim before covering it with the hood of her sweatshirt. "Let's go."

"Jennsyn—"

She held up a hand, cutting me off. "You're not driving to the hospital alone. I'll stay in the truck when we get there or sit in the waiting room or hide in a corner so no one realizes we're together. But you're not driving there alone."

It hit like a sledgehammer to my chest.

There wasn't time to absorb it. To let it sink in, not tonight. Not while my head was spinning and there was fear rising from my bones. A fear that I'd buried years ago. A fear born from experience. From losing a mother. A father. An uncle.

All three at the Mission Medical Center.

If Jennsyn was willing to ride along so I didn't have to go alone, then I'd let her tonight. Even if that meant going to a very public place together on a Wednesday night where there'd be no pretending we were strangers.

My family couldn't lose another person. I wouldn't survive another anniversary date to remember each year, not yet.

And I wasn't too proud to admit I didn't want to go to the hospital alone.

"Okay." I clasped Jennsyn's hand, pulling her with me into the garage.

When we got to the ER, she offered to wait in the truck.

But I reached for her hand instead. "Go inside with me?"

She laced our fingers together. "Absolutely."

CHAPTER FIFTEEN

TOREN

F aith was in the waiting room when we walked through the emergency room's double doors. She had her phone pressed to her ear as she paced along the back wall, her eyes glued to the linoleum as she walked.

Jennsyn wiggled her fingers, trying to slip free from my grip, but I held tight.

Other than Faith and the nurse stationed at the reception desk, the waiting room was empty. Tonight, I didn't care that they'd see us together. I was using Jennsyn's hold to keep me steady until I knew that Abel was okay.

"We'll be home in a bit," Faith said into the phone. She glanced up as we came closer, relief flooding her eyes when she spotted me. Her gaze flicked to Jennsyn, to our hands clasped, but if she was surprised to see me with a woman, she didn't let it show.

I held out my free arm and she walked straight to my side, sagging against me.

"It's all right, Beck. Everything will be fine," she said.

"Toren just got here, so I'm going to hang up. I'll call you when we leave the hospital. I love you."

Whatever he said made her nod and sniffle. Then she pulled the phone from her ear and shoved it in a pocket.

"Hi." I finally let go of Jennsyn's hand so I could wrap my aunt in a hug.

"Hey." Her voice was raw, like she was trying not to cry. "Thanks for coming."

"Of course. You okay?"

"Not especially." Faith let me go and stood, wiping beneath her eyes. She was dressed in red-and-blue flannel pajama pants and an old sweatshirt that had been Uncle Evan's. Her feet were covered in the UGG slippers I'd bought her for Christmas last year.

"Can I see him?" I pointed to the wooden doors that led into the emergency room.

"Yeah. I just came out to call Beck. Make sure everything at the house is okay. He's freaked."

"Want me to go there? Stay until you get home?"

"No, I think he's okay. Dane and Cabe are asleep. And the doctor said we should be able to leave soon."

"Okay. What happened?"

Faith walked to the nearest chair and slumped on its edge, her shoulders curling forward.

The seat beside hers was more like a bench with enough room for two, so I sat on one end and patted the navy vinyl for Jennsyn.

She hesitated for a moment, then gave me a sad smile and squeezed in beside me, tucking her hands in between her knees.

I snagged one, threading our fingers together while my other arm went around Faith's shoulders.

"The kids don't have school tomorrow or Friday," she said. "Professional development days for the teachers. So Abel asked if he could spend the night at Robbie's house. And apparently, Robbie asked his parents if he could spend the night at our house."

"Shit," I muttered. Idiot kids. "Where'd they actually go?"

"Into the mountains for a bonfire. They were going to camp out but I guess Abel's ex-girlfriend was there and some drama happened. I couldn't catch the exact specifics because my *son. Is. Drunk.*" Faith's voice shook, either from fear or fury. Probably both.

I blew out a long breath. "Shit."

"Robbie wasn't drinking. He was the one to drive home. They were on a gravel road, took a corner too fast and rolled Abel's Explorer."

"Fuck," I muttered as Jennsyn's hand tightened on mine.

"It could have been so much worse." Faith swallowed hard, staring at an invisible spot on the floor. "Robbie is fine. He's got a cut on his forehead and another on his arm from the broken windows. He left with his parents about ten minutes ago."

"And Abel?"

"He has a nasty gash on his head and a minor concussion. The doctor was just finishing the stitches when I came out to call home." She buried her face in her palms, but instead of crying, she let out a muffled, angry huff.

When Faith dropped her hands, she sat ramrod straight and sucked in a fortifying breath. Then she glanced past me to Jennsyn. "Hi. I'm Faith."

"I'm Jennsyn." She gave my aunt a sad smile. "Nice to meet you. I'm so sorry about your son."

"Me too." Faith sighed.

This was not the time or place that I'd wanted them to meet. Hell, I hadn't planned on them ever meeting. Later, I'd explain to Faith the situation. I'd have to ask her to keep a secret. But that was for another night. That was for after Abel was out of the ER.

"Okay." Faith shoved to her feet and clenched her fists. "I'm so mad at him I can hardly see straight. His car is totaled. They were extremely lucky not to each get an MIP, but Robbie got a reckless driving ticket. His parents are livid and blaming this on me. I just . . . he could have killed himself."

As a fresh sheen of tears filled her eyes, I stood and hauled her into another hug. "He's okay."

"He's okay." Her body shook as she began to cry. "I can't . . ."

"I know." She couldn't lose another person. She couldn't lose a child. "Let's go see him."

She nodded, sucking in a breath. Then she wiped at her face and walked toward the doors.

"Would you like me to wait out here?" Jennsyn asked.

I didn't want her in this drafty, depressing waiting room alone. She was in the mix of it now, whether either of us was ready for it or not. Tomorrow, we'd need to figure out where to go from here. Tonight, I just wanted to survive this.

If she wanted to stay out here, I wouldn't blame her. But if she was up for it, I wouldn't mind having her along.

"Your choice." I held out my hand.

She locked her fingers through mine without hesitation.

I let myself savor that single, calming touch for only a moment before we followed Faith to find Abel.

The ER was empty other than for a few nurses working.

We walked past a row of dark rooms until we reached an open area divided with pale-green curtain partitions. Only Abel's space had the curtains closed.

My cousin was lying in a narrow hospital bed. As we slipped through a slit in the curtains, his eyes popped open. One look at his mother's face and Abel's face paled. His gaze widened when he saw me behind her.

Faith crossed her arms when she came to a stop at the foot of his bed.

Jennsyn let go of my hand, lingering outside the curtain, as I went to stand beside my aunt and crossed my arms too.

Well, he was alive. The knot in my gut loosened a bit. "Hi."

Abel swallowed hard. "Hey."

"Are you all right?" I asked.

"Not really." His bloodshot eyes flooded and he laid his head back against the single pillow, staring up to the ceiling. "I'm so fucking stupid."

Faith scoffed, her jaw working as she blinked back another round of tears.

I sighed and moved to sit on the edge of his bed.

His chin began to quiver, so I reached for his shoulders, hauling him up and into a hug.

"I'm sorry." He sagged against me, sniffling as his voice cracked.

"I know."

"I just wanted to have fucking fun with my friends and fucking relax and not give a fuck about fucking football and fucking school and all the other fucking bullshit."

That was a lot of fucks. Each was slightly slurred.

"I get it." I held him closer, absorbing the shudders that racked his body as he began to cry.

"I fucked up," he sobbed. "I fucked up so much."

"Take a breath," I ordered.

The air hitched in his throat. "I'm s-sorry."

"I know you're sorry. We'll figure this out."

"My life will be over if I can't play. Over. Dad's rolling over in his grave."

"We cremated him," Faith muttered, dabbing beneath her eyes.

At her voice, Abel pulled away, looking past me to his mother. "I'm sorry, Mom."

"I know you're sorry, kid."

His mouth turned down in a frown. His hair, the same brown as mine, flopped into his eyes. The older he got, the more he looked like Uncle Evan.

"Mrs. Greely?" A nurse slid through the curtains and held up a stack of papers in her hand. "We can go through this and get him discharged."

"All right." Faith slipped out of the space as Abel lay back on the bed, eyes downcast.

I put my hand on his arm, giving it a squeeze. "The important thing is that no one was seriously hurt. You guys made the right choice in letting Robbie drive if he was sober. Your car, the rest, we'll figure out."

"What about football? Coach is gonna kick me off the team. Robbie too. I just know it. We're fucked."

"You don't know that yet. You're not the first kid to get in trouble during football season."

"He already said, Tor. If any of us get caught drinking, we're out."

That sounded like Coach. He'd said the same thing ages ago when I'd been one of his kids. Knowing him, he'd follow through and Abel would learn a hell of a lesson.

"Then you're out for the rest of the year. You'll play next season."

"I can't miss a year. I can't. My whole life will be ruined. I'll never get a scholarship to play." He broke down into a fresh wave of sobs as he covered his face with his hands. "Dad would be so disappointed in me. I have to play."

Where the hell was this coming from? Yeah, Evan had loved football. But he'd never been the type of man who'd made a sport his entire personality. He wouldn't have given a damn if his kids played.

All he'd ever cared about was that they were happy.

"Abel." I pulled his hands from his face, waiting until he looked at me. "Your dad wouldn't have cared about a scholarship. He wouldn't have cared if you quit football altogether. He only ever wanted you and your mom and your brothers to be happy."

"But football was our thing. It was our fucking thing. It's our thing too, you and me."

My heart squeezed. Not *his* thing. *Our* thing. "Do you even like football, Abel?"

"Um." His hesitation was answer enough. "Yeah. I like it. Just . . . not as much as I used to."

Then it was time to move on. Expand his interests. Before he stopped loving to toss a ball around for fun. Before he changed the channel whenever a game came on.

"Maybe this is a blessing in disguise," I said. "Not the drinking. We'll be talking about that. But if your coach does kick you off the team this year or put you on the bench, then maybe it's the break you needed. If you don't love it, stop. It's okay. I don't care. Your mom won't care. Your dad wouldn't have cared."

His face crumpled, like the idea of quitting would break everyone's hearts.

Abel had changed a lot these past four years. He was growing into a young man. But at the moment, he looked like the sad, broken boy who'd held my hand during his father's funeral and cried into my shoulder when his mother had stoically stood in front of the crowd to thank them all for coming.

"Hey." I took his face in my hands and dropped my forehead to his. "It's just a game."

"My car is fucked."

"It's just a car."

He only cried harder. "I'm sorry."

"I know." I hauled him in for another hug, holding him close until Faith came back with the nurse.

"We can go home," she said, looking more exhausted than she had all night, like the stress of this was finally over and all of the emotions had drained her dry.

"I'll drive." I stood and fished my truck keys from my pocket.

Faith shuffled into the room, picking up Abel's coat that was draped over the chair at his bedside. She gave her son a slight smile, then held out her hand to help him to his feet.

He gulped as he stood, four inches taller than his mother. "I'm sorry, Mom."

"I know, baby." She hauled him into a hug, holding him tight.

I slipped past the curtains to give them a moment alone.

Jennsyn was standing against a nearby wall, her arms wrapped around her waist. There was something in her expression that made me pause. Something hard and guarded.

But before I could ask if she was okay, Faith and Abel appeared at my side. His arm was looped through his mother's like she was holding him up. That boy probably had no idea that his mother was the strongest person I'd ever met.

She was stronger than she should have to be.

"Ready?" I asked.

Faith nodded. "Thanks for coming down."

"I'll drive you guys home. Jennsyn can take my truck."

"We're okay," Faith said. "Head on home."

"Are you sure?"

"Yeah." She smiled up at Abel. "We're good."

He nodded, looking like he was about to cry again, but when she urged him forward, he walked at her side down the hall, past the nurses' station and the empty ER rooms to the exit.

I breathed, the pressure in my chest loosening, then held out a hand for Jennsyn.

She pushed off the wall and took hold, then together, we left the hospital too. When we climbed into my truck, she shoved the hood off her head, then stripped off my hat.

There was no need to keep hiding, not when we were alone.

The drive home was in silence, the weight of everything that had happened tonight settling heavily in the truck's cab. Not just Abel's accident, but everything.

The movies she'd brought over. The hospital.

That kiss.

We'd broken all the rules. The Fourth of July party had been one thing. For that, I could claim ignorance.

But tonight? Everything had changed.

Now what? Where did we go from here?

I didn't have an answer and doubted Jennsyn did either,

so I didn't ask. I just drove down the quiet streets of Mission until I was parked in my garage, the door closing us in.

"Thank you for coming with me," I said.

"You're welcome," she whispered. There was a sadness in her eyes that made my heart hurt.

"What's wrong?"

She lifted a shoulder. "I heard what you told him. About football. I wish I'd had you when I was his age."

She wanted someone to tell her that it was okay to quit volleyball. To ask her if she even liked the game.

The night I'd found her in my yard after her game, the night her dad and I had both been at Upshaw to watch her play, she'd mentioned quitting. Was that what she wanted?

Over the past few weeks, I'd broken down and spent way too much time on Google learning about volleyball. Stanford was one of the best universities in the country, and they had one of the best volleyball programs. Why would she trade that caliber of education, that level of play, for Treasure State? We were a good school but we weren't Stanford. And she'd been so close to graduating, just one year away. So why had she left California?

"Why'd you transfer this year?" It was the question I'd wanted to ask for weeks.

Was this move her way of coming to a slow stop? Not a cold-turkey quit, but a gradual exit from the game?

"Because I didn't have you to tell me I could stop," she whispered.

"You can, you know. You can quit."

"Not yet. I don't even know if that's what I want."

And too few people had asked her what she wanted.

Jennsyn forced a small smile, then reached for the door's handle. "Goodbye, Toren."

All I had to do was take her hand. All I had to do was lead her inside. We could pick up where we'd left off. But I stayed motionless behind the wheel, watching as she hopped out of the truck.

Jennsyn walked to the door that led inside, stepping out of my Crocs. Then she walked to the side door, the one that would lead her home.

And she disappeared into the night.

"Goodbye, Jennsyn."

THE PARTY
TOREN

Jennsyn drew swirls around my nipple with a fingertip. Most women I knew had manicured nails with shiny polish, but hers were cut short and clean.

Her body was stretched out long beside mine. She was propped up on an elbow, and beneath the sheets, she dragged her foot up and down my calf.

I had an arm behind my head, my heart still pounding from the last orgasm.

"Have you ever stayed up all night with someone before?" she asked. "Like this?"

Like we were so into each other we'd fight sleep for as long as possible. Like we couldn't get enough. Like we couldn't stop, even to rest.

"No." With any other woman, it had never even crossed my mind. "Have you?"

"Nope."

With every stroke of her foot, my body seemed to thrum, my cock springing to life for another round. That finger of hers kept circling my nipple.

"We're going to run out of condoms if you keep that up," I murmured.

She smiled, so beautiful and bright it lit up the dark room. "That seems like a challenge."

I chuckled and pounced, rolling to trap her beneath me so quickly she gasped. "I like a challenge."

CHAPTER SIXTEEN

JENNSYN

My professor picked up a stack of papers from his desk, waving it in the air as he paced the length of the room. "Midterms. In general, I was underwhelmed."

A collective groan echoed through the class.

This Small Business Management course should have been an easy A, except this professor seemed determined to torture us all. Not only did he continually veer off course from the syllabus, he'd throw us assignments without context or supporting material. Our textbook had been irrelevant so far—a hunk of weight I was forced to cart around campus two days a week in the off chance Professor Smith changed his mind and wanted to use it.

Our midterm exam had been about funding sources for small businesses. It was a subject we'd only touched on briefly. According to our pointless syllabus, we were supposed to spend the next two weeks discussing the topic.

Of course he was underwhelmed with the grades.

I was underwhelmed with his teaching.

None of us knew what the hell he wanted.

Thankfully, I'd already taken a small business course at Stanford, so I'd used what I'd learned last year and slogged through the test.

"Review the syllabus over the weekend," Professor Smith said. "We'll be starting a section on exit strategy Monday."

Exit strategy was supposed to be discussed in November. Did he know what was on his own syllabus?

Smith walked to his desk, setting the stack on its corner. Then he sat in his chair and flicked a hand in the air.

Class dismissed.

The room burst into action, everyone shoving books and notepads into their bags before standing and shuffling to the front of the room. A line stacked up to collect our tests, so I didn't rush to leave. I pulled on my coat and slung my backpack over a shoulder, then walked from my seat in the front row to the last spot in line.

Smith didn't so much as glance my direction as I collected my test and flipped past the cover sheet with my name in the corner.

I blinked at the letter scrawled in red ink.

C

What? I leaned in closer to the page, triple-checking that this was my paper and that was my grade.

My stomach plummeted as I scanned my own handwriting.

He'd given me a C? No. That couldn't be right. I'd never gotten a C in my life.

"Professor Smith?" I approached the corner of his desk.

He glanced up over the rim of his black-framed glasses. "Ms. Bell."

"I, um . . . I'm a little surprised by my grade."

"So was I." He pulled off those glasses, letting them

dangle in a hand as he stared at me. "I'm slightly concerned with what they taught you at Stanford."

Wait. He knew I'd transferred from Stanford? It wasn't exactly a secret. Maybe he followed the volleyball team or something.

"My notes are in the margins," he said.

My stomach sank deeper and deeper as I flipped through the pages, his red scrawl coloring nearly every question on every page. My answers weren't wrong, but they weren't right. At least, not for what Smith had wanted.

I could argue with him. But I doubted it would do any good. He wasn't going to change his mind. Which left me stuck with a C.

No, damn it. This couldn't be happening. I didn't get Cs. I didn't fail at school.

Maybe I wasn't sure what to do about volleyball, maybe my future was as clear as a brick wall, but I was good at school. I *needed* to be good at school.

My hands began to shake, the paper crinkling softly. There was that rattle in my bones.

"Don't worry." Professor Smith refitted the glasses on his face. "I grade with a curve."

———

"WATCH IT," a girl hissed at me as I stepped through the library's door.

She'd been walking backward, clearly not watching where *she* was going. Until the moment she'd spun around, a scalding hot latte in her hand, and run straight into me.

Coffee dripped down the front of my coat, steaming and sticky and sweet.

She shot me a glare as the liquid dripped off the side of her cardboard cup to the tile floor. "Thanks. I just bought this."

My mouth was too busy hanging open to reply.

With a sneer, she shoved past me and outside, not once apologizing for the fact that I was covered in her coffee.

A guy passing by gave me a sideways glance, probably because I was standing with my mouth agape and my arms lifted, frozen at my sides.

I'd come to the library to study. To pore over my midterm in Smith's class and figure out where I'd gone wrong or if I could find a way to argue a few points.

Except the coffee was soaking through my coat, so I unglued my feet, backed away from the puddle and stripped off my jacket. With it wadded into a ball, I turned and left the library, heading for the fieldhouse. There was a hoodie in my locker I'd planned to wear after tonight's game.

I was shivering by the time I made it across campus. The long-sleeved tee I'd worn beneath my coat wasn't exactly warm, and the late-October weather was so cold my teeth chattered. I was ten feet from the warmth of the fieldhouse when the door opened.

Toren walked outside with Coach Ellis.

The air rushed from my lungs. Nerves. Joy. Relief. Fear. They all hit at once. We rarely crossed paths on campus, but every time, the warring emotions caught me off guard. I faltered a step.

He looked gorgeous in a gray pullover and a pair of dark-wash jeans. He grinned at whatever Coach Ellis was saying, neither of them having noticed me yet.

It had been nine days since I'd seen Toren. Nine days

since Abel's accident. Nine days since Toren had held my hand and kissed me in his kitchen.

Nine days where I'd convinced myself this had to end. Once and for all.

Before the rattling ruined my season. Before another kiss got us caught and he lost his career.

Both men spotted me at the same time.

Coach Ellis gave me a slight smile, dipping his chin. "Morning."

"Good morning," I said, my voice hoarse.

Toren swallowed hard, then mirrored his boss, pretending like I was just another student. He held the door open, not saying a word as I slipped past them both inside.

As they walked away, he didn't look back.

I stared at his back for a long moment, my feet still moving forward though my eyes were aimed over my shoulder.

My toe caught on the corner of the doormat.

And then I was just looking at concrete while I splayed on the floor with a throbbing ankle.

"Fuck."

———

I ROLLED my ankle in a circle, testing it from earlier. It was fine, just a bit tender. Twisted but not sprained or broken.

This was not my day.

I was more than ready for it to be over. Except first, we had a game to play.

"Is something wrong with your ankle?" Stevie asked as we both sat in front of our lockers.

"I tripped earlier but it's fine." I waved it off as my phone buzzed on the bench between us.

Mike Simmons.

I sent his call to voicemail, wincing the moment my finger tapped the button. Not sixty seconds later, an email notification popped up. It was the fourth email Mike had sent me since our phone call last week, and all four were waiting for a reply.

The first had been to trade contact information and summarize our call. The second had been a contract. The third had been a reminder to sign that contract. I suspected the fourth was the same.

Not once during our call last Monday had I agreed to move forward with him as my agent. Not once had I accepted his offer of representation.

Either my mother had done it for me. Or Mike thought if he pushed hard enough, I'd cave. It was probably both.

He'd said all the right things. He'd made it sound so freaking tempting. But something was holding me back. The same something that had been plaguing me for a while. Something I'd ignored at Stanford.

Something I hadn't ignored at Treasure State.

Was this really what I wanted? To play volleyball professionally? To make it my life's ambition?

The answer was there, deep in my gut. Waiting for the moment when I was brave enough to say it out loud.

Today was not that day.

The locker room was noisy, the energy for our upcoming game infusing the air. Megan was chattering about something with a few of the girls. Coach Quinn had just walked in with the trainer to talk to Liz, who'd been struggling with her knee all week.

And I couldn't stop staring at the notifications on my phone.

Mike was waiting for an answer.

What if I signed the contract, just in case? What if I bought myself more time to figure this out? Worst-case scenario, I hired him as my agent, and when the time came to accept a job offer, I turned it down.

We could break up later, right? Did I really have to decide now?

Dread crept through my veins, pooling in my stomach and making it churn. The rattling was worse than ever. I was about to come apart.

I picked up my phone, my hand shaking as I shoved the device in my locker.

"Are you okay?" Stevie asked.

I swallowed hard and adjusted the waistband of my shorts. "Yeah."

I didn't have any other choice but to be okay.

We had a game to play.

———

THE LOCKER ROOM WAS SILENT. Other than the sound of clothes rustling, of bags being zipped and shoes being tied, not one person dared to speak.

We'd lost.

I couldn't seem to wrap my head around it.

We'd lost tonight's game.

In my mind, I knew it wasn't my fault. This was a team sport and we'd all played like shit, me especially. There'd been no rhythm. We'd made stupid mistake after stupid mistake. And the other team had been on fire.

It wasn't my fault.

It *was* my fault.

I'd let all of these girls down tonight. I'd let myself down. All because I'd let myself get distracted by a C. By a spilled cup of coffee. By tripping over a doormat, a missed phone call and an email.

By a man.

By a coach who was wholly off-limits and who I couldn't get off my mind.

The rattling had manifested into the game.

Just like before.

A hand landed on my shoulder, making me jump.

Stevie's gaze was laced with concern but she didn't disrupt the silent mourning of our perfect season.

Neither did I.

I stepped away from her touch, picked up my bag from the floor and walked out the locker room door.

———

SWEAT BEADED at my temples as I wiped my rag back and forth across the inside windshield of Liz's Subaru. The squeak of clean glass filled the inside of her car along with the scents of leather conditioner and ammonia.

The last time I'd checked the clock, it was twelve thirty in the morning. That was before I'd started cleaning Liz's car. After I'd detailed my own BMW and Stevie's red Jeep.

My roommates were inside, asleep and oblivious to me in the garage. I'd wondered if they might hear the vacuum when I'd hauled it out to clean the carpet in each of our vehicles, but if the noise had bothered them, neither had come to check it out.

So I kept cleaning, needing the distraction since I couldn't sleep.

I'd driven home after tonight's game and locked myself in my room, licking my wounds. I'd hoped that after some rest, the rattling would stop. Except I'd tossed and turned, unable to shut it off.

We'd lost. We'd lost a game we should have won.

It wasn't my first loss but it was the hardest I'd ever had to swallow.

There was too much energy flowing through my veins. Too many thoughts racing through my mind.

It was too cold and too dark to go for a run. I'd almost driven to campus and hit the weight room. Instead, I'd settled for cleaning my car. Except when it was finished, I'd still been brimming with jitters and this insatiable need to move. Like if I sat still for too long, I'd fall apart.

So I'd moved on to clean Stevie's car next. Then Liz's.

It should have been enough. Contorting my body into tight spaces to clean plastic and leather. Dusting air vents with cotton swabs. Vacuuming crumbs from crevices.

After a long day, after a loss and a C and a coat that would probably always reek of coffee, I should have been exhausted.

But the moment I climbed out of Liz's Subaru and stood, that urge to keep moving, keep pushing, was as strong as ever.

There were no more cars to clean.

My insides knotted. Now what?

That question boomed in my head, so loud I might as well have screamed it in the quiet garage.

Now what?

It was bigger than my next move. Than the next five minutes.

Now what did I do with my life?

My throat burned with this sharp, aching need to cry. I refused to cry.

The last time I'd shed a tear over a lost game had been my junior year in high school when we'd lost the state championship.

Mom had gotten mad, and on the drive home, she'd lectured me about my tears. She'd told me that losers cried. Winners got better. Winners worked harder.

I wouldn't cry over tonight's loss. Not when I could clean cars instead.

Except there were no more cars.

Unless . . .

Twisting around, I stared at the garage's wall. Beyond it, past the stretch of grass that separated our homes, was a filthy vehicle. Inside and out, Toren's truck was a wreck.

I was supposed to be staying away from Toren. Steering clear until this rattling vanished. But before my better judgment could stop me, I collected my cleaning supplies, clasping bottles with one arm while the other carried a handful of rags. I shoved a handful of cotton swabs into the pocket of my sweats and swept out the garage's side door, walking to Toren's in my bare feet. My toes were instantly cold from the frost coating the ground.

Please be unlocked.

I reached for the knob to his own garage, turning it slowly, expecting to be met with the stop of its lock. But the door popped open with a slight whoosh of air.

The relief was so crippling I whimpered.

Careful to keep my steps light, I stepped inside his

garage and closed the door behind me, crossing the space to his truck.

The outside was dirty, the sides so covered in dried mud there wasn't a bit of shine to the silver paint on the bottom half. It was in desperate need of a wash and wax, but tonight, I'd have to settle for the interior only, like I had with the three cars at my house.

I wouldn't even be able to vacuum Toren's, but at the moment, I didn't care. So I opened the rear door, set my supplies on the floor, and got to work.

I'd just finished the back seat when a throat cleared. The sound made my entire body jolt so fast I whacked the back of my head on the truck's roof.

"Ow." *Shit.* I dropped the rag in my hand, pulling myself out of the truck as I rubbed my skull.

Toren stood in the doorway that led into the house. His arms were crossed as he leaned against the frame. His hair was a mess, sticking up at odd angles. The dark scruff on his face was thick enough all I had to do was squint and it was practically a beard.

He was wearing a pair of black boxer briefs and nothing else. Every muscle of his ripped body was on display. His gaze darted to the truck, then back to me. Toren didn't utter a word but his expression spoke volumes.

What the fuck was I doing?

"I lost my game tonight," I said.

He nodded, like that was all the explanation necessary before he shoved off the door, walking down the two steps to the cement floor.

My breath lodged in my throat as I waited for him to show me out. For him to tell me to go home and go to bed.

Except Toren didn't walk toward me. He crossed the

219

garage to the large shop vacuum stowed in the corner. Its wheels scraped across the floor as he dragged it over.

And when my eyes flooded with tears, it wasn't because I'd lost a game.

It was because I'd missed him. Because somehow, this man understood me better than anyone else in my life.

"Hey." He took my face in his hands, his thumbs stroking across my cheek.

"Ugh." I sniffled, blinking away the tears. "Sorry. I'm a disaster, and I'm so tired of being a disaster. What is wrong with me? Who cleans cars in the middle of the night?"

Toren's eyes softened. "You're not a disaster."

"The fact that my hands smell like Armor All suggests otherwise."

He dropped his forehead to mine, his hands firm on my cheeks. "Want some help?"

"Do you even know how to clean a car?"

His low chuckle was a balm to my aching heart. "Bet you can teach me."

CHAPTER SEVENTEEN

TOREN

With the vacuum stowed in the corner, I snagged a jacket from the coat hooks on the wall, then pointed to the truck's passenger door as I walked for the driver's side. "Hop in. We'll finish this up."

"We are finished," Jennsyn said, tossing the last dirty rag into the pile with the others.

"Not quite." I shook my head and pulled on the coat. "This is the cleanest my truck has been in years. We might as well clean the outside too. We'll go hit a car wash."

Jennsyn's eyebrows lifted. "At two in the morning?"

"You're the one who started this."

A flush crept into her cheeks as she tried to hide a shy smile. "Sorry."

"Don't be." I chuckled and climbed in the truck, closing my door as she did the same on her side.

"You're in your underwear." Her gaze flickered to my bare thighs before darting to her lap.

So she had noticed I was in my boxer briefs. She'd barely

glanced my way while we'd cleaned the truck, her focus so locked on the task at hand.

Meanwhile, I'd cleaned at a fraction of her pace because every other minute I'd catch a glimpse of her and stop to stare.

She was dressed in a pair of sweatpants that were rolled at the waist. They were long and baggy, a pair that might fit me, but they were thin, and every time she moved, the fabric would mold to those perfect legs. All she had covering her breasts was a thin-strapped sports bra. Every time she'd had her back to me, I'd followed the long line of her spine to those sexy dimples above her ass.

I'd been fighting an erection for an hour.

"There's a drive-through car wash at the gas station by campus," she said.

"I know."

She smirked. "Do you?"

I grinned and hit the remote to open the garage door. As it lifted, I started the truck and reversed out of the driveway.

Her seat belt clicked into place, then she relaxed and propped her elbow on the console.

"Tired?"

"No." She glanced over, her expression less frazzled than it had been when I'd found her in the garage.

I'd been upstairs, reading in bed, when I'd felt a shift in the house, like an air seal had been broken. I'd listened for a few moments, thinking it was nothing. But the hairs on the back of my neck had stood on end and a hunch had sent me downstairs. I'd watched Jennsyn clean for at least fifteen minutes before finally clearing my throat so she'd notice.

Then she'd almost started crying. And damn if it hadn't

ripped me into shreds. I'd seen plenty of people cry. Yet her tears might have hit the hardest.

If she needed to clean my truck, if she needed a distraction tonight, then we'd go to this car wash at two in the morning.

"You okay?" I asked as we rolled down the quiet street, stopping at the first main intersection that would take us to town.

"Yeah." She inhaled, holding it in for a long moment, then exhaled. "Thank you."

"You're the one who cleaned."

A smile toyed on her mouth. "I still can't make sense of how a man who has such a neat and tidy house has such a messy truck."

"Mysterious, isn't it?" I stole the word she'd tossed at me months ago.

She giggled, leaning her head against the back of the seat.

"Want to talk about tonight?" I asked.

"Not especially. We lost. I don't handle losing very well. And it was . . . a strange day."

I looked over, blue eyes waiting. "It's always strange to see you on campus."

Every time, I'd forget for a split second that we weren't possible. That she was there because she was a student. And for that split second, when my heart stopped, I wanted to smile and move closer, like she was reeling me in. Then I'd remember and get pissed. Paranoid.

Today, Ford and I had decided to get outside and away from the fieldhouse for our weekly meeting. We'd gone to the student union for a change of scenery. I'd convinced myself on the walk over that he'd noticed my reaction to Jennsyn.

There'd been no need to worry. Ford was so keyed up about everything happening with Millie and having his ex-wife in town that he was locked in his own bubble at the moment. If he wasn't with his daughter, he was immersed in football.

Which suited me just fine. We'd spent two hours talking about the other team's offensive plays after an extensive session watching film. Then we'd talked about how we'd tailor defensive plays to stop their running game.

Tomorrow—or today, since it was well after midnight—was going to be a long fucking day with no sleep. But I kept driving, weaving through the deserted streets of Mission on my way to the car wash.

If these late hours were all I'd get from Jennsyn, I was taking them. I was taking every minute.

"How is Abel doing?" she asked.

"He's okay. His coach didn't boot him off the football team entirely. He gets to practice with the team as second string. But he can't dress for games and he's on the bench. He's working off the cost of his car on the farm. He gets to ride the bus to and from school like his brothers. That was an ego bruiser. But he knows he got lucky. And even though I wish it would have happened differently, I think it sparked a conversation he's been scared to have."

With Faith. With me.

Abel missed his dad. And in Evan's absence, all his son could do was wonder. Abel had built up this idea in his head about what Evan would have wanted for him. We'd work through it all. Mostly Faith and Abel. But I'd be around for whatever he needed too.

"I'm glad." Jennsyn lifted her hand, like she was going to

reach across the console for me, but stopped herself, pulling it back and into her lap.

My hands strangled the steering wheel because it was the only way I could keep them to myself. With every block, the temperature in the cab spiked, the tension between us growing tighter. Hotter.

She shifted, crossing and uncrossing her legs.

The cab smelled like leather conditioner and glass cleaner, but beneath it all was Jennsyn's subtle scent. Citrus and summer sunshine.

I wanted it in this truck for good. In my house and in my bed.

My grip on the wheel tightened, holding firm, to keep from reaching for her thigh.

We hadn't talked about the kiss. We should talk about the kiss.

Except I was worried she'd say it was a mistake. Hell, it had been a mistake. But that didn't mean I wanted to hear it from her mouth.

When we reached the car wash, I rolled down the window to swipe my credit card. Chilly night air flooded the cab, chasing away a bit of the heat. I sucked it into my lungs, hoping it would cool the fire simmering beneath my skin.

It wasn't right how much I craved this woman. How much I wanted her around.

"Don't be cheap," she murmured. "You need the works."

I chuckled, shaking my head. And instead of getting the economy wash like I usually did whenever the Tundra was so dirty I could hardly stand it myself, I bought the works.

As the car wash beeped and flashed a green light for me to enter, the tall overhead door sliding open, I rolled up my window and eased inside, stopping when I was in the right position. The jets started, the spraying water deafening against the glass and metal.

Jennsyn's gaze snared me. Everything I was feeling, every frustration and hesitancy and desire, shined in those blue eyes.

She wanted this, as much as I wanted this. *Fuck.*

God, I was tired of fighting this. So fucking tired.

"It's not fair," she said, barely loud enough to be heard over the spray.

I swallowed hard. "No, babe. It's not fair."

It wasn't fair that we'd met before. That we'd been tempted by what we couldn't have. It wasn't fair that she was perfect and that every moment together made me crave ten more.

It wasn't fucking fair that I'd take her home, and while I slept alone in my bed, she'd be tucked away in hers.

Disappointment weighed like a thousand bricks on my shoulders as the car wash finished. The drive home was silent. Maybe Jennsyn knew I was attuned to her every move, her every breath, because she sat so still at one point, I glanced over just to make sure she was still awake.

Her eyes were locked straight ahead, her expression exhausted and worn.

I wanted the chance to chase that look away. To be around when she smiled more often than not.

Was she staying after graduation? Would she stick around Mission?

Probably not. She'd likely leave Montana, and for the rest of my life, Mission was home.

By the time we pulled into my garage, I was so worn down that even my bones felt weary. Months of wanting

Jennsyn when I knew I shouldn't had frayed every one of my nerves.

I killed the engine but didn't move for the door. I breathed in that sweet scent one more time, closing my eyes to savor having her close. Then on a sigh, I shoved open the door and climbed out.

Jennsyn did the same, walking to where she'd left her cleaning supplies on the floor. But she didn't bend to pick them up. She stared at them, her shoulders sagging.

"Toren." Her whisper filled the garage.

I braced, ready for her to say goodbye. Ready for the moment when she meant it, just like I'd asked.

But she didn't leave. A tiny laugh escaped her mouth as she unglued her feet from the floor, closing the distance between us. She stopped so close our toes were nearly touching. Then her hands fitted to my sides, her fingers molding to the cut at my hips as she dropped her forehead to my heart. "I don't want to go home."

"Then don't." What the fuck was I saying? Whatever it was, I didn't care.

I craved Jennsyn Bell beyond reason or rationality.

My palms settled on her shoulders, my thumbs tracing across her collarbones.

"What are we doing?" she asked.

"I don't know." I hooked a finger beneath her chin, tilting up her face until I was drowning in stunning blue eyes. "Stay anyway."

The words had barely left my lips when she rose up on her toes, like she'd planned to kiss me no matter what I'd told her.

The moment her mouth was on mine, a hum vibrated

through my chest, coming from deep in my bones. It was the sound of my will breaking. My resolve shattering.

She pushed at the open lapels of my jacket, sliding it off my shoulders.

As it pooled on the floor, I swept her into my arms, holding her tight as I hauled her off those bare feet. Then I carried her toward the house, my mouth never breaking from hers as I shoved open the door and stalked through the mudroom.

Jennsyn's legs wound around my waist, her ankles locking behind my back as her arms linked behind my neck. Then this fucking woman ground her center against my cock.

I almost came in my underwear. "Fuck." I tore my lips from hers, slowing my steps but not stopping.

She was panting as she leaned away, her eyes searching mine. "Toren."

It was a plea, and any chance at stopping this vanished into the ether. Tonight, she was mine. Tomorrow, well . . . we'd figure it out later.

With a quick spin, I pinned her against the hallway's wall and bent to nibble her neck. "What do you want?"

"You." Her hands threaded into my hair as she arched into my touch.

She'd have me. Every fucking inch.

I growled against her throat, then ripped my mouth away before I fucked her against the wall. Why the hell was my bedroom so damn far away? With her in my arms, I couldn't walk fast enough, so I set her on her feet and clasped her hand in mine, dragging her through the living room and past the kitchen until we were both jogging up the stairs.

The second we crossed the threshold of my bedroom, we

were on each other, mouths fusing as hands grappled with the scraps of clothing keeping us apart.

Her hands dove beneath the waistband of my underwear, and she palmed my ass, squeezing so hard I hissed.

I tore at the straps of her bra, trying to get it off her shoulders, but the damn stretchy thing was tight. "Off," I ordered.

She huffed and pulled her hands free, then tore the bra off her torso as I stripped the sweats off her hips, taking her panties with them.

Jennsyn kicked them free from her legs as I made quick work of my boxer briefs.

"Bed." With a hand on her heart, I urged her backward until her legs collided with the mattress.

With a quick sweep, I bent and picked her up behind the knees. We fell together onto the mattress, hammering hearts and naked limbs.

My mouth crushed hers, my tongue sliding past her teeth to tangle with hers, as I pressed her into the mattress. God, she tasted good. Sweet and warm like honey. Like a summer night. Like mine.

Somehow, it was better than the night of the party. A night I would have said couldn't be topped. But this kiss was different than any from July. This kiss was the start of something. Something that could ruin my life, and as my tongue dueled with hers, I didn't fucking care.

I sank into her, savoring every lick and suck and the quiet mewls that came from her throat. Her hands roved my back, her fingers digging into the muscles of my shoulders before they trailed down my spine.

She widened her legs, rocking against my cock as it throbbed against her soaked center. Fuck, she was drenched.

I trailed my lips along her jaw, kissing lower and lower

along her neck until I hovered over her breasts, my tongue darting out to flick her nipple. "Jennsyn."

"Tor," she moaned. "Fuck me."

All night. I'd fuck her all night. To hell with sleep. I'd be a wreck for our game tomorrow and didn't give a damn.

She arched into my touch, searching for more. "I need you inside. Right now."

I captured a nipple and sucked it into my mouth, rolling it against my tongue.

"Oh God." She writhed, her legs wrapping around me as her heels dug into the backs of my thighs, like she was trying to pull me in.

I shifted to the other breast, cupping it before I squeezed, then devoured that nipple too.

"You have to stop that." Her voice was breathy. "Or I'm going to come."

"Then come," I murmured against her skin. She could come again and again and again.

"With you." She tugged on my hair, forcing me up until our eyes locked. "I want to come with you."

That wasn't the plan. I'd wanted to taste her first. To hear her scream my name before I drove inside her tight body. But there was a longing on her face. Her resolve had shattered too.

We'd gone long enough.

So I shifted to bracket her head with my elbows, settling into the cradle of her hips.

I stretched for the nightstand, feeling for the drawer because I didn't want to look away. Not when I was scared to blink and have her disappear.

Except before I could find the drawer where I kept a box of condoms, her hand settled on my forearm, stopping me.

"I don't want anything between us," she whispered. "If you're okay with it. I'm on birth control. And there hasn't been anyone since you."

Holy fuck. She wanted me to fuck her bare?

"I haven't been with anyone either," I said.

"Good." She pulled her bottom lip between her teeth as satisfaction danced in those blue eyes. As her heel slid higher on my thigh, her knee extended, bringing my cock closer to her pussy.

I fitted myself at her entrance, holding her gaze as I slid home.

Sheer ecstasy roared through every vein in my body. It turned to fire the minute I was rooted deep, my jaw clenching as I fought for control. "Fuck, you feel good."

Her head lolled to the side, her eyes fluttering closed. "Toren. Move. Please."

"Say it again."

"Please."

Not please. I buried my face in her neck, pressing even deeper until the base of my cock rubbed against her clit. "Say my name."

She made a sound that was part moan, part cry. "Toren."

"Fuck, I missed you." I eased out and thrust inside, burying myself deep.

It earned me another one of those sexy-as-fuck sounds from Jennsyn's throat.

I closed my eyes, savoring it for a long moment. Then I set a steady, deliberate rhythm, pumping in and out as her hands clawed at my back.

Over and over I brought us together until our bodies glistened with sweat. Until we were breathless and my heart threatened to beat out of my chest.

She clung to me as her limbs began to tremble. She writhed beneath me, matching my pace with the tilt of her own hips. Glide after glide, we moved in perfect tandem. Like lovers who'd spent countless years in this bed together, not two damn nights.

But with every stroke, it took us higher. This was better than before. Better than ever.

The pressure in the base of my spine built and built, my orgasm threatening. But I held it off until she began to shake, until those sounds were coming in a steady stream. The flutter of her inner walls was pure bliss as she got closer and closer to the edge.

Jennsyn Bell was ruining me.

She'd ruined me in July.

Her mouth parted on a soundless cry, then she detonated, toppling over the cliff as her body quaked and clenched.

She pulsed around me, and because she'd wanted us to come together, I let go. I came apart, shattering on a roar as everything turned to white. Stars consumed my vision. The air rushed from my lungs and the world disappeared.

There was nothing but Jennsyn.

I poured inside her, draining myself dry of all my strength until I couldn't hold myself up and collapsed on top of her, utterly spent and boneless.

"Oh my God." She shoved her hair out of her face. The tie she'd had in earlier was lost somewhere. "Did that just happen? Or am I dreaming?"

I chuckled into her neck. "Not a dream, babe. That was . . ."

The best sex of my life. Phenomenal. Life changing.

And I wanted to do it again.

232

So I did.

I kept her in my bed for as long as possible, until the time on the clock couldn't be ignored.

"I wish you could stay," I said.

"Me too." She kissed my stubbled jaw, then climbed out of bed.

As she pulled on her sports bra and those sweats, I pulled on a pair of faded, soft jeans, then walked her to the garage.

I opened my mouth to say goodbye, except I couldn't seem to say it out loud. We'd said it enough.

"Good luck at your game today," she said.

"You too." I'd all but memorized their schedule. They had a game at seven. If not for a mandatory postgame event for the coaches, I'd be there to watch. Instead, I'd have to catch highlights on the team's social media account.

"Thanks." She smiled, her cheeks flushed and perfect. Her feet bare. God, I liked that. "Good—"

"I'm going to the farm on Sunday." I cut her off before she could say goodbye. I didn't want to hear it as much as I didn't want to say it. "Go with me."

She blinked. "Are you sure that's a good idea?"

"No," I admitted. "But it's a safe place."

She didn't hesitate. "Then yes. I'd like that."

CHAPTER EIGHTEEN

JENNSYN

My car was parked at the grocery store. My roommates thought I'd left to study on campus all day. And I was riding in Toren's truck, a smile tugging on my lips as I tried not to stare at the gorgeous man driving me to his aunt's farm.

Deep down, I knew this thing between us was more than a casual hookup. I knew that we were more than two secret nights in his bed. But I hadn't realized how much I'd needed this day.

A day in the light. A day together. A day where he'd bring me to meet his family.

If we got caught, if we were found out, our lives would implode. I didn't care. When Toren had texted earlier and asked me to meet at the store to ditch my car in the lot, I hadn't even hesitated to say yes.

"What did you tell Faith about us?" I asked. It was probably something we should have talked about Friday night. Instead, we'd cleaned his truck and fucked all night long.

When he'd invited me to come with him today, I'd been too lost in the haze of our orgasms to ask for details.

"I told her that things between us were complicated. That we'd appreciate it if she'd keep it between us."

And the farm was a safe place. I didn't really have a safe place. Today, I guess I'd get to borrow his.

"Does she know that I'm a . . . student?" The title tasted sour.

I *was* a student. For most of my life, I'd always wished people would refer to me as a student first, then an athlete, though it had always gone the other way.

But at the moment, I loathed that term. I wanted to be anything else.

"Yeah," Toren muttered. "She does."

"And what does she think about that?"

He glanced over with a wry grin. "That I'm a fucking idiot."

"She's not wrong." I laughed. "We're both idiots."

But we were here anyway.

Toren reached across the console, shifting to steer with his other hand.

I laced my fingers through his and savored the warmth of his skin.

"She also knows that I've never brought a woman to the farm before," he said.

Wait. What? My eyebrows lifted. What about past girl-friends or lovers? "Never?"

"Never."

"But you're bringing me."

"Yeah." His fingers squeezed mine tighter, like he wanted to make sure I knew he wasn't going to let go.

DEVNEY PERRY

Toren drove us through town, taking turns and streets until the houses and buildings became fewer and farther between. Then we turned onto a narrow highway, heading for the mountains that stood tall and proud against the blue sky.

Trees with leaves in shades of orange and yellow and red decorated sweeping meadows of gold grasses. The foothills were thick with evergreens. It was the scene from a travel magazine or postcard. It was so beautiful it didn't seem real.

I hadn't spent much time exploring Mission or the surrounding area. I went from school to home with the occasional stop at the grocery store. But after today, I'd make it a point to wander. To soak in this little corner of paradise while I was in Montana.

With every mile, Toren seemed to relax, like out here in the countryside, he could breathe.

"Someday, I'd like to get a place out here," he said, slowing to turn off the highway and onto a gravel lane. "I don't mind living in town, but eventually, I'd like some breathing room."

A mental image of him living in a quaint country house popped into my mind. Of him driving home from work each day down these gravel roads in his dirty truck.

Part of me wanted to insert myself into his dream. To steal it so I'd have something too.

Except it wasn't mine. Toren wasn't really either.

He was thirty-three years old. He was settled in Mission. He'd built a life and career here. Even if I wanted to keep him, how would that work?

I was twenty-two and my future was as cloudy as the dust kicked up by the truck's tires.

What happened when—if—I signed that contract with

236

Mike Simmons? What happened if I played volleyball in Europe? What happened when I left Montana?

Toren would move on to the woman who'd share his country house. The woman who'd sleep in his bed every night. The woman who wouldn't have to hide beneath hoods and hats when they were together in public.

I'd be a fool to think I could keep Toren Greely. But I would remember him. For the rest of my life.

But I wasn't gone yet. Today, he was mine. So I shoved the doubts, the dread for our inevitable end aside and let him hold my hand as we drove to his safe place.

To a place where we wouldn't have to hide.

The drive to the farm took twenty minutes, and by the time we turned off the main gravel road and onto a narrow lane, my heart had climbed into my throat.

The last time I'd met a boyfriend's family had been my sophomore year in high school. His mom had needed to drive us on our one and only date to a movie. That boy had dumped me because I wouldn't kiss him in the theater.

Toren wasn't my boyfriend. I wasn't sure what label to use. Important, maybe. He was important. This connection between us was special.

The lane was bordered by barbed wire. In the meadow out my window, a pretty brown horse grazed in the grass. Ahead of us was a tall, wooden archway with a hand-painted sign dangling from its center that read *Greely Farm*.

"The horse is George," Toren said. "The goats are Hetty, Izzy and Jessy."

"Goats." I scanned the fields, not seeing any goats.

Toren pointed over the steering wheel to the barn. Beside its whitewashed wood siding were three goats.

Their jaws worked as they chewed, a look of sheer

annoyance on their faces as they watched us come to a stop outside a white farmhouse with a sweeping front porch and a swing.

A golden retriever came bounding around the corner of the house, tail wagging. Its paws were covered in mud and its fur was wet.

"That's Kelly." Toren shut off the truck. "Looks like she's been in the pond."

"There's a pond?" I glanced around, taking it all in as I climbed out of the truck.

Next to the barn was a small shed with a ramp leading to a door big enough for the chickens pecking around the wide gravel driveway that separated Faith's home from the other buildings. Beside the house were various gardens, some fenced and others open.

The raised flower beds were made from wooden boxes and large, corrugated metal tubs. Most were empty, probably cleaned up for the fall, but a few still had autumn flowers that hadn't frozen completely. There were lights strung over one section of the garden where the planters had been sepa-rated by wide, walking rows. A planter beside the porch was brimming with tangerine mums.

"This is charming," I said, joining Toren in front of his truck. The air was clean and cool, infused with the scents of earth and pine and sunshine.

He took my hand, lifting it to kiss my knuckles. It was so natural, so easy, like we'd done this a hundred times. Like we weren't hiding from the world.

So I leaned into his side, rising up on my toes to press my lips to his smooth cheek.

When he'd parked beside my BMW at the grocery store

earlier to pick me up, I'd done a double take at his clean-shaven face. He looked sexy and rugged with the short beard, but I think I preferred this Toren better. I liked the chiseled lines of his jaw.

I put a hand on his cheek, my thumb tracing along his cheekbone. Then I flicked the brim of the gray Wildcat hat he was wearing today. "Goodbye, whiskers."

"I'm not a beard guy, babe."

"Turns out, I'm not a beard girl either."

He chuckled and kissed my forehead, then tugged me toward the house. But before we could climb the porch stairs, the front door blew open and a boy dashed outside, his footsteps pounding as he raced down the steps.

"Toren!" The kid launched himself at Toren's body.

Toren let me go just in time to catch the boy. "Ooof. What have you been eating?"

"Cheeseburgers. Do you want—" The kid noticed me and his eyes bulged. "Who's that?"

"Meet Jennsyn," Toren said, setting him on the ground. "And this is Dane."

"Hi, Dane." I waved. "Nice to meet you."

"You too." He leaned in closer to Toren. "Is she your girlfriend?"

Was I his girlfriend?

Toren glanced to the house, not giving Dane—or me—an answer. "Where's your mom?"

"She's making us work in the garden today to get the rest of the pumpkins loaded. I had to pee but she said I couldn't go outside." Dane pointed toward the open field as his little forehead furrowed. "Isn't that weird? She made me come all the way inside when I could have just gone in the grass. I had to take my boots off and everything."

Toren laughed as he ruffled Dane's strawberry-blond hair. "Let's go find her."

"'Kay." Dane took off like a shot, racing around the side of the house.

"He's adorable," I said.

"That he is." Toren winked, then went to the truck, reaching inside for two pairs of leather gloves.

He tossed me a set, then set off on the same path Dane had taken around the house.

The farm was a sweeping meadow that stretched to a grove of trees in the distance. Faith and the boys were working in a massive fenced garden. At the back were rows of corn stalks, their tan tips swaying in the breeze. There were rows of tilled dirt from where she'd already harvested the bulk of her vegetables except for the pumpkins she was piling in a red wheelbarrow.

"Hey." Toren jerked up his chin as he slid on his gloves.

I did the same, stepping through the gate in the fence and following him to where Faith and the kids were working.

He'd told me to dress in clothes that could get dirty, so I'd paired a blue T-shirt with a pair of old, soft jeans. Toren was dressed like Faith, in jeans, boots and an untucked flannel shirt.

"Hey." Faith smiled, her eyes shielded by a pair of mirrored sunglasses. "Hey, Jennsyn."

"Hi, Faith. Your farm is absolutely enchanting."

"Thank you." Her smile widened. "Toren, give her a tour."

"We'll help you finish up here first."

"No." Faith cut her hands through the air as she shook her head. "You're not coming out here to work today. Besides, I've got my crew."

The boys all stopped what they were doing and walked over.

Abel wouldn't meet my gaze as he muttered a quiet, "Hey."

"Guys, this is Jennsyn." Toren started pointing at the boys. "You know Abel."

"She does?" Dane looked up at his older brother. "How?"

"She just does," Toren said, continuing introductions. "This is Beck, Cabe and you already met Dane."

"Nice to meet you." I fought a laugh as Cabe studied me, trying to figure out exactly who I was and why I was here.

Beck narrowed his eyes and puffed up his chest, making sure I knew that Toren was his first.

I liked them all instantly.

"Go." Faith jerked her chin toward the gate. "The canoe is still down by the pond. I was going to haul it back to the barn later today, but you can take it for a final voyage. Bring it back for me when you're done."

"You sure you don't want help with the pumpkins?" Toren asked.

"I'm sure. We're almost done anyway. We've got the ones I'll take to the Wednesday farmers market. The rest will be compost."

"Okay." He clapped his hand on Abel's shoulder. "You all right?"

"Yeah." Abel shrugged and gave his mom a soft smile. "I'm okay."

"Good man." Toren flicked the tip of Beck's nose, earning a scowl. Then he hauled Cabe into a sideways hug before letting them get back to work. "We'll be back in a bit."

"Take your time." Faith waved us away before joining her sons to harvest the pumpkins.

I walked beside Toren as we left the garden and started through the meadow toward the trees. We meandered in easy silence, in no rush to cross the meadow. I fell in step behind him when we came upon a trodden path that led through a gap in the trees. And beyond their branches was a small, clear pond that mirrored the landscape and reflected the clouds floating through the sky.

"Wow," I whispered.

This would be my safe place too.

Toren walked to a hunter-green canoe turned upside down. He flipped it over and pushed it to the shoreline before setting its oar inside. "Hop in."

"Okay." The boat wobbled as I climbed onto the front seat, holding carefully to the sides as I sat down, facing Toren's spot, not the front.

With a steady shove, he pushed us into the water and climbed inside the canoe. Then with a graceful stroke of the oar, he steered us toward deeper water. "I come out here when I want to get away. Forget the world and just breathe. There's always something going on. Drama with players. Rumors spiraling. You've probably heard the latest about Rush Ramsey."

I shrugged. "There's always talk, but I ignore it. It's not my business."

Toren stared at me for a long moment, so intensely I squirmed and the canoe rocked.

"What?"

"Nothing." He shook it off. "I forget sometimes that you're only twenty-one."

Twenty-two. But I kept that correction to myself as he

paddled us farther. The water lapped against the hull and the oar splashed as he brought it in and out of the pond.

I inhaled the scent of water and tilted my face to the sky, letting the sunshine warm my cheeks.

There was a gentle smile on Toren's lips. A light in his eyes. And the way he stared at me made my heart flutter.

What if I didn't let him go? What if I kept him for myself? I let go of those ideas before I could get attached.

"Abel, Beck, Cabe, Dane and Faith," I said. "George. Hetty, Izzy, Jessy and Kelly. What was your uncle's name? It starts with an E, right?" A. B. C. D. Then their names skipped to F.

"Yeah." His voice dropped. "Evan. He died four years ago."

"I'm sorry." For him. For Faith. For those boys. It explained why Toren came out here so often. Why he was so close with the kids. "If you don't mind me asking, how did he die?"

"Heart attack." Toren swallowed hard. "He'd head into the mountains this time of year before the heavy snow came and cut up a fallen tree for firewood. He went up one morning, and by dark, he still wasn't home. I was living in Oregon at the time. Otherwise, I probably would have gone along. Search and Rescue found him the next morning. They said it looked like he'd sat down for a break, leaned against a tree trunk to close his eyes and never woken up."

"Toren." I pressed a hand against my heart.

"He was healthy and active. No signs of heart disease. His heart just stopped. It was how my father died too."

"Oh my God." My voice cracked.

Toren stared out across the water, the oar resting across his knees. "Uncle Evan loved the mountains. Faith always says she's glad that's where he went. Knew he'd be at peace out there in his final moments."

He'd lost his mother. His father. Then his uncle. I didn't need to ask if they'd been close. The pain in his voice gave it away. "I'm so sorry."

"Me too. I moved back to Mission that next year. I would have moved anyway just to be back home, but the timing worked out so I could get a job with the team."

A job he couldn't lose because of me. A job he was putting at risk by rowing me around this pond.

This had to stop.

How did we stop?

I didn't have that answer, so I leaned toward the canoe's edge and let my fingers tickle the cold, clear water. I let myself have today with Toren.

———

WHEN WE FINISHED with the canoe, we carried it back to the barn, Toren on one end and me on the other.

Cabe and Dane introduced me to their chickens and let me help gather the eggs while Abel, Beck and Toren played catch with a football. Faith sent us off with a loaf of fresh pumpkin bread.

It was the most normal, relaxing day I'd ever had in my life.

There was no talk of volleyball or school. No mention of yesterday's game. It was like escaping my life and living someone else's for an afternoon.

I lived the life of a girl who smiled more often than not.

That smile lingered until we reached the grocery store

parking lot and my car, sitting alone as the sun began to creep toward the mountain horizon in the distance.

"Thank you for taking me out there," I told Toren.

"Thanks for coming."

If this was a real date, if we were a real couple, this was the part of the night when we'd go home together. When we'd cook a meal and eat and talk and laugh and kiss. When I'd park in the space beside his and crawl into his bed after dark.

Except I needed to drive myself home. I would lie to my roommates and pretend I'd spent the day studying at the library.

I couldn't bring myself to reach for the door's handle. I didn't want to get out of his truck. I didn't want this to end.

"That was the best day I've had in a long time." I leaned across the console and pressed my lips to his, not letting myself linger. Then I forced myself to open the door. "Goodbye, Toren."

"Goodbye, Jennsyn." He didn't mean it. Neither did I.

Because later that night, while my roommates were asleep in their beds.

I was in Toren's.

CHAPTER NINETEEN

JENNSYN

I sprinted past Toren's garage and raced over the sidewalk, legs and arms pumping as I leapt onto his front porch the moment his door whipped open. My laugh filled his entryway as I launched myself into his open arms.

It was tricky to kiss when you smiled this wide. I attempted it anyway.

Toren grinned, his eyes crinkling as we kissed with our gazes locked.

"Hi," I murmured against his lips.

"Hi." He banded an arm around my lower back, keeping me pinned against his body as he used his other hand to close the door.

The second it clicked shut, the smiling stopped and this kiss wasn't tricky at all. It was as easy as breathing. Our mouths molded and my lips parted so he could sweep his tongue inside. He tasted like Toren and a hint of cinnamon gum. He tasted like home.

I slanted my mouth over his, kissing him like he was the air in my lungs and I'd been suffocating for days.

A hum rumbled through his chest, the vibration running beneath my skin and pooling in my core.

I tore my lips from his and bent to the crook of his neck, latching on to his pulse as I licked and sucked his skin.

"Fuck, babe." Toren slammed me against the closest wall, trapping me with that strong chest.

His hands roved across my ribs, his touch firm, like he was memorizing my curves. His palms slid around my hips to grip my ass. He gave it a hard squeeze before reaching lower, taking my legs and spreading them apart. Then he positioned one of those bulky, sexy thighs against my center, pressing up until the friction against my clit was dizzying.

I whimpered, rocking against him. "I missed you."

He growled and nipped at my bottom lip as I kept grinding against his thigh. "Missed you too."

I'd left on Wednesday last week for away games through Friday. The football team had traveled for their game Saturday. I'd planned to sneak over last night, but Stevie and Liz had decided on an impromptu Sunday movie night and both of them had fallen asleep on the couch.

So I'd endured a long day on campus, trying to catch up on schoolwork, then spent the evening in my bedroom as I'd counted down the hours to midnight, praying that everyone would sleep in their own fucking beds tonight so I wouldn't have to stay in mine.

The minute I'd been sure my roommates were asleep, I'd silently bolted out the door.

"I need you." I tugged frantically at his T-shirt, attempting to rip it off his shoulders.

He leaned away barely an inch to reach behind his nape, and with a yank, the fabric was gone.

My hands pressed against his hot, smooth skin, my

fingertips digging into those solid, hard muscles of his back. I kept rocking against his thigh, the need in my lower belly coiling tighter and tighter with every swivel of my hips.

Toren stripped away the sweatshirt I'd pulled on, his jaw clenching as it sailed over his shoulder for the floor.

No tee. No tank. No bra. Tonight wasn't about a slow strip and tortured foreplay, not when I'd been waiting nearly a week to feel him inside me.

"Fuck me," I breathed. "Please. Hard. Now."

He growled again, the sound nothing more than primal male desire. My nipples were already hard, but that sound turned them to stone.

We broke apart only long enough for me to shove down my sweatpants and him to kick off his jeans.

Toren kept me pinned against the wall as he reached for my knee, lifting one of my legs to circle his hip.

He positioned the blunt head of his cock at my entrance and I closed my eyes, waiting for him to sink inside. But he stopped, his grip on my knee locked so I couldn't shift.

"Toren." I tried to tilt my hips, to take what I needed, but the way he had me against the wall meant I couldn't move enough.

He had me pinned at just the right angle so that only a thrust of his hips would bring us together.

"Keep your eyes closed." His command was a murmur over my lips.

I obeyed, letting them drift shut. My chest heaved as I dragged in desperate breaths, my body thrumming with desire. With every inhale, that coarse dusting of hair over his pecs tickled my pebbled nipples.

It was torture and bliss. It was agony and perfection.

It was temptation and fire that would singe us both.

But I couldn't stop myself from reaching for the flames. Not yet.

"Did you think about me this week?" His voice was sex and sin as he bent to speak low in my ear.

"Yes."

"Did you touch yourself when you thought of me?"

I gulped. "Yes."

He groaned but still didn't move. "Every morning, every night, I thought about you when I took my cock in my hand. I thought about your mouth. Your body. Your pussy. I thought about all the ways I want to fuck you."

"Oh God." My entire body quivered, my arms cinching tighter around his broad shoulders. But no matter how hard I pulled, he refused to move. "Tor, please."

"Say it again." His lips skated across mine, his breath hot.

"Please."

"Tor. Call me Tor."

My entire body shuddered at the pleasure in that dark voice. "Tor."

He thrust inside me before his name was off my tongue.

I cried out as I clung to him, savoring the feel of my body stretching around his. God, he was big. So fucking big it took my breath away every time. He filled me in a way no man ever had before. Ever would.

"Fuck, you're tight," he clipped, like he was trying to keep control.

But I wanted him to lose it. I wanted him to be as undone by me as I was by him.

With one hand, I reached between us and cupped his balls.

The hiss that blew past his teeth was the sound of triumph.

He took my lower lip into his mouth, holding it in his bite as he pulled out and slammed inside again.

Over and over, he drove to the hilt, fucking me exactly the way I'd been dreaming about all week. Hard and fast and deep and perfect.

"You feel so good." He groaned and quickened his pace, the sound of our bodies slapping together filling the hall.

My inner walls fluttered. We'd only just begun, but I'd spent a week aching for this, for Toren. And the orgasms I'd given myself in the shower were nothing compared to sex.

Heat spread through my veins and my limbs began to shake. My head fell back against the wall and lolled to the side, exposing my neck. "Oh God. I'm going to come."

"That's it, baby." He bent to my throat, his teeth grazing across my skin. "Come for me."

Two hard strokes of his cock and I shattered. My orgasm broke and sent me hurdling into the heavens, flying toward the stars.

"Tor." I gasped for air as I came apart. Unable to stand, I sagged against him as I lost control of my body. Head to toe, every cell shook and pulsed. I couldn't breathe. I couldn't think. I couldn't do anything but feel as it rolled into me wave after wave.

Toren didn't slow his pace. He fucked into me hard and fast, chasing his own release. His roar was a dull murmur beyond the pounding of my pulse in my ears. He tipped his head to the ceiling, and with my name on his lips, he poured into me, his come hot as it leaked down my thighs.

My throat felt raw, my lungs burning like I'd run ten miles, when my orgasm began to fade and I managed to crack my eyes open.

Toren had collapsed against me, his chest rising and

falling with heavy breaths as his forehead rested on the wall beside my hair. Aftershocks zinged through his body, the muscles in his back spasming beneath my touch.

He was still buried inside me, his cock twitching.

I used the leg already around his hip to pull myself closer, then I wrapped my arms around his shoulders and buried my face in his neck, drawing in the masculine, clean scent of his skin.

"I missed you." More than was rational.

His arms wrapped around my waist, holding so tight it was almost hard to breathe, as he shifted his face into my hair. "I missed you."

We held onto each other even as the fire in my veins banked and the sweat on my skin cooled. Only when goose bumps broke out across my forearms and an involuntary shiver rolled over my shoulders did he finally break our connection.

He pushed the hair off my face and his eyes searched mine. Toren opened his mouth but, before he could speak, clamped it shut. Then he kissed the tip of my nose before taking my hand and pulling me into the house and straight for the stairs.

Straight to his bedroom, where we fell into each other again, taking our time to explore until we were both spent.

"Don't fall asleep," he warned, lying face down on a pillow. He lifted a hand to my face, his thumb tracing a line across my cheekbone.

"I won't," I promised as a yawn stretched my mouth.

The clock on his nightstand glowed. It was after three. All I wanted to do was crash and sleep in his plush bed for a few hours, but before that clock turned to four, I needed to be home. I needed to sneak back into my world, where I'd pretend that I wasn't entirely addicted to Toren Greely.

"Did you read that book I left?" I asked.

"Yes."

Last week, before we'd left for our games, I'd stopped by the bookstore on campus and picked out a thriller I'd hoped he'd like enough for his shelf.

"And?" I perked up, lifting off the pillow an inch.

"It's in the office."

"Yes." I did a fist pump, Toren's low laugh my reward. "What else have you been doing?"

"Working mostly. Lying low."

We hadn't talked or texted in our time apart. These were all questions I would have asked a boyfriend over the phone, but somehow, we'd settled into an unspoken agreement. These stolen nights were what we had together. Other than the occasional text to trade plans, we kept communication to a minimum.

The last thing I needed was to have someone get curious and ask who I was texting so often.

I'd made that mistake once and wouldn't do it again.

"Did you watch any good movies?" I asked.

"I watched the ones you bought me."

"Did you get scared?"

He grinned. "No, babe."

"Be honest. Did you like them?"

"I don't think horror is my genre."

"Dang." Maybe I could change his mind if we watched one together. Rather than bury my face in a blanket when I got scared, I could curl into his chest. "Just eighties and nineties movies, then, huh?"

Something passed across his gaze, something I'd seen

before but hadn't questioned. Something like pain. It happened so fast it was gone in a blink.

"What?" I asked, waiting as silence settled between us, even though his thumb never stopped moving on my cheek.

"I'm not really into those eighties and nineties movies either."

I blinked, then shoved up on my elbows, moving out of his touch to stare down at him. "What? Then why do you have them?"

"They were my mom's favorites. She had a whole collection of VHS tapes that I kept for years. I've still got them in the storage room in the basement, but when I was in college, I decided I wanted to get the DVDs too. In case I ever wanted to watch something she loved."

My heart pinched. "Oh, Tor."

"I don't watch them much," he said quietly, rolling onto his back to stare at the dark ceiling. "I'm glad you did though. She would have liked that."

I shifted across the bed, curling into his side. VHS tapes. Those were old. Hell, so were DVDs anymore. "How long?"

"She died when I was sixteen. Breast cancer." He closed his eyes, like saying the words was physically painful.

I pressed a kiss to his chest. "I'm sorry."

"She was only forty-eight." When he opened his eyes to look at me, the sadness in his irises was so raw, so deep, it sliced to the bone. "Everything changed after that."

"I can imagine."

He was quiet for a long moment, staring at the ceiling until, "It broke my dad. He was this big guy, about my size. She was five feet tall but had this fiery spirit. She was his spark, and he loved her with everything he had. When she

253

was gone, he became a shell. He had a heart attack a year later, when he was fifty-four."

So within a year, he'd lost them both. "I'm so, so sorry."

"It's been a long time."

"So? That doesn't mean it still won't hurt." That he wouldn't have days that were hard to bear, like the anniversary of her death.

"Yeah. I guess so." He blew out a long breath. "I went to live with Evan and Faith when I was seventeen. Stayed there for a year until I graduated and went to college. Evan and Dad were brothers but there were fifteen years between them, so I'm sort of in the middle. I was the older cousin to visit and play with the boys when they were little. Those kids gave me an escape from the grief. They gave me a reason to keep going. When Evan died . . ."

Toren had stepped into his shoes. He'd made sure those boys kept going. Faith too.

"You became the one who takes care of everyone now."

He shrugged. "I help."

Toren did more than help. He was the one who Faith called during an emergency. He was the guy who'd fill the role of father for four boys. He'd give himself to everyone, even if that meant not keeping anything for himself.

"Who takes care of you?" I asked, more to myself than to him, but his silence was all the confirmation I needed.

Toren was an anchor to everyone in his life. He was the steady. The rock.

I swung a leg over his body and pushed up to straddle his hips. Then I bent down to take his mouth as his hands came to my sides.

He could take care of everyone else.

And I'd take care of him.

THE PARTY
JENNSYN

"Toren," I whispered.

He hummed, his eyes closed and his face nestled in a pillow. He was seconds from crashing, but before that happened, I wanted to say goodbye.

We'd been awake for hours, talking and kissing and fighting sleep. But we'd finally worn each other out.

"I'm gonna go." I kissed his cheek. "Bye."

His eyes flew open, wide for a minute before they narrowed. Then the sexiest, most endearing frown I'd ever seen in my life turned down the corners of his mouth. His eyes drifted closed again as his arm snaked around my waist, hauling me close. He buried his nose in my hair, drawing in a long inhale. "Say goodbye in the morning."

"It is morning." Well, almost.

"Don't say goodbye," he murmured, holding tight. "Not yet."

"Okay." I snuggled deeper into his arms.

And as dawn kissed the horizon beyond his bedroom window, we finally fell asleep.

CHAPTER TWENTY

TOREN

My stomach knotted as I read over the text I'd drafted an hour ago. It was short, a few quick sentences to the head coach at the high school. My former coach. There were no specifics, just a greeting and question to see if he had time to meet up in the next few weeks.

He'd probably assume I wanted to talk about Abel.

I doubted it would even cross his mind that I was going to ask him for a job. Maybe take his place when he retired soon.

Was I really doing this? Was I really considering giving up my career for a woman? A student?

"Fuck." I dragged a hand over my face and deleted the text, then set my phone on my desk and sagged in my office chair.

Not yet. It wasn't time to explore other options yet. Not until I knew where this thing with Jennsyn was going.

Most likely, it was pointless to worry about my career.

She'd probably be done with me by spring. By the time she graduated, she'd probably want to find a guy her own age. A guy who'd follow her around the world and watch her play in Europe, if that's where she was headed next. A guy who hadn't already put down roots and who was ready for them to grow.

I wanted a family. Kids of my own. It was a selfish desire, considering that Dad and Uncle Evan had both died young. Chances were, I'd suffer the same fate.

There wasn't a damn thing wrong with my heart. I made sure to have a thorough checkup every year with my doctor. But Dad and Evan had both been healthy men, which meant there was always a chance, even if it was slim, that I'd be dead before I reached sixty.

That was not a loss I wanted for my children. I didn't want them to know what it felt like to lose a father.

Except I wanted the promise of them more.

I wanted toys scattered through my living room. I wanted noisy, chaotic meals at the dining room table. I wanted to look into the stands at Saturday football games and see my family cheering on the Wildcats. Cheering on me.

But I wasn't getting any younger. I'd spent a long time fucking around with casual hookups and one-night stands. I'd always figured that eventually a woman would come along who'd make me want to give up the playboy routine.

I guess I'd been right.

I just hadn't expected it to be a student. A woman over a decade younger. A woman who still had adventures to live.

A woman I wasn't sure how to let go.

Jennsyn and I needed to have a serious talk. A talk that wasn't clouded with the haze of sex. A talk aimed more toward the future than the past.

Except the nights when she'd sneak over to my house,

the last damn thing I wanted to do was talk. She walked through the door and all I could think about was her. Kissing her. Touching her. Fucking her.

No matter how many times I had her in my bed, it wasn't enough.

Over the past two weeks, any time that we were both in town, she'd come over after midnight. I'd lost countless hours of sleep worshiping her body until she crept home before dawn.

The volleyball team had a game tonight in Upshaw. Maybe I'd go to the gym, pretend to be there to support the Wildcats program as a whole. Afterward, before her naked body stole my attention, maybe Jennsyn and I could have that talk.

We were leaving tomorrow for an away game. If we talked tonight, it would give us both a few days to think about what was coming.

Or a few days for me to lick my wounds if our conversation didn't go the way I hoped.

What if she wasn't looking for anything serious? What if she was at that stage where she only wanted casual hookups and one-night stands? What if she realized that I was falling and she was not?

My head began to throb like it did every time I let myself wander down this mental road. God, I'd really fucked myself, hadn't I? I'd put myself in the worst possible position.

Falling for a fucking student athlete.

How much longer could we keep up this charade? How much longer did Jennsyn and I have until one of her roommates caught her leaving at night? Until someone realized it was me she'd text from time to time?

Would Faith let me move into the barn when I was

unemployed? My reputation would be in shambles, and I'd never coach again. Maybe I should retype that text after all, quit this job while I still had the chance.

While it was still my choice.

I was about to stand from my chair and head outside the fieldhouse for some fresh air when Aspen walked through my open door.

"Toren, are you busy?" she asked, already closing the door before I could respond.

This wasn't the first time Aspen had swung in to talk. She hadn't been with the Wildcats for long, and given my history with the school and in Mission, she stopped by at times for advice. Usually when she couldn't track down Millie.

But now that I had this thing with Jennsyn, every time I saw Aspen, my stomach churned.

Did she know? Had she found out about Jennsyn and me? Was today my last day as a coach?

My heart clawed its way into my throat as it hammered, dread leaching the color from my face.

"Sorry to bother you. I need advice and Millie is nowhere to be found." Aspen collapsed into a chair across from my desk.

Advice? The air rushed from my lungs. She wouldn't be coming in here for advice if she'd caught on to the fact that I was fucking one of her players every chance I could get.

"What's up?"

Aspen opened her mouth, about to speak, but a knock came at the door. Before I could say a word, Ford barged inside.

"Oh, shoot. Sorry," he said. "Figured you were alone. Hey, Aspen."

"Hey, Ford." She waved, glancing over her shoulder.

"Swing by my office whenever you're free?" he asked me.

"You got it."

"Thanks." He gave me a tired smile, then closed the door behind him.

Aspen hooked a thumb over her shoulder. "Is he okay? Do you need to go?"

No, Ford wasn't okay. Neither was Millie. Both were walking around the halls pretending to be fine when they were anything but.

"I'm sure it's just about travel plans for tomorrow." I waved him off. "What's going on?"

"I don't know what to do." She closed her eyes, drawing in a long breath. "We just finished practice for today. It was, well . . . awful."

"What happened?"

Bad practices happened during a season. Players would show up unfocused. Plans would go awry and everyone would leave in a shit mood. It was part of managing a team, but those were the worst days as coaches, second only to a devastating loss.

"I can't even articulate it. But the team is . . . off. We all feel it. And I know why, but I have no idea what to do about it. Well, I have one choice, but it sucks."

"What's that?" I asked even though I had a hunch what she was going to say. Who this was about. The dread was instant. It settled onto my shoulders like ten thousand bricks.

This advice she needed. It was about Jennsyn, wasn't it?

Aspen sighed. "How do I bench my best player?"

CHAPTER TWENTY-ONE

JENNSYN

Our lockers didn't have doors. They were open compartments where we could stash our bags and hang our coats, but if we wanted to lock anything up, there was a safe at the base of each column for us to key in a code.

Probably a good thing. I would have slammed a door otherwise.

The tension in the locker room was as thick as a concrete wall.

The buttons on my safe beeped as I punched in my code —one, three, five, seven. I wanted to scream with each number.

I took out my phone and keys, tossing them into my bag. Then I stripped off my sweaty shirt and changed clothes in rushed, hurried jerks, balling up my shirt before throwing it into my bag.

No dawdling for me today. Coach Quinn was expecting me in her office at five.

It was asinine that I was getting summoned. That *I* was the person in trouble.

I wasn't the one who'd slacked on the court all week. I wasn't the one who'd been more concerned about trivial gossip than running our plays. I wasn't the one who'd started crying so dramatically that the coaches had called practice quits fifteen minutes early.

That would be Megan.

Her sniffles echoed through the locker room along with the murmured assurances from the other girls. Even Stevie and Liz were huddled over her shoulder.

Which left me to change alone. I hadn't even bothered with a shower.

I hadn't missed Stanford much since I'd moved to Montana. I hadn't missed the pressure and expectations of playing at that level. I hadn't missed the California weather or the grueling class schedule.

But today was the first time I'd missed the Stanford team.

Not a single player would have acted like Megan had during practice. If another girl had thrown the kind of tantrum that Megan had thrown today, every other girl would have said exactly what I'd told Megan.

Shut the fuck up and get to work.

Apparently, that sentence made me the bitch on the Treasure State Wildcats volleyball team.

I was fairly certain I'd had that title for months, even before I'd moved. Megan, and some of the other girls, would have hated me no matter how I acted. No matter how I played.

I'd taken their friend's spot on the team, which made me the enemy.

Whatever. I wasn't here to make friends, especially with Megan. We were nothing alike.

There'd been a time my freshman year when I'd been

complaining about the workouts and practice schedule. When I'd been the girl in the locker room acting like a brat. One of the seniors had told me to shut the fuck up.

I'd become a better player because of it. Because she'd reminded me that there was a string of girls ready and waiting to take my place. So either I could gripe about how hard it was to be a student athlete. Or I could suck it up and play.

I hadn't cried in the locker room that day. No, I'd saved my tears for when I was alone, knowing that if I'd called Mom, she would have told me to suck it up too.

And today, I'd acted just like my mom.

The realization hit me so hard I winced. Damn it.

Maybe I was the problem. Maybe I was taking volleyball too seriously. That's what I'd been taught to do, after all.

I didn't regret calling Megan on her bullshit, but I could have been gentler.

Closing my eyes and sucking in a deep breath, I finished putting away my sweaty clothes, then walked to where the team was clustered.

"Megan," I said, forcing as much kindness into my voice as possible. "I'm sorry for being harsh."

Her shoulders shook as she buried her face in her hands. She kept on wailing.

So I took that as my sign to leave.

On a sigh, I turned and walked out of the locker room, shoving the door open too hard before I marched down the hall, straight for Coach Quinn's office.

She was sitting behind her desk, elbows braced on its surface as she rubbed her temples. When I cleared my throat, she straightened and gave me a tight smile. "Come on in, Jennsyn."

I closed the door behind me—this would be a private conversation—and set my bag next to the chair's legs as I took a seat. "I apologize for losing my temper with Megan."

Coach Quinn's shoulders sagged. "This isn't Stanford."

"No, it's not."

She winced, like I'd struck a nerve. "I agree, Megan should have been taking practice more seriously. I'll be having a discussion with her about that and the gossip."

This was all over Rush Ramsey and speculation about the woman he'd gotten pregnant. Rumors were running rampant through the fieldhouse, and every time I heard someone whisper his name, I cringed. It wasn't Megan's business. It wasn't mine.

"I hate gossip," I said. "Especially when it takes place during a practice."

"I wish I had heard what she'd said. I would have called her on it myself. But you beat me to it."

And if it happened again, I'd still call Megan on it. Though next time, I'd try to be softer in the delivery.

Coach Quinn blew out a long breath and leaned forward on the desk, hands clasped like she was begging for some answers. "Why are you here, Jennsyn? You are so talented. Too talented. You belong on a team like Stanford's, where you won't have to harass the girls to focus. Where everyone on the team is as dedicated to a win as you are. Why would you transfer to Treasure State of all places when you were at Stanford?"

Gossip. A broken heart.

Those were the simple answers. Rather than suffer through them, I'd left.

But not a soul in Montana knew the truth, and I had no plans to change that now.

"You aren't a part of this team," she said. "You sit alone. The girls talk about getting together, but they say you never go."

"Is that required?"

Something like defeat crossed her face, like she'd hoped I'd have a different response. "No, it's not required."

"I live with Stevie and Liz. I see them every day."

"And Liz says you stick to your bedroom."

My hands curled around the chair's armrests as my molars ground together. "Liz has no reason to be talking about me."

Coach held up her hands. "I asked her how things were going at home. Please don't be upset with her."

It wasn't like Liz was wrong. I rarely left my bedroom unless I was here on campus or sneaking to Toren's in the middle of the night. At least Liz couldn't report that to Coach Quinn.

Though why was she reporting anything? Why had Coach Quinn asked Liz how things were going in the first place?

"Is this about the game we lost?"

She blinked. "Huh?"

"I'm sorry. I had an off day. It won't happen again." And it hadn't happened again. Every game since that loss, we'd won. I'd shoved past the rattling, tamped it down with my iron will, and when I walked onto the court, I was wholly focused.

We wouldn't lose again, at least not in our conference. In the playoffs? Against better teams? Yeah, then we'd lose. But I was determined to claim the conference championship title.

"It's not about the loss," Coach said, her eyes softening.

"This is a winning season. The most successful season in the program's history, Jennsyn."

"Okay," I drawled. Then why was she talking to Liz and why was she calling me into her office for a spat with Megan?

"You are destroying your opponents," she said. "You leave everything on the court. You said you were here this year to play."

I nodded, not sure where she was going with this.

"You say you want to play, but today, you looked like you wanted to be anywhere else."

"Megan pushed all the wrong buttons. I'm sorry."

She gave me a sad smile. "*Before* Megan started gossiping. I watched you pick up the ball earlier and look at it like it weighed a thousand pounds."

My stomach dropped.

Yeah, there'd been a moment today when I hadn't wanted to be there. When I'd known there'd be a text from Mom and an email from Mike Simmons waiting when practice was over.

Apparently, I wasn't as good at hiding my indecision, my exhaustion, as I'd thought.

"This is a team sport," Coach Quinn said. "My best friends are the girls who I played with in college. You don't have to love all the girls. I get it. But . . . try. Please. I can't do much to coach you on the court. You're already ahead of me. So if I can coach you off the court, I'll take my shot. The season is almost over. Most of the girls look at you like they're staring at the sun. They so desperately want you to be on their team. Give them a chance. They might surprise you."

Or they might stab me in the back.

They might break my heart and ruin it all.

"I'm sorry about practice," I said. "If having me on the team is an issue, then I'll understand if you need to make a change."

Part of me wanted her to kick me off the team. Part of me longed for her to be the reason I had to quit. Because then it wouldn't be my choice.

Coach Quinn shook her head. "No, of course not. Though, I'll admit I thought about putting you on the bench for a few games."

I'd never been benched before. The blow to my ego might actually be worse than being kicked off the team. To sit and watch everyone else play, especially if they lost, would be crushing.

Something Coach likely knew.

"I'll see you tomorrow at the game," she said, her gaze flicking to the door.

In the scope of ass chewings, that hadn't been all bad. Not great. But it could have been worse.

I stood and collected my bag, then walked out of the fieldhouse, wishing more than anything I could go back in time and tell past Jennsyn to keep her mouth shut.

But I'd said what I'd said. It was too late. I'd apologized to Megan and all I could do now was move forward.

When I fished my phone from my bag, as expected, there was an email waiting in my inbox from Mike Simmons and a text from my mother demanding I call her immediately. I ignored both and drove home, finding both Liz's and Stevie's cars already in the garage.

They must have left not long after I'd gone into my meeting with Coach Quinn.

I braced for glares and the silent treatment, except as I

walked into the living room where both my roommates were waiting, they shot off the couch.

"Are you okay?" Stevie asked.

"What did Coach say?" Liz's eyes were wide. "She didn't put you on the bench, did she? Because you told Megan what we were all thinking."

I blinked. Okay. Not the reaction I'd expected. "No, she didn't put me on the bench."

"Thank God." Liz slumped back into the sofa. "Megan stopped crying the second you left the locker room."

"I actually believed she was upset." Stevie rolled her eyes. "I guess that makes me the chump. As soon as the door closed behind you, she stood up and gave everyone this nasty smirk, like she was intentionally causing drama. I'm done with her. I told her that to her face too."

"Same." Liz nodded. "She needs to grow the hell up."

"Wait. What?" It wasn't the idea of Megan putting on an act that surprised me. It was that they'd both . . . defended me.

It had been a long time since anyone had chosen me, at least when it came to friends.

"She's such a brat." Stevie plopped back on the couch beside Liz, stretching for the remote.

"Yeah," I muttered, not sure what else to say.

So I started for the stairs, about to hide away in my room like normal. Except before I made it to the bottom step, I paused, turning back.

"I've been into these old eighties and nineties movies lately," I blurted. "I don't know if you have homework or anything tonight, but I was going to watch one."

Liz and Stevie shared a look and the silent conversation that passed between them made me feel an inch tall.

Was I really so withdrawn that a movie invite was shocking news? *Yes.*

"Sounds good to me," Stevie said. "I don't have anything to do tonight."

"Me neither," Liz said. "I'm in. Maybe we could order pizza or something. Thursday night is ten-dollar pizza night. We could get delivery."

"Sure." I shrugged. "I'm not picky."

"Good." Liz smirked at Stevie. "Because she's one of the pickiest eaters on the planet. No pepperoni. No bacon. Extra sauce with extra green peppers, and if there's a mushroom in sight, you might as well throw the entire thing in the trash."

"Whatever." Stevie scrunched up her nose. "I know what I like."

Her statement was spoken with such confidence. It was stated so definitively, like she'd known what she liked for ages.

Meanwhile, I was still figuring it out. What *did* I like?

I liked to read. I liked cheesy movies. I liked a clean car.

I liked Toren.

I liked him enough to risk my scholarship. My spot on the team. My future. I liked him enough to risk his career.

It was one of the most selfish things I'd ever done, but I couldn't stop.

No matter how often I told myself to let him go, for his sake, if not mine, I couldn't stop. So after pizza and a movie, when Stevie and Liz had retreated to their bedrooms and thought I was sleeping in mine, I slipped out of the house and raced to his.

Like usual, he was waiting. The door flung open the moment my bare foot touched the porch.

Except he didn't greet me with open arms. There was a

crease between his eyebrows, a tension in his frame that turned my run into a walk.

"What?" I asked.

"Are you okay?"

I sighed. "You talked to Coach Quinn, didn't you?"

"Yeah." He opened his arms.

And I fell into his chest.

"You good?" His hand came to the back of my head, stroking my hair as he used a foot to kick the door closed.

"Meh." I shrugged, burrowing into his T-shirt as I drew in the scent that smelled like mine.

"Talk to me. What's going on?"

The truth, the whole truth, was on the tip of my tongue. But the reason I was in Montana, the reason I'd left Stanford, meant I might lose Toren. I could barely stomach the truth. How would he?

I wasn't ready for a real goodbye, not yet.

"Just a bad day," I said, rising up on my toes to kiss the underside of his jaw.

He opened his mouth, like he wanted to ask for more, but it was late and we didn't have long. Just a few stolen hours before I had to run back home.

Where I'd pretend like I could hide the truth forever.

CHAPTER TWENTY-TWO

TOREN

The problem with being six four was that I stood above everyone in a crowd. It meant people spotted me before I spotted them.

Somehow, I'd managed to go unnoticed when I'd come to watch Jennsyn's game earlier this season. Tonight? Not so much.

Millie weaved through the crush of people filtering into the Upshaw gym, her attention locked on me. When she stopped in front of me, her forehead furrowed. "What are *you* doing here?"

Watching the woman I was in deep with play in a volleyball tournament.

"I was working late. Thought I'd come watch the game and support Aspen and her team." Did half-truths count as lies when they were given to one of your oldest friends?

"Ah." She nodded. "Want to sit together?"

"Love to." Now that was a blatant lie.

Hell. I probably should have suspected Millie would be

here tonight. I definitely should have worn a hat and tried harder to blend.

When Jennsyn was around, it wasn't exactly easy for me to pretend she was just another Treasure State student. If I was lost in the stands surrounded by strangers, no one would notice if I stared too often at a certain player. But Millie? She'd notice.

Which meant I'd be on edge all night. Great.

Millie smiled and led the way into the gym, taking a seat in the first row of bleachers marked as reserved. We were behind the chairs set up for the team, so close that it would be impossible for Jennsyn not to see me when they came out of the locker room.

So much for being inconspicuous. I didn't want my presence here to pull Jennsyn's focus from the game, hence why I'd planned to sit in a dark corner alone.

Damn it. Maybe I should just leave. Make up an excuse and head home.

Except this was my last chance to watch Jennsyn play. Tomorrow, the football team was leaving for an away game and we wouldn't be home until Sunday. This tournament would be over before we returned.

We'd be gone while they played for the conference championship too. If—*when*—they won, they'd earn a slot in the playoff bracket. But those games would all be on the road against big schools. And while they were a force to be reckoned with in our conference, they'd likely lose out to a larger school with a more prestigious program—like Stanford.

So this was it. This was my last chance to watch Jennsyn play college volleyball. Maybe I'd get another chance to watch a game if she kept playing after graduation. Maybe, somehow, we'd figure this thing out.

But if not, if this was my shot to cheer her on, then I wouldn't miss it.

"Ready for the trip tomorrow?" Millie asked, nearly shouting over the noise in the gymnasium.

I nodded. "Think so. Ford's got everything organized."

She was quiet for a long moment, tucking a lock of her dark hair behind an ear. Then so quietly I strained to hear, she said, "How is he?"

Ford was awful. The man was a wreck. Whatever was going on between them had turned him inside out, and he was in a bad mood more often than not.

"Not great," I admitted.

She swallowed hard, her shoulders curling inward. There were dark circles beneath her eyes, circles I hadn't noticed at first. We hadn't gone to dinner lately, not since tacos over a month ago. Since Ford had asked me to watch over her. It hadn't been for lack of my trying. Each time I'd text her and ask if she was free for a burger or tacos, she'd have an excuse.

It was a busy time of year with fall sport activities nearly every night. But I suspected she was avoiding me and anyone else who reminded her too much of Ford. And it wasn't like she could escape him entirely, not when they worked in the same building.

"Sorry." I put my arm around her shoulders, hauling her into my side for a quick hug.

Millie leaned against me until most of the spectators were seated and the visiting team emerged from their locker rooms.

My heart rate spiked when the Wildcats emerged, and I scanned every face for Jennsyn's.

Aspen took the lead, walking to her chair with her

assistant coaches on her heels. Then came the players, each wearing a stoic game face. Liz was in the middle of the group. Then Stevie. And at the end of the line, slightly separate from the rest, walked Jennsyn, her chin held high and her eyes narrowed.

That granite expression was such a contrast to the woman who ran from her house to mine in the dark, her smile so bright it lit up the night.

Her posture was perfect, tall and lean and intimidating. She was in the zone, ready to dominate. She looked past her own team once she reached the court, her gaze drifting to the opposing team's bench. She scrutinized every opponent, one by one. They each withered beneath her icy stare.

A swell of pride, of want, stretched in my chest. That shouldn't have been sexy, but damn if it wasn't.

"I don't know why she came here," Millie said, like me, watching Jennsyn. "But I'm not complaining."

I should know the reason. I should know the details of why Jennsyn had left Stanford. Weeks we'd been together and she had yet to confide in me. Why? What was she hiding?

We couldn't keep avoiding the hard topics. We couldn't keep getting lost in each other. Last night, after she'd told me about what had happened at practice with Megan and getting called into Aspen's office, I'd hoped she'd confide in me. I'd hoped we could talk about the future and what we were doing.

Except she'd sealed her lips over mine, and rather than put a stop to it, I'd taken the easy road and kissed her back. We'd spent a few wild hours in my bed. Then it had been too late to have a long, serious conversation, so I'd walked her to the door and watched as she tiptoed home.

We'd have to talk soon. But not tonight. When she came over later, the only talk I wanted was her screaming my name and begging for more.

The players shifted together in a huddle around Aspen. Jennsyn's gaze must have felt mine because she glanced past the chairs, straight to where I was sitting.

Those blue eyes widened, not by much, but enough. Then she looked away too soon.

I did the same, dropping my chin to stare at an invisible spot on the floor.

Fuck, this was such a bad idea. I should be across the gym, sitting in a sea of faces, not right behind the team's bench.

When I looked up, it was to Millie first. A small smile tugged at her mouth that meant she'd caught Jennsyn's reaction. *Shit.*

"What?" Could I bluff my way out of this? Feign ignorance?

"Maybe we should have sat somewhere else." Millie's gaze flicked toward the team, where another player, this one wearing a different color shirt, was staring my way.

The moment she realized I'd caught her gawking, she jerked and looked to the ceiling, her cheeks flushing.

"You'll have the whole volleyball team crushing on you before the night is over," Millie said, leaning close as she smirked.

I frowned. "I'm just sitting here."

"I'm teasing."

"Yeah," I muttered.

If Millie thought Jennsyn was crushing on me, well . . . she wasn't wrong. She just didn't realize that the crush went both ways.

That this thing between us felt like a lot more than a crush.

"Hi, Millie. Toren." A hand landed on my shoulder. Kurt, the athletic director, stood at my side.

The last person I wanted to see tonight. My boss's boss. *Awesome.*

"Kurt." I stood and shook his hand.

"You guys got room for one more?" He glanced past Millie to the empty spot beside her.

Say no, Millie.

Her smile was forced as she nodded. "Of course."

"Damn," I muttered under a breath.

As we squished together so Kurt could sit at my side, her lip curled. It was brief, something he wouldn't have seen with my body blocking his view. But Kurt wasn't Millie's favorite person, though she tolerated him as her boss.

Ever since last spring's scandal with the former coach, he'd been hovering over everyone like a helicopter, Millie especially. But every coach too. Without question, if he left this game with any suspicions I was involved with a student, he'd fire me first and ask questions later.

Which meant I kept my gaze locked anywhere but on Jennsyn. I didn't so much as glance her way as she walked out to the court. I made sure not to stare. Not while she played. Not when she came over for water during a break. Not even when she delivered the final kill on each set.

I watched the game, and any time I felt that pull to Jennsyn, I forced myself to look away. Until finally, the game was over and the crowd was cheering for a Wildcat victory.

And I felt like I was finally able to breathe.

They'd won. And now I could get out of this gym.

"That Jennsyn Bell." Kurt whistled as we all stood. "Sure

wish she wasn't a senior. We could use her for another few years."

"Yep," I muttered. "Darn."

Thank fuck Jennsyn was a senior. I wasn't sure where this relationship was going, but my only salvation was that she'd no longer be a student by the end of the spring semester.

"That was a great game." Millie gave Kurt a smile that didn't reach her eyes, not that he noticed. He left without a goodbye, too busy making his way over to the team to congratulate them on the win. "I'm going to head home. It's been a long day."

"See ya." I pulled her into a sideways hug, then watched as she disappeared into the mass of people making their way to the exit.

There was no reason for me to linger. Not when I couldn't exactly approach Jennsyn. So I tucked my hands in my pockets, about to fall in line and shuffle for the doors, when a blond woman walked in front of me and strode onto the court.

It was the shape of her nose and mouth that made me look twice. They were familiar.

She was tall with an athlete's build. She had on a pair of stiletto heels that lifted her higher than anyone around except me. She wore a pair of gray slacks and a navy sweater that accentuated her blue eyes.

Jennsyn's eyes.

The woman glanced around, waiting for the team to break from their talk with Aspen. When she finally faced me fully, I knew who she was without needing to ask.

Jennsyn's mother.

Was this a surprise visit, like her father's? Or had this been planned?

Those questions would have to wait. Because Kurt walked over and gestured for the door.

"I'll walk out to the parking lot with you. Had a thought about Saturday's game."

"Can't wait to hear it," I lied.

And as we left the gym, I didn't let myself look back.

CHAPTER TWENTY-THREE

JENNSYN

Toren's seat was empty. Not that I'd expected him to wait around after the game, but my heart sank when I glanced to where he'd been sitting all night with Millie, and he was nowhere in sight.

Did he know how much it meant to me that he'd come tonight? It was the last night we'd both be in town for one of my games. When I'd spotted him earlier, I'd been so happy I couldn't breathe.

He'd come for me. Besides the occasional visit from my father and the games Mom would watch to pick apart, no one had ever come just for me. Just to support me without any other motivation.

I wished he were still here. But at least I'd get to see him later tonight.

"Nice job, ladies," Coach Quinn said into our huddle. "Back at it tomorrow. Get some rest tonight. Great game."

As she held out her hand to the center of our huddle, we all joined in and on the count of three yelled, "Wildcats."

We broke apart to collect our things and head to the

locker room, except before I could fall in line with the other girls, a figure appeared at my side.

"Mom?" I did a double take, then leaned in for a hug. "H-hi. What are you doing here?"

There might be a rift between us at the moment, but it was still good to see her. For most of my life, it had been only the two of us. I hadn't realized until I stared into her blue eyes, the same color as my own, how much I'd missed her lately.

She gave me a squeeze, then let me go, probably because I was a sweaty mess. She was dressed like usual in a pair of slacks and sweater. Solid colors were her staple. And sky-high heels. Mom liked that she stood so much taller than the average person.

She gave me a slight smile as she pushed an errant strand of hair off my temple. "Your form is slipping."

I blinked, not sure I'd heard her correctly.

Your form is slipping.

We hadn't seen each other in months. We hadn't spoken in weeks, not since the call when she'd informed me of my meeting with Mike Simmons.

She'd sent texts I hadn't acknowledged. Messages I'd ignored. I'd missed her. And instead of saying hello, instead of asking if I was all right or congratulating me on a win or telling me that she'd missed me too, her first comment was to critique my form.

My heart splattered on the shiny, honey-colored gym floor beside Mom's four-inch Jimmy Choos.

"Oh," I muttered as my head spun around her words. My entire chest cavity ached, like someone had hit me with a baseball bat. "I, uh, need to shower and to change."

"I'll wait." She nodded. "Then we'll talk."

Without another word, I slipped away, chin tucked as I made my way out of the gym and toward the locker room, trailing behind the team. The burn in my throat felt like someone had shoved a red-hot iron past my lips. The sting in my nose made it hard to breathe.

Your form is slipping.

Hot tears flooded but I managed to keep them at bay, hidden from the other girls, as I swept up my toiletry bag and a towel, then disappeared into a shower stall.

That's when the tears shook loose. They mingled with the warm water and I slapped a hand over my mouth to smother a sob.

I didn't want this anymore. I didn't love playing enough to do this for another five or ten or fifteen years. When I quit, this flimsy relationship I had with Mom would probably disintegrate. I would lose her, wouldn't I?

It was the reason I'd been so hesitant to quit. The reason I hadn't told Mike Simmons no.

When I gave up volleyball, I would give up my mother.

And tonight, for the first time, I was okay walking away from them both.

Done.

I was done.

The relief was so staggering I had to brace my arm against the tile, giving myself a moment to let it sink in.

Volleyball wasn't my dream. I was done pretending that it was.

It was time to figure out what I wanted. Who *I* wanted to be. Where *I* wanted to live. It was time to create dreams of my own.

It was scary and exciting and daunting and grounding, all at the same time.

DEVNEY PERRY

I was done. I was ready to be done with volleyball.

And it was time to tell Mom.

So I rinsed off my face, sniffling away the last of the tears. And with my body wrapped in a towel, I padded out of the showers and to my locker, where I pulled on a pair of leggings and a thick hoodie.

Most of the girls were already dressed, each smiling after tonight's win. Even Megan seemed to be in a good mood, this week's spat long erased by tonight's victory.

"My mom and dad are taking Liz and me out for tacos," Stevie said as she stood in front of her locker space beside mine. "Want to come?"

"Actually, my mom surprised me with a visit," I told her. "But thanks."

"Sure. That's cool your mom came."

I nodded. "Yeah."

Stevie's parents were constants in the Upshaw gym. They never missed a home game and traveled to some away tournaments too. Granted, they lived in Mission, so watching their daughter play and taking her out for dinner afterward was easy. But I suspected that even if she'd moved away for college, they would have been just as supportive.

"Have a good time." Stevie zipped up her coat. "See you at home."

"Yep. See ya." I headed for a mirror and a blow dryer. When I was finished with my hair, I put on a bit of makeup, some mascara and blush with my favorite lip balm. I took my time, dawdling so that I was the last person to leave the locker room.

As expected, when I emerged into the hallway, Mom was waiting.

There was disappointment etched on her pretty face. For

282

years, I'd done so much to try and make her proud. But it wasn't my face to change, was it? It wasn't my responsibility to make her happy.

I was letting go of a sport and letting go of her expectations too.

Mom shoved off the wall where she'd been leaning, her phone in hand. "Mike Simmons has decided you're not a good fit for his services. He prefers clients who return his emails."

I shrugged. "Good for Mike Simmons."

"Jennsyn," Mom hissed, pinching the bridge of her nose. "What is wrong with you? How could you throw away this opportunity?"

"Is that why you came tonight? To scold me for not signing Mike's contract?"

"Yes. And to sit down and figure out how we can get your career back on track."

I sighed. "No, Mom. I quit."

She blinked. "What?"

"Will you love me when I stop playing your favorite game?" My voice didn't wobble, even though my entire body began to tremble.

It was the question I'd been too much of a coward to ask for years.

I didn't let her answer. I was still too raw and fragile to handle the truth.

"I don't have any dreams, Mom. Not dreams of my own. I want the chance to make them. I want a life not centered around volleyball. I want friends, not teammates. I want . . . my own life. I don't want yours."

"Excuse me?" She recoiled, like I'd slapped her across the face.

"I'm not going to play in Italy. I'm not going to be on another national team. I'm not going to the Olympics. I'm done. My last game will be as a Treasure State Wildcat."

"Jennsyn." There was horror in Mom's voice, like I'd stabbed her in the back.

"I love you, Mom." My heart twisted as a fresh wave of tears made the world go blurry. "We don't say that very often. We should fix that."

"Jennsyn." The shock on her face morphed to sorrow.

Maybe we'd both leave here tonight with broken hearts.

"I hope you can find a way to love me just because I'm your daughter," I whispered. "Without volleyball."

She stared at me, her mouth agape. Tears in her eyes too.

This was my fault. For too long, I'd pretended. I'd hidden my feelings and doubts. I'd let her take charge, and when our conversations always steered toward volleyball, I'd never hit the brakes.

There were probably a thousand better, gentler, ways to break this news. Maybe if she'd told me hello tonight instead of informing me that my form was slipping, I would have softened the blow.

But it was out there now. It was finally free.

There wasn't much more to say to Mom, so I gave her a kind smile, adjusted the strap on my backpack and walked down the hall toward the exit.

"Jennsyn?" Mom stopped me before I could push open the door.

I met her gaze, hating that I was the person who'd put tears in her eyes. Knowing it was unavoidable. "Yeah?"

"I do love you. Very much. I don't . . ." She swallowed hard. "I don't know who I am without volleyball."

"Maybe we can figure that out together."

"Maybe." Mom pressed a hand over her heart. "This is a lot to think about and process."

"I understand." While I'd had most of this season and my time in Mission to come to this conclusion, she was still reeling.

"I'd like to come and watch your other games this weekend," she said. "My flight isn't until Sunday morning."

It was on the tip of my tongue to tell her that I'd love to have her around as long as she didn't pummel me with critiques. That my form was not slipping, and even if it was, who cared? We were winning, weren't we?

But I simply nodded. "I'd like that. I'll see you tomorrow."

Mom didn't follow me as I left the fieldhouse. She'd hang back and give herself some space to absorb that news. I wasn't sure what to expect from her through the rest of this tournament's games, but I hoped if the Wildcats won, she'd at least be happy for this team. For me.

A numbness settled into my limbs as I climbed in my car and I drove home through the quiet night. I hoped that come dawn, I'd still have a relationship with my mother. But whatever she decided, it was done.

I was done.

Oh my God. I was done.

Countless hours practicing. Years of games. Tournaments and teams and travel.

It was almost over. I was nearly finished with volleyball. What now?

An emotional tidal wave crashed forward the moment I parked in the garage. It crushed the breath from my lungs and ground my ribs together. Tears burst from my eyes, streaming down my cheeks and landing on my lap. Sobs racked my entire body as I tried to gulp down air.

With a shaking hand, I managed to open the car's door. My knees wobbled when I shoved to my feet, crying harder than I'd ever cried in my life.

I was done.

It was sad. It was a relief. It was terrifying and thrilling.

The person who'd dedicated her life to the sport regretted every word to Mom. The person who wanted to do anything other than play, who'd buried her feelings for years, was so incredibly glad to have the truth out in the open. Those two people were at war, and even though I knew who'd win, it still hurt.

Another sob shook loose. The tears showed no signs of stopping, so I clapped a hand over my mouth and walked.

Not inside to my house. Not upstairs to my bedroom.

I walked out of the open garage door and across my driveway to Toren's. I marched right to his front door.

It was unlocked.

He came walking down the entryway the moment I stepped inside. One look at my face and his arms opened. "What happened? Was it your mom?"

"I quit." Saying it out loud only made me cry harder as I fell into his chest, hiccupping as I attempted to explain. "I-I told my mom I was done. That this was my l-last season."

"Baby." One hand cupped the back of my head as the other splayed across my lower back, shifting me even closer. "Breathe."

I nodded, attempting to suck in an inhale as his hand moved up and down my spine. "I knew it was coming. I just . . . it hurts and it doesn't. I can't figure it out."

"You will."

"Who even am I without volleyball?"

Toren shifted, taking my face in his hands. His thumbs caught the tears that wouldn't stop, wiping them dry. "You're my Jennsyn."

My eyes searched his, sure that he was too good to be true.

Why did Toren even want me? He could have a woman who knew herself. Who had a career and a life and her shit together. He could have a woman closer to his age. Why me?

My heart was too heavy to ask. To delve into a conversation that would undoubtedly lead to questions about my past that I wasn't ready to answer.

We needed to talk about the future. We needed to figure out what exactly we were doing together.

But what happened if we decided there was no future? What happened if we ended that conversation not together?

I wouldn't survive the loss of volleyball and Toren all in the same night.

So I fell into him again, stealing from his strength as I soaked the front of his shirt with my tears. And when they finally subsided, I pulled away and dried my face. "The girls will be home soon. I should go."

"You okay?" He tucked a lock of hair behind my ear.

"Yes. No." I sighed. "I'll be okay."

"Come back later?"

There wasn't any place I'd rather be than in his arms, but tonight, I didn't trust myself to leave before dawn. "I think I need to be alone for a bit. Sleep and absorb all of this."

He tucked a lock of hair behind my ear. "I get it."

"I wish you weren't leaving tomorrow. I wish I could have hugged you after tonight's game."

The sadness in his gaze said he wished the same. "Me too."

"Good luck at your game this weekend."

"You too." He kissed my forehead, then walked me to the door.

"Goodbye, Toren."

Toren winced, so slightly I barely caught it. Then he lowered his voice as I stepped onto the porch and into the night. "Goodbye, Jennsyn."

How many times had I said goodbye since we'd met? The first had been the morning after the party.

If I could go back in time, if I could do that night and the next morning all over again, there was only one thing I'd change.

I wouldn't say goodbye.

THE PARTY
TOREN

Jennsyn smiled over the rim of her coffee mug. "Fun party, Toren."

Her hair was a mess, thanks to my hands and a sleepless night. There was a slight mark on her throat, thanks to my teeth. And her cheeks had a freshly fucked glow, thanks to the last round we'd gone this morning before she'd finally climbed out of my bed.

Last night had been . . .

Wild. Absolutely fucking wild. That was the best time I'd had with a woman in years.

"Do you need a ride home?" I asked, leaning against the counter in the kitchen, my own coffee cup in one hand.

She shook her head. "I can walk."

"In bare feet?"

"It's not far."

How far? Where did she live? Part of me wanted to ask which house in the neighborhood was hers, but I liked the idea of a mystery. Of hunting for her a bit. To see how long it would take before I spotted her getting the mail or walking down the block.

Last night had been about sex, nothing more. Incredible, unrestrained, wild fucking sex. But damn if I didn't want to do it again.

"I've never crashed a party before." She let out a quiet laugh, more to herself than to me.

"Glad you did."

"Me too." Jennsyn set her mug on the counter and walked over, grabbing the pen that I'd left out on the counter. She stretched past me, her hand brushing my arm before she ripped a paper towel from the roll.

After folding it in half, she wrote down her phone number.

"You could just put it in my phone," I said.

"You can put it in yourself." She smirked. "I like the idea of you doing a little work."

"I thought I did a lot of work last night."

She laughed, her blue eyes dancing. They were brighter in the morning light, even more dazzling than they'd been last night.

Yeah, I'd be looking for her. I'd give this a few days, maybe a week. Give myself a chance to come up for air, to think this through a little. Find out if I actually missed her or if I was just in a sex haze. See if I could track her down and be the one to just show up at her door. If not, then I'd probably call.

"Goodbye, Toren." She flicked the pen in the air, walking away as I caught it with my free hand.

Damn, she really was something. "Goodbye, Jennsyn."

CHAPTER TWENTY-FOUR

JENNSYN

My alarm startled me awake. I reached for my phone on Toren's nightstand, turning off the noise, then shoved the hair out of my face.

Four o'clock in the morning was the actual worst.

I didn't want to get dressed. I didn't want to go outside. I didn't want to crawl into my own empty bed where the sheets were cold.

But four o'clock was already later than I normally left, and I needed to get going.

It had been a week since my mother's visit, since I'd decided to quit volleyball, and Toren and I had fallen into our normal routine.

Any night that we were both in town, I was in his bed. We hadn't talked much. We hadn't so much as glanced at the elephant in the room that was our future and this relationship. We'd skipped the conversations we probably should have had in favor of orgasms and early-morning alarms.

On Monday morning, I'd snuck home around three. On Tuesday, 3:15. Wednesday, 3:20. Every day, I gave myself just a few more moments with Toren, but I was reaching the limit of how far I could push it.

Time to go home.

He was asleep beneath me, head turned slightly into his pillow. His lips had a slight sheen from the lip balm that he'd put on before we'd crashed.

I kissed the corner of his mouth. "I'd better go."

The hand he had splayed across my lower back slid over my hip before his hold tightened. He trapped me on top of his chest. "Not yet."

"You need to get some sleep." We both needed sleep. And if I stayed any longer, there was a chance I'd pass out and wake up with the sun streaming through the windows.

He growled, his lip curling before his eyes opened. Then I was spinning. He moved so fast I gasped.

"Tor—"

His lips crashed onto mine, and my only protest was a hum as his tongue swirled against mine. He settled into the cradle of my hips, and my fingers wove into his hair as his cock pressed against my slit.

There was no fanfare or foreplay before he slid inside, driving to the root.

My pussy clenched around his length.

He tore his mouth away and gritted his teeth. "Fuck."

"Tor. Move," I whimpered, arching my hips to send him deeper. Then I reached between us, placing my hand over his chest.

His heart raced beneath my palm, the beat an echo of my own, speeding faster and faster as he eased out and slammed inside. "You feel so good."

I slid my hand up his pec to his neck, then around to his nape, tugging him down until his mouth was on mine. Then

I kissed him while he fucked me, gliding in and out in an unhurried, steady pace that made my entire body quake.

My orgasm came without warning. Our breaths mingled, our lips locked, as I came apart, crying down his throat. The trembling in my limbs, the pulsing in my core, went on and on and on. It wasn't hard or fast. It wasn't a release that made me scream his name. But it touched every muscle, every bone, every cell, as it spread through my veins in a lush, heady wave of tingles.

These early-morning orgasms were my favorite of them all.

Toren's body tensed as he continued to slide in and out. Then he buried his face in my neck and came on a groan that curled my toes.

I splayed my hands over his back, loving how the muscles racked and bunched as he came, knowing I was the woman who made this man lose control.

He collapsed against me when he was spent, his arms banding tight to hold me close. With a spin, he reversed our positions, our bodies still connected, so I wouldn't be crushed beneath his weight.

"We should talk," he murmured.

My body instantly went taut.

Toren sighed. "But you have to go."

"I have to go."

The clock on his nightstand had crept dangerously close to five.

I got dressed in a rush, pulling on the leggings and sweatshirt I'd worn to sneak over. November was coming to a close and the temperature had plummeted with winter's first skiff of snow. There'd be no more bare feet for months, and my tennis shoes were waiting downstairs.

After quickly tying back my hair, I went to the bed where Toren was hugging a pillow, lying on his stomach. I brushed his dark hair off a temple and kissed his forehead. "Bye."

"I'll walk you out." He made a move to sit up, but I placed a hand on his shoulder.

"Sleep. Good luck today."

He pushed up on an elbow, his free hand coming to my cheek. "You too."

The Wildcats were playing the University of Montana Grizzlies today at the stadium. Like it had been for the volleyball team, the rivalry was fierce and campus was buzzing.

Kickoff was at noon.

We had a volleyball game tonight too, but it didn't start until seven. Coach Quinn wanted us dressed and ready by six, and she'd also told us to skip the football game. The forecast for today was eleven degrees and calling for snow this afternoon. She wanted us to stay loose and warm.

So I wouldn't be going to the stadium today to watch Toren coach. I'd be stuck at home, watching the football game on television. We'd have to celebrate later, hopefully victories for us both.

"Tonight?" I asked.

"Yeah, baby. Tonight."

I kissed him again, then quickly headed downstairs, navigating the house in the dark. With my shoes on and the sleeves of my hoodie tugged over my fingertips, I braced for the icy blast that hit me the moment I opened the front door.

A shiver raced down my spine as I jogged across the sidewalk, making my roundabout trip down Toren's driveway to the street, where I followed a tire track until I was at my own driveway and jogging for the door.

My house was quiet as I slipped inside, holding my breath as I tiptoed past the living room toward the stairs.

"Jennsyn?"

I jumped at Stevie's voice and let out a panicked squeak. *Shit.* "Stevie? You scared me."

Her eyelids were droopy as she shuffled out of the kitchen, a glass of water in her hand. "What are you doing?"

This was bad. Oh God, this was bad. Why hadn't I set my alarm for three? Why had I let Toren keep me up so late? My heart climbed into my throat as I scrambled for a lie. "I, um, couldn't sleep. So I went out for a run. Or tried to anyway. It's really cold."

Maybe she'd think the flush in my cheeks was from the cold or exercise, not sex. Maybe she wouldn't get close enough to smell Toren's scent on my skin.

"Yeah." She nodded, rubbing an eye still groggy with sleep. "I couldn't sleep either."

"I'm going to take a shower," I said, too brightly as I took another step for the stairs. "Then maybe crash for a while."

"Okay." She yawned, then blinked, her eyes narrowing as she took in my shoes.

They were not my running shoes. Those were in the tray beside the door.

Before she could ask, I moved quickly for the stairs, taking them two at a time.

Her gaze was hot on my back.

She knew I was lying, didn't she? She could tell I wasn't wearing a bra and there wasn't a chance I'd ever go running without one.

I raced up the stairs, not stopping until I was safely in my room, sagging against the closed door. "Shit."

My pulse pounded in my ears as I closed my eyes, adrenaline coursing through my veins.

That was close. Too close.

I should have been more careful. "Damn it."

It took a hot shower and three hours of sleep to shake it off. When I woke up, I dressed in a pair of thick joggers and my warmest Treasure State sweatshirt before heading downstairs. My breath was lodged in my throat when I spotted Stevie at the dining room table, textbooks and papers spread out around her.

If she did suspect anything, she didn't let on. She smiled as I walked into the kitchen. "Hey. Did you go back to sleep?"

"Yeah. You?"

She shrugged. "For a little while."

I filled a glass of water from the sink, then glanced out the windows that overlooked the street.

The rumble of an engine sounded from outside, and even without seeing his truck, I knew it was Toren. He'd be leaving for the fieldhouse to get ready for today's game.

Stevie glanced over her shoulder, leaning in her chair as she peered outside. "I really wanted to go to the football game today."

"Me too."

She bit her lower lip when she faced forward. "I know Coach told us to skip it. But Liz and I were thinking of going anyway. It's our last year. This is probably the last chance we'll get to watch a game because we'll be in the playoffs at the same time. So I got tickets. Three of them in case—"

"I'm in," I blurted, my heart swelling. "I want to go."

"Okay." She smiled wider. "Leave in an hour?"

I nodded. "I'll be ready."

———

THE NOISE in the stadium was deafening. The sound waves were so strong they pushed me around. Or maybe the concrete beneath my boots was actually swaying with the weight of the bodies crammed into the stands.

Stevie, Liz and I were surrounded by thousands of Wildcat fans, just three more faces in the crowd decked out in silver and royal blue.

Besides my nights with Toren, it was the most fun I'd had in years.

Each of my exhales was a puff of white, floating up toward the clear blue sky. My gloves muffled my clapping, but I smacked them together anyway, yelling until my throat had gone raw.

We were ahead, ten to seven. The score had been as frozen as the air since the first quarter, but with only minutes left in the fourth, victory was in hand. We just had to hold off the Grizzlies for a few more minutes.

The defense, Toren's defense, had to stand strong.

Stevie, Liz and I had come to the stadium early, all three of us wearing hats and hoods and sunglasses with our winter gear. I had on so many layers I was sweating, but I didn't want to get cold and stiff. Stevie had found hand warmers for our fingers. Liz had bought the first round of hot cocoa.

Most likely, we'd get our asses chewed out by Coach Quinn when we showed up for our game tonight, but this, to watch Toren and enjoy a football game like any normal student, would be worth it.

We'd been here so long that we'd managed to get second-row seats in the student section, right behind the team.

Toren paced the sidelines, shouting and pointing as the Griz offense shuffled on the line.

My heart was in my throat, attention locked on him.

I wasn't a Wildcat, not really. I hadn't spent enough time here to feel like this school was mine.

But *he* was mine. And I wanted this win for him. I wanted this more than I cared about my own game tonight.

The ball snapped and the Griz ran it for a first down, the students around us muttering curses under their breaths.

"Dang it."

Toren smacked his hands together, as frustrated as the crowd. He stood in profile, which gave me a straight shot to see his jaw flex.

He had no idea I was here, but I watched him, sending him all of my support with every clap of my hands.

His defense was getting tired. I recognized the trudging steps as they moved to the next formation. Their panted breaths were as cloudy as my own. But they held the Grizzlies on the next attempt until they could finally jog off the field.

"Um, does that mean we're going to win?" Stevie asked.

Liz shrugged. "No idea."

"I think so?"

Maybe by next year, Toren would have taught me all about football. Next year, I wouldn't be watching from the student section.

A smile tugged at my lips.

There'd been plenty of moments over the past week when I'd second-guessed my decision to quit volleyball. We weren't even finished with the season yet, but I was mourning it all the same. There was a hole in my heart. It would probably double in size after our last game.

But I had a feeling that it wouldn't be hard to fill. Not when I had the man on the sidelines.

Toren clapped each of his players on the back before pulling a few aside to talk while the offense jogged onto the field.

Something happened with the offense, some sort of delay, because everyone around us began yelling about the play clock.

"I really need to learn about football," I said, more to myself than Stevie.

She laughed. "I'm just going to cheer along with everyone else."

"Good plan."

On the field, Rush Ramsey had the ball positioned and ready to throw, except he couldn't find an open player, so he tucked the ball under an arm and took off running. He didn't make it far enough for a first down, but it was a gain.

They all hurried to line up again and, this time, made the first down.

The announcer's voice boomed through the speakers. "First down, Wildcats!"

"Go Big Blue!" a guy behind us screamed.

There was a carelessness in how he cheered. A freedom. It was so loud, the stadium was chaos, and if he wanted to scream, he could scream.

So I tipped my head to the sky and yelled.

When I found Toren on the sidelines again, he was clapping for the offense, but his attention was mostly locked on his players, making sure that if the defense had to go back on the field, they'd stop any attempt at a last-minute win from the Grizzlies.

The clock was ticking. Time was running out. The chains moved and the teams took their position.

"Don't fucking fumble!" the guy behind me screamed and the scent of booze drifted my way.

Stevie and I shared a look, then both burst out laughing.

A hush rolled over the student section as the ball was snapped and Rush took a few steps back, poised to throw.

He didn't hesitate. He found his receiver and launched the ball like a bullet.

The receiver caught the ball and raced for the end zone.

Touchdown.

The stadium erupted.

Toren did a fist pump and yelled, his face splitting into a wide smile. Free and victorious and happy. It was a smile I wanted to see every day. On his face. And mine.

Special teams jogged onto the field, and as the Wildcats scored their extra point, the clock flipped to zero.

"We won." Stevie grabbed my forearm, jumping up and down with everyone else in the stands.

He'd won.

I laughed and threw my hands into the air. "Go Wildcats!"

Toren's players descended on him like a swarm. One guy smacked him on the shoulder before another hefted him off the ground. They huddled so closely around him that for a moment, I lost him in the sea of shoulder pads and helmets.

His players loved him.

I loved him.

The air rushed from my lungs.

I'd never been in love before, not really. But I knew I

loved him as surely as I knew the sky was blue and the Wild-cats had just beaten the Grizzlies. It filled me so full I felt like I could float on the breeze.

I was in love with Toren Greely.

Like he'd sensed my stare, he turned slightly, his gaze drifting toward the stands. The moment he spotted me, his throat bobbed. Then his eyes crinkled at the sides, that smile getting just a little bit brighter.

For me.

I pressed my hand to my heart, holding his dazzling eyes for only a moment before he turned and jogged onto the field to shake hands with the Griz coaches.

The crowd around us began to shift, people making their way down the stairs and aisles to leave the stadium.

I looked to my roommates, about to ask if they were ready to go, but my question lodged in my throat.

Liz was talking to the girl on her other side, totally unaware of the smile I'd shared with Toren.

But Stevie stared at me with a slight furrow to her forehead.

She looked to the field, finding Toren's back. Then she turned to me again, and as the confusion in her gaze morphed to suspicion, my stomach dropped.

The blood drained from my face.

No. No, this couldn't be happening.

Not again.

CHAPTER TWENTY-FIVE

TOREN

With my phone pressed to my ear, I paced my dark living room while Parks shouted over the noise at whatever bar he'd picked for tonight.

"Get downtown! Let's party!"

"Nah. I'm tired," I lied, glancing out the windows that overlooked the front yard.

Where was Jennsyn? She'd texted over an hour ago that she was coming over. Had something happened with a roommate?

"Come on, Toren," Parks groaned. "We should be celebrating."

"You celebrate. I'm going to chill."

"Need me to come get you?" he asked. "I'll be there in ten."

Fuck no. He was the last person I wanted to see tonight. "Don't come over."

"I'm coming over."

"Parks," I warned. "I'm going to bed. If you wake me up, I'll pummel you."

He scoffed. "Whatever. Where's the Toren who was always up for a good time?"

That Toren had met a woman who had consumed his life. That Toren only wanted to celebrate with Jennsyn.

"Good night, Parks."

"Loser!" he called before I hung up.

Rounding the couch, I walked toward the windows, glancing outside. No sign of her. I'd opened up our text thread, about to send her a note, when a streak of black raced across my driveway.

A grin tugged at my mouth as I hurried to the door, opening it just as she leapt onto the porch and flew into my open arms.

"Hi." I wrapped her up tight, burying my face in her neck.

"Hi," she murmured, her arms circling my shoulders.

I kicked the door closed, intent on holding her for a while and breathing her in, but she wiggled free and dropped to her feet.

Bare feet.

I frowned. It was too cold for her to be running over without shoes, whether she liked the socks that went with them or not. But before I could say anything, I got a glimpse of her face and my stomach dropped.

Her skin was too pale and she looked on the verge of tears.

"What happened? Was it the game?"

The volleyball team had won by a landslide tonight. But maybe Aspen had found out that she'd gone to the football game.

Yeah, she'd disobeyed orders. I'd be pissed if my players had done the same. But selfishly, spotting her in the second row of the student section had been the best part of my day. It had made the win over the Griz that much sweeter.

"Did Aspen find out you came to the game today?"

Jennsyn shook her head, walking past me and into the house. She wrapped her arms around her middle when she reached the living room and began to pace.

"Babe, talk to me."

Her chin started to quiver. "Stevie knows about us. Maybe. I'm not sure. She suspects something. Probably."

"Fuck." I dragged a hand through my hair as the world disappeared from beneath my feet. *Fuck. Fuck. Fuck.*

"She was awake this morning when I got home," Jennsyn said. "I lied and told her I'd tried to go for a run but it was too cold. Then she was there at the game and I couldn't stop staring at you and then you looked at me and I'm such an idiot because I smiled and ruined everything because I was so happy for you."

Well, damn. That was the best and worst thing she could possibly say.

"I'm such an idiot." Her hands flew into her hair, pulling at the strands. Then they flopped at her sides again, her fingers shaking before she once again tucked them in her armpits to keep pacing.

"You're not an idiot." I'd forgotten too. I hadn't schooled my expression. I hadn't pretended she was just another student. I'd found her in the crowd and smiled. Because her face made me smile. It was automatic.

"I was getting ready to come over here and was about to sneak down the stairs when I saw her in the living room. Liz is always the one who stays up late to watch TV. Stevie will too sometimes, but only if Liz is up. Except tonight it was just Stevie and maybe I'm being paranoid but I got this feeling like it was because of me."

Hell. "Did she say anything after the game?"

"No." Jennsyn shook her head so wildly her hair swished into her face. "I sort of didn't give her the chance. After we left the stadium, I went straight to the fieldhouse and took a hot shower to warm up for our game."

"And tonight when you got home?"

"We drove separately. I beat them home and was in my room."

I sighed. "Let's not get ahead of ourselves. Maybe she doesn't know."

"Maybe." Jennsyn worried her bottom lip between her teeth. "But what if she does?"

What if Stevie knew?

She stopped walking, her arms cinching impossibly tight around her waist. The dread on her face made my stomach bunch. "I like Stevie. But I don't trust her. I don't trust any of the girls on the team."

"Why not?" Something had happened that had kept Jennsyn apart. Were they mean to her? Did they blame her for the girl who'd been cut?

"Experience," she said.

"Your team at Stanford." It was a guess, confirmed when she swallowed hard and nodded.

"I thought they were my friends. We were more than teammates. Or . . . I thought we were. I confided in a few of them. Told them about my mom and dad and everything else friends tell friends."

Things she'd confided in me.

Had she told them that she wasn't sure she wanted to

keep playing? Maybe those girls had seen it as their opening. A weakness to exploit.

I'd seen the same thing happen with certain football players. Those with the most talent were usually the most popular. But their skills meant they'd have a target on their back. Others might get jealous. Look for an opening to get that player in trouble.

It didn't always happen. Rush Ramsey was loved by his teammates, and his friendships were genuine. But he'd also been with this team since his freshman year.

Jennsyn wasn't just better than the other girls on the Wildcats team. She was extraordinary.

If Stevie knew about us, if she wanted to knock Jennsyn down a peg, all she'd have to do was tell Aspen.

"This is my fault." I'd been the one to keep her late this morning. I'd been the one at the game who hadn't maintained enough awareness. I'd been the one taking risks with Jennsyn from the start.

"No." She shook her head. "We're in this together."

Hell yes, we were.

I crossed the room and blocked her path so she had no choice but to stop pacing. Then I took her face in my hands and dropped a kiss to her lips.

"What are we going to do?" she whispered.

"Talk."

She dropped her gaze to the center of my chest and nodded.

It was time for the serious conversation we'd both been avoiding. The discussion that might make Stevie's suspicions irrelevant.

I let Jennsyn go, then walked toward the windows, staring out into the cold, starry night. After she'd texted earlier to say she was coming over, I'd shut off the lights inside. That way, no one driving by would see her here.

Hiding her, hiding us, was getting damn old. But tonight, I was glad the lights were off. It was easier to bare your soul in the dark.

"My life is in Mission. This is where I want to live. Where I want to raise my family. Soon, I want children of my own. I don't want to be an old man when my kids are growing up. Not if I end up . . ." The words lodged in my throat. *Like Dad. Like Uncle Evan.*

Not a soul on this earth knew I was afraid to die young. Except Jennsyn.

"Tor." The gentleness in her voice made it better and worse at the same time.

"You've got so much ahead of you. I don't ever want you to feel rushed or trapped."

"Who says I'd feel trapped?"

I lifted a shoulder. "You're twenty-one. You shouldn't be tied down to an old man."

"Twenty-two," Jennsyn whispered. "I'm twenty-two."

"Wait. What?" I whirled. "I missed your birthday. When? Why didn't you tell me?"

She crossed the room and stood at my side as she stared through the glass. "Don't feel guilty for missing a milestone you didn't even know existed. Be around for the next one and we'll call it even."

Her next birthday.

If she wanted me around, I'd be there. "Deal."

She shifted closer, resting her temple on my arm. "I haven't thought a lot about having kids."

Because she was only twenty-two. Her life had been

centered around volleyball. She had plenty of time to think about kids, and with another guy, she'd have years.

"I should let you go."

She slipped her hand into the back pocket of my jeans. "Please don't."

"You sure?" If she was willing to stick this out, give me a chance at a future, I'd do everything in my power to make her happy. But she had to be sure.

"Someone needs to be here to watch your mom's old movies and buy you books and make sure your condiments stay color coordinated and clean your truck in the middle of the night. I happen to be good at all of those things."

There wasn't a woman in the world who'd do it better.

We moved in tandem, shifting away from the window and toward each other. Our mouths collided in a kiss that was like coming up for air. Every bit of tension melted from my muscles as I swept her into my arms and hoisted her off her feet.

There was no chance I'd make it to the bedroom, not when her tongue tangled with mine. So I walked to the couch, laying her down on the leather. Then I covered her body, tasting and licking and devouring her mouth until the need to sink inside her tight heat thrummed through my veins.

"Tor." She ripped her mouth away, panting as she moved her lips to the shell of my ear. "Fuck me."

This woman. My dick was so hard it ached.

We stripped each other bare, our clothes piling on the floor next to the couch, and when I drove hard into her body, her moan echoed off the walls.

"Damn, the way you make me feel." I dropped a hard kiss to her mouth as I eased out and slammed inside.

"Yes." She hooked a leg around my hip, sending me deeper.

I worked us together over and over until she began to tremble. But I wasn't ready for her to come, not yet. I wasn't ready for this to ever end. So I eased away and hauled her off the couch, spinning us so she was straddling my lap.

There was a grin on her face as she sank onto my cock.

"Fuck." I tipped my head against the back of the couch, jaw clenched as she rolled her hips.

Her fingertips dug into my shoulders as she rode me, faster and faster until she whimpered.

My hands gripped her waist, my arms working to help her move.

Not that she needed it. The strength in her body was a marvel as she chased her own release.

The flutter of her inner walls was nearly my undoing. Each time she sank down, I fought the pressure building at the base of my spine. "Get there, baby."

"I'm close," she said, breathlessly. "Come with me."

I reached between us, finding her clit with my thumb. All it took was a single circle on the bundle of nerves and she threw her head back and clenched around me as my name spilled from her lips.

Her orgasm triggered my own and the world faded into a blur as I poured inside her. My pulse roared in my ears as I came hard, my entire body spent by the time she collapsed against me, sated and limp.

I was still hard inside her as I buried my nose in her hair and inhaled.

"Tor." She nuzzled into my neck as I held her close with both hands splayed across her spine.

I loved her.

I wanted nights like this for the rest of my life. I wanted her in my arms, in this house, in my bed. I wanted to go shopping at the store together. I wanted to eat breakfast with her in the mornings and dinner with her at night. I wanted her clean car parked beside my dirty truck in the garage.

We'd get there. We just had to wait a little while longer.

"I should go." She sighed and kissed my cheek before easing us apart. "If Stevie does suspect something, I don't want to risk that she's up early again tomorrow."

"All right." As much as I wanted her in my bed, that was probably the smart move.

Before she could bend to pick up her panties, I snatched them from the floor and held them out as she stepped into them, then her sweats.

When the hoodie she'd worn covered her naked torso, I swiped my jeans from the floor and shoved to my feet, pulling them on and tucking myself away. Then, with her hand clasped in mine, I walked her to the door.

"Good—"

I put my finger over her lips, cutting her off. "I'm so fucking tired of saying goodbye to you."

Her blue eyes softened.

"Sweet dreams, Jennsyn."

She lifted on her bare toes and kissed the corner of my mouth. "Sleep tight, Toren."

CHAPTER TWENTY-SIX

JENNSYN

"Leave your final papers on my desk. Grades will be posted online by Friday." Professor Smith flicked his wrist toward the door. Class dismissed.

Everyone stood, most of us still wearing our coats. There'd been no point in coming to class this afternoon. It was four o'clock and campus was nearly deserted. We could have dropped off our finals at his office, but Smith had such a God complex that he wanted to exert his control over us one last time.

There was a chance that his Small Business Management class would be the only B I received in my entire collegiate career. I hadn't even gotten a B in high school. But at this point, I didn't care. I'd graduate and never have to see Smith's pinched face again.

Wearing a fake smile, I walked to his desk and set my paper on the stack with the others. "Thanks, Professor Smith. I really loved your class this semester."

Yeah, I'd survive a B, but I wasn't above blatant ass-kissing in the hopes of an A.

"Thank you." His smirk was so arrogant I nearly gagged. Whatever. With any luck, I'd never cross paths with this man again.

The moment I was out the door, my entire body seemed to exhale.

Semester over.

Only one more to go.

Then . . . something.

I wasn't sure what that something was quite yet but I was excited to figure it out. With Toren.

Tugging my phone from my coat pocket, I sent him a text.

Done!

His reply was instant. *Congrats baby*

The past three weeks had been the best of my life. It had been a whirlwind of school and sports and secret nights.

The football team had made it to the playoffs but lost in an early round. Our volleyball team had won the conference championship, but we'd lost to Oregon during the first round of the tournament.

I hadn't cried after the game. I'd traveled home with the team, not shocked at the loss but almost numb. That numbness had lasted until I'd walked through Toren's front door. One step past the threshold, and I'd started bawling.

Never before in my life had I cried as much as I had over the past couple months, but it was like I'd finally found my safe space to let go.

He'd held me while I'd mourned the loss of a sport that had been my entire life. And when I'd finally pulled myself together, he'd asked me if I was sure I wanted to quit.

There wasn't a doubt in my mind that he would have supported me with any decision. Yet nothing had changed.

I'd need time to find my footing, to find a different path, but I was ready for a new adventure. With him.

My phone vibrated with another text. Toren's number was saved under James, his middle name. In his phone, my number was saved under Marie.

Are you going home?

I replied as I walked across campus. *Coming to the field-house for a workout first*

Meet you there

We wouldn't talk. We'd barely acknowledge each other. But being in the same room with him was enough.

The sidewalks were quiet, only a few other students out this late. In the distance, through the gaps in brick buildings, the sun was dipping past the mountain horizon, and the evening light was a soft blue tinged with orange and gold. It was the most beautiful campus I'd ever seen, and for one more semester, it was mine.

I still had access to the weight room for the rest of the year. The team would start practicing again in the spring, but since I wasn't going to play professionally, I wouldn't be joining them. Neither would the other seniors. There might be a few scrimmage games, and if Coach Quinn asked us to play, I'd gladly participate. But for the most part, I was finished.

I made it to the fieldhouse and was about to walk into the locker room when my phone rang.

Unknown number.

"What's with the spam calls today?" I muttered to myself. That was the third so far.

I sent it to voicemail, then hurried to change. It rang again as I was tying my shoes. This time, Mom's photo popped up on the screen. "Hey," I answered.

"Oh, hi. I was expecting to get your voicemail. How are you?"

"Good. I just handed in my last final for the semester."

"That's great." There was a smile in her voice. There was one in mine too.

Our conversations were more awkward than not, but as we ventured into other topics beyond volleyball, it was getting easier. Unless I was in class, I answered Mom's calls. I'd asked her to try. So I was trying too.

"Are you sure you don't want to come home for Christmas?" she asked.

"I'm sure. It will be nice to relax and not travel."

It was partially the truth. I didn't feel like flying to Nebraska for the break, not when there wouldn't be much to do at home. Mom was spending the holiday as a special guest commentator at an invitational tournament. She'd be busy doing exactly what she loved, and I didn't want to tag along only to get asked a thousand times where I was playing next.

"Have you spoken to your dad?" she asked.

"No."

She huffed but otherwise made no comment.

Maybe Dad would call me on Christmas. If he didn't, I'd send him a text. I'd already sent gifts for the boys, and Tina had mailed me their family's holiday card.

"All right. Then, um, I guess we'll talk later," Mom said.

"Sure. Bye."

"Goodbye."

Mom always said *goodbye*. Never *bye* or *see ya later*. Always goodbye. Maybe that was why I'd said that to Toren for so many months. I was used to saying goodbye.

Not anymore.

Every night when I slipped out of his bed, I'd say, "Sleep tight," while he'd wish me, "Sweet dreams."

Starting Friday, there'd be no sneaking to or from his house. Stevie was spending the break with her parents in Hawaii. Liz was flying home to Ohio.

Both thought I'd be spending my holiday at home alone.

Instead, I'd be at Toren's, spending every night in his bed and waking up in his arms each morning. We'd be going to Faith's for Christmas and celebrating with his family.

I couldn't remember a time when I'd been more excited for a vacation.

If Stevie did suspect something, nothing had come of it in the past three weeks. We'd been more careful, my stays at Toren's shorter than ever. There'd been nights when I hadn't risked going over at all because Stevie or Liz had stayed up late.

But none of that would matter starting Friday.

I dug my earbuds from my bag before heading into the weight room.

Toren was already inside, standing beside the water fountain and filling up a bottle.

I bit back a smile as I walked over with my own empty bottle.

He screwed on the lid, then walked away, and as we passed, his knuckles brushed my arm.

I smiled so wide I had to tuck my chin so that the three guys lifting wouldn't notice.

With my water bottle full, I weaved through the equipment to an open stair machine directly beside Toren's.

He was already moving, climbing infinite steps.

I matched his pace, and in just minutes, sweat beaded at my temples. Neither of us risked a glance. We exercised to our own music, tuned out from the world. But every few steps I'd catch a subtle hint of his cologne.

I'd draw it into my lungs, hold it for a moment, then exhale.

When he increased his pace, I did the same. Every beep from his machine was echoed by a beep from mine.

We pushed each other in a silent competition until one of us tapped out.

My thighs burned as he hit the button again, and when I risked a glance, there was a grin toying on his mouth.

He wasn't even close to quitting, was he? I might have him on the treadmills, but on the stair climber and the elliptical, he beat me every time.

I gritted my teeth and punched *stop*.

My lungs were on fire as I plucked out my earbuds and snagged my water from the cup holder, tipping it to my mouth.

A low chuckle came from his direction as he kept climbing.

I plucked my phone from the machine's tray and typed out a text.

You win. Name your prize.

He picked up his phone as I walked to the station for the cleaning solution, spraying down the machine. When I finished, his reply was waiting.

I'm fucking your mouth tonight

A shiver ran through my entire body as my core clenched.

God, I loved our dirty texts. By the time I made it to his place tonight, I'd be throbbing and wet. And I wanted nothing more than to take him in my mouth.

I want to be on my knees when you come down my throat

There was a thud behind me, then the thump of his footsteps stopped.

When I glanced over my shoulder, he had his phone in hand, his knuckles white as his jaw ticked and he made an adjustment to his cock. He shot me a glare as I faced forward and hid a giggle in my hand.

I'm in shorts, babe. Not a great time to get hard.

My workout for today was cardio followed by my favorite yoga routine. So I made my way to the mats as I typed out my next reply.

You started it.

He crossed to the farthest end of the space, putting nearly the entire weight room between us. It was his chest, shoulders and triceps routine today.

You'll pay for that later.

I put my earbuds back in, then smiled as I typed another text. *Promise?*

We went quiet for a while as we each focused on exercise. When I was finished, my muscles were warm and loose. I headed for the locker room after a quick glance to find Toren doing pullups.

He'd taken off his shirt.

That man. I opened the camera on my phone, and pretending to take a selfie, instead, I took a picture of him.

Someday, that would be the wallpaper on my screen. Someday, when we didn't have to hide in plain sight.

With a quick flip of the camera, I took a selfie of myself blowing a kiss to the camera. It was a photo I texted him as I disappeared into the locker room for a shower.

By the time I was dressed and finished blow-drying my hair, it was well past five. Every office I passed in the halls was dark. Every office except one.

I slowed my pace, checking behind me to make sure no one was watching, then passed Toren's open door. My plan was only to wave, but as I raised my arm, a hand clamped around my wrist and hauled me into his office.

Toren was on me the second the door swept shut, pressing me against the wall as my bag landed with a plop beside our feet. He brought both of my arms above my head, trapping them against the concrete at my back.

"Tor—"

He silenced me with a kiss, his tongue sweeping inside to tangle with mine. Then he sucked my bottom lip between his teeth and any protest about making out in his office vanished.

I hummed as he kissed me deeper, one hand still locked around my wrists above as the other came to my ass, squeezing tight through my leggings.

He'd changed into jeans after his workout and he positioned one of his bulky thighs between mine so I could rock against him. God, the friction was incredible. I whimpered as I ground against his strength, already wet and aching for more.

Toren's kiss wasn't soft or gentle. It was the punishment that he'd promised for turning him on in the gym. It was hard and wet, and when he finally broke his mouth from mine, I was left with a smile.

"Hi." I laughed.

He grinned. "Hey, baby."

"I like this. Making out in your office. But . . ."

"Probably shouldn't make a habit of it." He wiped his mouth dry, then loosened the hold he had on my arms. But before he let me go, he brought them between us to plant a kiss on my wrist. "Someday, I'm going to bring you in here after a game and we'll fuck against the wall and on my desk. We'll go wild, just you and me."

Someday. "You and me."

His hand came to my face, his thumb dragging across my cheek as he stared down at me. His eyes searched mine for a long moment before he opened his mouth, like he was going to say something serious.

Like maybe he was going to say what I'd been hoping to hear for weeks.

A knock came at the door.

And before Toren could stop him, before I could hide under the desk, Ford Ellis walked into the room.

CHAPTER TWENTY-SEVEN

TOREN

Ford's expression was unreadable as we walked from my office to his.

Fuck.

Fuck fuck fuck.

A steel door slammed shut, the sound carrying through the hallway behind us. That was probably Jennsyn leaving the fieldhouse. She'd wasted no time grabbing her bag, and the moment Ford had moved out of the doorway, she'd shot me a panicked look, then swept out of the room.

That was seconds ago. Minutes. It felt like hours. Time had slowed to a crawl.

Panic boomed, and with its every thundering beat, my heart sank lower and lower.

This was it. This was the end. The years I'd spent at Treasure State were spiraling down the drain. My career was over. My reputation ruined.

All because I'd wanted to kiss Jennsyn, just once, before she left the fieldhouse for the day.

What the fuck had I been thinking? What was wrong

with me? A kiss on campus. I deserved to be fired for being a fucking dumbass.

Everyone had left the building. I wouldn't have pulled her into my office otherwise. When I'd come out of the gym, every office had been dark. Everyone had gone home for the night.

Except Ford.

His office light had been off. I'd checked. But he must have been upstairs with Millie.

Shit. Ford could fire me, but somehow, she had to be allowed to stay in school. She deserved to graduate. Even if she lost her scholarship, I'd find a way to pay for her last semester.

I dragged a hand over my face as we walked into his office.

He closed the door behind us and its soft click was like a knife through my ribs.

I was about to be fired by my oldest friend in the world. This was not how I'd envisioned today ending, but if this was the end, I guess . . .

I'd rather it be Ford than anyone else.

We stared at each other for a few long, miserable moments until Ford arched his eyebrows. "Are you going to explain or what?"

I sighed and my entire frame sagged. "Not sure what there is to explain."

"That was a student, right? The volleyball player?"

"Yeah." I gulped. "Jennsyn Bell."

"Lie to me. Tell me you were giving her CPR."

I huffed a laugh. "Can't do that."

"Fucking hell, Toren." Ford groaned and walked behind his desk, plopping into his chair. He pointed to the empty seat in front of me. "Is this really happening? Are we actually having this conversation? She's a *student*. What the hell are you thinking?"

Where did I even start? I sat down, elbows dropping to my knees as my hands clasped together, like a silent plea that maybe not all hope was lost.

"I'm in love with her."

It felt wrong to tell him before Jennsyn, but it was the truth. And the truth seemed like the only place to begin.

"She's it for me."

Ford blinked, shaking his head like he'd heard me wrong. But then the confusion vanished, and he looked at me with such pity it hurt.

We both knew I was absolutely fucked.

"I met her this summer," I told him. "Before you moved to Mission. I had no idea she was on the volleyball team. She didn't know I was a coach. We hit it off. When I realized she was a student, I tried. I swear, Ford. I tried to stay away from her."

But she was it for me.

Whether Jennsyn wanted to travel the world or grow old with me here in Mission, I wasn't letting her go.

Weeks ago, when I'd told her I wanted a family, this image had popped into my mind of a little girl running around in the backyard. Blond hair. Blue eyes. A smile that could command my every move.

I didn't just want kids. I wanted them with Jennsyn. It was all or nothing.

She was my life.

If it came down to choosing her over my job, then I'd find a new career. Maybe I'd open a car wash so she'd never need to worry about my dirty truck again.

Ford dragged a hand through his hair, staring blankly at the smooth surface of his desk. "I don't know what to say."

"You're fired?"

He frowned. The shake of his head was so subtle, I might have dreamed it. But hope surged, straightening my spine and lifting my heart off the floor.

Ford's eyebrows came together as he leaned forward, eyes hard. It was his game face. The face he'd worn as a player, first for the Wildcats and then in the NFL. It was the face he now wore as a coach on the sidelines.

"Kurt won't care that you met her this summer," he said.

"Nope. Not after the scandal from this spring."

Ford sighed. "She's a senior?"

I nodded. "Yeah."

"Twenty-one?"

"Twenty-two."

If Ford thought the age gap was too big, he didn't let it show. "Damn it, Toren. What am I supposed to do?"

Fire me. That was his only choice. "It's okay," I said. "Just . . . do it."

He scoffed. "I can't exactly condemn you for a secret relationship when Millie and I spent most of the fall sneaking around."

Hold on. Was he . . . okay with this? My breath lodged in my throat as I waited for him to continue. "What are you saying?"

"These are not rules I can change," he said. "You're a coach. She's a student."

"So I'm fired." Fuck.

"No, shithead, you're not fired. But you need to be more careful. Keep it quiet. Nothing here on campus." He shot a pointed glare to the wall and my office beyond. "Get her to graduation."

I blinked, then shook my head like this was a dream. "Ford. If anyone finds out that you knew—"

"Don't let anyone find out. Take a pause if you have to. I don't care. Just don't get caught."

Holy fuck. Was this really happening? If any other person had walked in on us, it would be over. But Ford?

Asking him to keep this secret was asking a lot. But I was going to do it anyway.

"You're sure?"

"I'm sure." He nodded. "In all our years as friends, you've never spoken about a woman like this."

"There is no woman like Jennsyn."

He scowled and flicked his wrist toward the door. "Then get out."

The emotion swelled so fast it was hard to breathe. I took a moment, then cleared my throat before extending an arm across his desk. "Thank you."

He clasped my hand for a quick shake. "You knew about Millie and me. You kept our secret. The least I can do is keep yours."

"This is a little different."

"Not really."

No, I guess it wasn't. "See you tomorrow?"

"Yes." He nodded as I shoved to my feet, then made my way to the door. "Toren?"

I turned. "Yeah?"

"Sorry I blew into your office earlier. I should have waited after I knocked."

I brushed it off. "Don't worry about it."

"No, that was my fault. Won't happen again."

"All right. Have a good night."

Ford waved. "You too."

I opened the door, ready to catch up to Jennsyn because she was probably freaking the fuck out. Except as I stepped into the hallway, Millie was rushing my way.

"Have you seen Aspen?" she asked, eyes wide and cheeks flushed.

"Uh, no." The panic on her face made the hair on the back of my neck stand on end. "Why?"

Jennsyn had already left the fieldhouse, right? She wouldn't have done something reckless, like go tell Aspen she was quitting the team or dropping out of school.

Millie frowned and pulled out her phone as Ford joined us in the hallway.

"What's up?" he asked.

"I need to find Aspen. There's a news article that's getting a lot of attention and one of her players is mentioned."

"What?" Ford shifted closer to peer over her shoulder as she showed him her phone.

I didn't need to read the article. My stomach dropped as the color drained from his face.

"Jennsyn?"

"Yeah." Millie nodded. "According to this, there's speculation that she had an affair with a coach at Stanford."

CHAPTER TWENTY-EIGHT

JENNSYN

Toren was getting fired. While I was walking to my car in the parking lot at the fieldhouse, Toren was inside losing his career.

Oh God. Why had we done that? Why hadn't we just waited until tonight? All that flirting and teasing in the gym and we'd lost our fucking minds.

Tears pricked my eyes as the lump in my throat made it impossible to swallow and hard to breathe.

Would he hate me when this was over? Would he regret everything that had happened between us? I'd just cost him his job. His reputation. I knew what we'd been risking. I knew the stakes. But I'd been an arrogant fool to think we wouldn't get caught.

When would I learn my lesson? When would I stop making the same fucking mistakes?

A tear dripped down my cheek, and I swiped it away. Another took its place.

"Damn it." I was seconds from turning into a sobbing mess, but somehow, I managed to make it into my car and

326

close myself inside before I gave up fighting the tears and just let them fall.

I couldn't lose him. When I looked into the future, I couldn't see the job I'd have or the friends I'd make. But I saw Toren. As clear as the moon shining in the night sky.

Maybe we'd figure a way out of this. Maybe I could call Coach Aspen and quit the team. If I dropped out of school, would they let Toren keep his job?

Probably not. My heart cracked as I reached for my phone, hoping to see a text from him or a missed call.

But it wasn't Toren's name that had filled up the screen with notifications. I'd missed two phone calls from my mother and a text to *CALL ME NOW*.

Was she hurt? Sick? My stomach dropped, but before I could call her back, I scrolled through the rest of the notifications.

Missed calls from numbers I didn't recognize. Texts from names I did.

The last was from Emily.

The shock of seeing her name made the tears stop.

When I'd left Stanford, I hadn't explicitly told her to forget my number, but it had been implied. I should have blocked her when she'd texted me on my birthday.

Except then I wouldn't have gotten the link she'd sent. What the hell?

I dried my eyes, clearing the tears, as an article loaded. The headline made my stomach drop.

Volleyball Coach Arrested for Relationship with Student

My gasp filled the car. No. *No no no*. This couldn't be happening.

Wait. I read the headline again, one word leaping off the screen. *Arrested*. Why would they arrest Christian for something that had happened months and months ago? There was no reason for him to be in jail. He'd lost his job, but why arrest him?

I blinked away the last remaining tears from my eyes and started reading. My heart seized when I came across two words in bold.

statutory rape

This wasn't about me. My time with Christian had been earlier this year. I'd been twenty-one years old, a legal adult.

Much older than the seventeen-year-old girl whose parents were pressing charges against Christian.

My stomach roiled as I kept reading.

Emily might have sent this to me out of spite, but the fact that my mother had sent a frantic text could only mean one thing.

In the second to last paragraph, I found my name.

An anonymous source has confirmed this is not the first time Christian Morris has engaged in an affair with a student athlete. According to those sources, Morris was rumored to have a romantic relationship with two former Stanford players, setter Rachael Keaton and outside hitter Jennsyn Bell. Both Keaton and Bell were coached by Morris and both have since left Stanford. Keaton denied the allegations. Bell has been unavailable for comment.

The phone slipped from my grip, plopping on my lap.

The calls earlier today. They'd been from reporters, hadn't they? And without question, Emily was that anonymous source.

My chest felt too tight, and I couldn't seem to fill my lungs as sweat beaded at my temples. I buried my face in my hands, torn between crying and screaming.

I chose to scream.

My voice cracked as my shout turned into a sob, those tears I'd banished for a moment returning with renewed force.

Why? This was supposed to be over. I'd left Stanford and that mess behind me. Would this ever go away? Or would my epic fuckup haunt me forever?

If I could take back every second spent with Christian, I would. There was nothing in my life I'd regret more than that first kiss.

My phone vibrated on my lap. *Coach Quinn.*

I sent it to voicemail, then buried my face in my hands as another cry broke free. If she knew about it, then it was only a matter of time until everyone at Treasure State did too.

And Toren.

My entire body crumpled into the steering wheel.

Tonight, he'd get fired. And then he'd find out he wasn't the first coach who'd lost his job because of me.

The pain that ripped through my chest was so fierce it stunned me for a moment, stopping the tears and the sobs racking my shoulders. It spread like poison through my veins until my entire body spasmed.

My hand rubbed against my sternum as another wave of torture stole the air from my lungs.

What if I lost him?

I wasn't good at losing, but I'd survived enough losses to know how to bounce back. But this? Losing Toren?

How would I ever recover from that?

The sound of a car door slamming made me jerk. Headlights flashed from the truck parked in front of mine, the light glaring through my windshield.

I couldn't stay here. Not when Toren would come outside eventually. Maybe he'd have a box of belongings from his office. Maybe they'd escort him from the building and tell him never to come back.

Because of me. All of this ruined, because of me.

When I managed to suck in an inhale, the air burned, but I gulped it down, fumbling to start the car and put it in reverse. Then I dried my eyes and drove off campus.

The last place I wanted to be was home, but there was nowhere else to go. As I rolled past Toren's dark house, my insides twisted into a knot.

How was I supposed to stay here? How was I supposed to live next door and not go to his house at night? Would he have to move? Would his name be tarnished throughout Mission?

I couldn't watch someone else live in his home.

My limbs were trembling when I finally came to a stop in the garage. There was no disguising the red-rimmed eyes or the splotchy cheeks. I didn't bother trying to hide my tears—they wouldn't stop. So I let them fall as I shoved open the door, leaving everything, including my phone, in the car as I walked on wobbling legs into the house.

Stevie was in the kitchen, filling a glass of water. When she spotted me, the pity on her face only made it worse.

So she knew about the article already.

"Hey," she said.

I ignored her and walked through the house for the stairs.

Liz was on the living room couch.

I didn't even bother with eye contact as I climbed the bottom step.

"Wait. Please." Stevie's plea made me stop. "You can talk to us."

There shouldn't have been more tears. They should be

running out by now. But they kept pouring off my face like a waterfall. "What's there to say?"

"I'm sure there's more to the story than what was in that article," she said. "We'll listen if you need to talk. No judgment."

I scoffed as my lip quivered. No judgment? Was that even real? It was almost as big of a lie as friendship. So I kept climbing the stairs until I was locked in my bedroom. Then I sank to the floor, the door at my back, as I kicked off my shoes and curled my knees to my chest and let the pain swallow me whole.

How had this happened? How had I gone from class to the gym to now this? How could I have been so stupid to think I could run away to Montana and forget? The truth was always going to catch up with me. And because I'd been so stubborn, because I'd kept it all a secret, I'd lose the only person who mattered.

Toren deserved the truth. He should have heard it from me months ago.

I'd been scared. I'd been a coward. And now everything was so much worse.

I wasn't sure how long I'd been on the floor when a knock came at the door.

"Jennsyn?" Stevie's voice was hesitant. "There's, um, someone here to see you."

There was only one person who'd come here. He shouldn't be here. He couldn't be here, not with Stevie and Liz. They'd know something was going on, and he'd get . . .

Fired.

Except he'd already been fired. The secrets, the sneaking around, had been for nothing.

It was over.

Part of me wanted to stay on the floor, to hide here forever, but Toren deserved an explanation. Then, if he was done, I'd watch him walk away. So I shoved to my bare feet and opened the door. The hallway was empty, Stevie having already retreated downstairs.

I sniffled, wiping my nose with the back of my hand, then wiped at my cheeks. There was no strength in my body to steel my spine or square my shoulders, so I trudged down the stairs, my heart clenching when I found Toren standing inside the entryway.

His gray-green eyes raked over my body, head to toe. His jaw ticked as he fisted his hands on his hips.

I couldn't make it all the way to the living room floor. I couldn't seem to force my feet off that bottom stair. "You shouldn't have come here."

"Then you should have answered your phone."

I deserved that cold, hard voice, but it cut a slash so deep I gripped the railing until my knuckles were white so I wouldn't fall. "It's in my car."

Toren's nostrils flared.

"Did you get fired?" I knew the answer but asked the question anyway.

My body started to shake, the rattling I'd fought weeks ago raging harder than ever. It started in my bones and came out through my voice. It came out with more fucking tears.

Like this wasn't hard enough, now I had to stand here while Toren watched me fall apart. While Stevie and Liz both stared from the living room.

"No," he said.

I flinched. "W-what? You didn't?"

"We get another shot to keep this under wraps until graduation."

My eyes flew to Stevie and Liz.

"You didn't lose your job?" Ford hadn't fired Toren? He'd agreed to keep our secret?

Toren nodded.

The entire world seemed to slip away from my feet. That secret might have been a possibility, Ford might have been our saving grace, except for the fact that Toren was standing in my living room. Where my two roommates were hanging on our every word.

Oh God. It was happening all over again. They'd tell the other girls or Coach Quinn and none of this would matter. Ford agreeing to ignore the fact that he'd walked in on us kissing earlier would be unnecessary.

Because Toren was standing in my living room.

"Why did you come here, Toren?" My voice filled the house as I threw a hand toward my roommates. "They will tell and it's over. We're ruined. And all of this would have been for nothing. You'll lose everything. I will have taken *everything* from you."

The hardness in his expression melted away. "Baby."

"Don't." I threw out a hand to Stevie and Liz. "They're *right there.*"

He glanced over and shrugged. "I don't care. I came here for you."

Because I hadn't answered my phone. Because he'd been worried.

"Tor." I crumpled, sinking to a stair as the sobs started anew.

He was a watery blur as he crossed the room and knelt in front of me, then hooked a finger under my chin, tilting up my face until our gazes clashed. "We're not ruined."

"Your job—"

"Is not as important as you." He brushed a tear away with a thumb. "We'll figure this out. Your scholarship. My job. None of it matters. The only way you could take everything from me is if you walk away."

"It's not about my scholarship. But there's no way this will stay a secret."

He gave me a sad smile. "Probably not."

Stevie cleared her throat, taking a careful step closer. "We, um, know where you go at night. We've known for a while."

So it was always going to end. I kept my gaze locked on Toren, expecting the same hopelessness in my heart to fill his eyes, except he almost looked . . . relieved.

"How long?" he asked, glancing over his shoulder to Stevie and Liz.

"A couple months?" Liz shrugged. "I saw you sneak out one night and watched you go to his house."

A couple of months? "But y-you didn't say anything? Why?"

They shared a look, then Stevie shrugged. "We're on the same team. We've got your back."

I stared at them unblinking, then shifted my focus to Toren. "I want to believe them."

"Then do," Stevie said.

Maybe it was that easy. Or maybe not.

"I don't have the best history with teammates," I admitted. The cloud of the article hung over the house, and though the person who deserved to know the most was Toren, I didn't ask Stevie or Liz to leave.

They might as well hear the truth too.

"I have to tell you something," I whispered.

He rose and took the space beside me on the stairs. Then

he took my hand in his, lacing our fingers together to hold fast while he waited. While I summoned the courage to say what I should have months ago.

"Last spring at Stanford, I started seeing an assistant coach." It was the first time I'd ever spoken the truth aloud.

"Christian Morris," he said.

I cringed, hating to hear his name, especially from Toren's lips. "Yeah. We'd been flirting for a while, and one night after a game, he asked me out on a date. I should have said no, but I didn't."

Toren's frame stiffened but he stayed quiet. So did my roommates.

"It went on for about two months. We took it slow. I was living with a few of my friends at the time. They were all on the team too. Emily, my best friend, knew I was seeing someone but wasn't sure who. She kept begging and begging for me to tell her who I was dating, but I held out. I never told a soul about Christian, but she must have suspected something because she started spreading rumors around the team that we were together."

"That bitch," Stevie hissed.

I dropped my gaze to my hand linked with Toren's. "She was grasping. I think she thought I'd eventually cave if she wasn't the only one asking. Except what Emily didn't know, what I didn't know, was that I wasn't the only one from the team Christian had pursued. He'd been sleeping with another girl, a sophomore, the winter before."

"Damn," Liz muttered.

"When Emily started the gossip about a coach and a player, the other girl thought it was about her. She went to the head coach and confessed. This was in May. Christian was fired immediately. And the next day, I went to the

335

compliance officer and asked to be put in the transfer portal. Guess who took my place as starting outside hitter?"

"Emily." Liz scoffed. "Wow. No wonder you have trust issues."

"That's the world I come from," I said. "If someone is better than you, then you do whatever you can to take them down."

"You're not at Stanford anymore," Stevie said.

Toren's fingers flexed around mine.

"Shouldn't something like that have made the news?" Liz asked.

"Yeah, except I'm sure everyone was forced to keep it quiet," Stevie said. "No school wants that kind of scandal attached to their name."

Except now that Christian had fucked up, again, there'd be no hiding from this.

"I was never with him," I whispered to Toren. "He wanted that. We came close. But I wasn't ready to go all the way. We'd meet for dinner. We'd kiss and fool around. Then I'd stop us and leave."

Maybe because a part of me had always worried about his interest. That relationship had been so wildly different than mine with Toren it was like night and day. Christian had pushed and pushed. He'd never once pulled back. He'd never once told me to walk away and say goodbye.

Maybe it was the thrill of breaking the rules that got him off.

My mother knew I'd been seeing a guy but we'd broken up when I'd moved to Montana. When she read that article, then I guess she'd have more of a clue as to why I'd left Stanford.

Mom and others would likely make Christian out to be a

predator. Maybe they were right. Maybe the only reason he'd paid me any attention was because he'd wanted to fuck a star player on the team. But for a time, he'd listened to my doubts about volleyball, telling me not to quit and throw away my talent. He'd let me vent my frustrations about Mom or the team.

But there hadn't been a real connection between us. Nothing substantial. Christian hadn't been man enough for me to risk it all.

He wasn't Toren.

"I didn't know how to tell you this," I said. "It's . . . humiliating. It makes me want to run far, far away. I'm sorry. Christian and I weren't . . . it wasn't like this. It wasn't like us. And I know it seems like the same thing, but it's not. I didn't love—"

I clamped my mouth shut before I went too far. Before I told Toren I loved him while I was a blubbering mess and my roommates were watching.

But he took my face in his hands, forcing me to face him. The emotion in his gaze stole my breath. "You didn't what, babe? Finish that sentence."

"I didn't love him," I whispered.

He dropped his forehead to mine. "You can't run far, far away. You promised to take care of me while I take care of everyone else. I need you here for that."

I sniffled and closed my eyes. "But what if—"

He silenced my question with a kiss.

It was soft and sweet, not much more than a brush of his lips against mine. When he pulled away, he took my face in his hands. "I love you, Jennsyn Bell."

"Are you sure?"

He huffed a laugh. "Pretty sure."

I sagged against him, still sniffling, still crying. Still the blubbering mess who loved this man with her entire heart. "I love you, Toren Greely."

He kissed me again, smiling against my mouth. Then before I knew what was happening, we were off the stairs and he'd swept me into his arms, crossing the length of the room to the entryway.

"Good night, Coach," Stevie said.

"Have a nice evening, ladies."

"Wait." I smacked Toren's shoulder, and when he was stopped, I looked at my roommates. Or maybe I needed to start calling them friends. "Thanks."

"You're welcome." Stevie smiled. "Now you can stop worrying about sneaking around in your bare feet. Your toes must be cold all the time."

"She likes bare feet." Toren chuckled as he dropped a kiss to my lips. Then, with one hand, he opened the door and carried me home.

EPILOGUE
TOREN

S even months later ...

"Toren, can I light these fireworks off in the street?"

"Toren, do you have any more cookies?"

"Toren, you're out of beer."

Three people were talking to me at once.

I ignored them all and walked across my backyard to the beautiful woman sitting on the edge of the lawn, legs stretched to bare feet.

Faith would stop Beck from lighting off fireworks in the street. Cabe would poke around in the pantry and find the pack of Oreos I'd hidden behind the cereal boxes. And Parks would hit the store for more beer.

My hosting duties for tonight were over. I'd barbequed burgers. I'd set out lawn games and camping chairs. I'd stocked my fridges and coolers with beverages for my annual Fourth of July party.

My work was done. Now I was going to sit next to Jennsyn and enjoy the rest of the night with her in my arms.

Laughter and conversation drifted into the night as the

stars began to pop in the darkening sky. The horizon was still bright with the fading orange and yellow rays of the sun.

Jennsyn was leaning back on her elbows, blond hair swishing as she swayed to the music we'd put on for the party. She must have felt my gaze because she sat up straighter, twisting to watch me weave through clusters of visiting people.

"Hi." I plopped on the grass behind her, inching close until my knees were straddling hers and her back was resting against my chest. "Having fun?"

"Yes." She snuggled deeper into my arms, staring into the distance and waiting for the fireworks show to start.

A familiar laugh drew her attention and she glanced next door to where Stevie and Liz were talking together.

This year's party had taken over our lawn and theirs. And now that they'd graduated, like Jennsyn, we could all just be neighbors. Friends.

Most people assumed Jennsyn was still living next door. She hadn't changed her address yet, but everything she owned was under my roof—our roof.

Or it would be ours, soon enough. There was an engagement ring in the pocket of my jeans. Before tonight was over, it would be on her finger.

"Glad your boss came by," I told her. "It was nice to meet her."

"Yeah. I'm glad she came too."

Jennsyn had taken a job at the local YMCA this spring after graduation. They'd been steadily growing over the past ten years, and now that they had year-round youth sports programs, they'd needed a full-time sports program director.

She loved working with the kids and coaches, and more often than not, she came home from work with a smile.

It was still a new role and she was still getting settled, but so far, she loved her job. She'd even managed to get Abel a part-time position as a summer camp counselor.

We'd spent a lot of time at the farm with Faith and the boys lately. It was our safe space, where Jennsyn and I could be together without hiding. We pitched in when Faith needed an extra hand. We shared movie and game nights. We went to the boys' games and concerts and plays. For most of the year, Jennsyn and I had driven separately and sat on opposite ends of the gym or auditorium. But the months of pretending, of making those sacrifices, had all been worth it to get us here.

Not everyone in the athletic department knew about our relationship yet. Those who did thought I'd started dating a former student this June.

Most people thought Jennsyn and I were one month into our relationship.

As far as I was concerned, the world could think we'd rushed into an engagement. I didn't give a damn.

We'd been blessed with a lucky few friends who'd kept our secret. We'd asked a lot of those people, and if we had to do it all over again, I'd ask the same. But Jennsyn and I were finally free to be together. No more hiding. No more secrets.

"Did you talk to your mom?" I asked.

"Yeah. I called her earlier." She blew out a long sigh. "It went . . . okay."

Jennsyn had told her mom about me today. How we'd started dating and how I was a bit older. She'd wanted to give Katy time to absorb the news before she flew in to visit us later this month.

"Give it time," I said.

We'd had months together. The rest of the world would need time to catch up. Especially Katy.

She was still adjusting to conversations with Jennsyn that didn't include volleyball. She'd gotten frustrated when Jennsyn had refused to tell her the details about that Stanford coach.

The same was true for the reporters who'd hounded Jennsyn for nearly a month this winter. But she'd stayed strong and silent, and eventually, people had realized that Jennsyn was moving on with her life. Whatever had happened at Stanford was over.

As much as I hated that she'd had to go through it all, the ordeal had brought her here. To Montana.

"I love you," she said.

"I love you too." I kissed her temple. "Are you set on staying right here?"

"Yes. This is my spot."

"But what if I want to take you inside?"

Jennsyn let out a soft laugh, then untangled herself from my arms. She stood from the grass and held out her hand.

The minute I was on my feet, she rose up on her toes and kissed the corner of my mouth. Then she laced her fingers with mine and led me to the house.

I'd sworn never to host this party again. But maybe it wasn't such a bad night.

While fireworks boomed above Mission, Jennsyn and I were locked in my bedroom, limbs tangled as I moved inside her. Her hand, wearing a sparkling diamond ring, was pinned to the headboard. And I gave Jennsyn, the love of my life, her very own fireworks.

ACKNOWLEDGMENTS

Thank you for reading *Blitz*! Every time I get to write in this fictional world at Treasure State, it feels like a gift. I hope you enjoyed reading Toren and Jennsyn's story as much as I loved writing it.

Thank you to these incredible individuals for all they do on each of my stories. My editor, Elizabeth Nover. My proofreaders, Julie Deaton and Judy Zweifel. My cover designer, Sarah Hansen. My publicist and agent extraordinaire, Georgana Grinstead. To Logan Chisholm for all you do and being a rockstar. And Vicki Valente for being so wonderful.

Thank you to Sarah Hansen and Maddy McCormick for all of their volleyball expertise and answering my thousand questions over the past few months.

Thanks to all the influencers who shout about my books from the rooftops. I am eternally grateful. To the Vegas Party Bus crew, I love you all to the moon and back. And lastly, thanks to my friends and family for your unconditional love and support.

ABOUT THE AUTHOR

Devney Perry is a *Wall Street Journal* and *USA Today* bestselling author of over forty romance novels. After working in the technology industry for a decade, she abandoned conference calls and project schedules to pursue her passion for writing. She was born and raised in Montana and now lives in Washington with her husband and two sons.

Don't miss out on the latest book news.
Subscribe to her newsletter!
www.devneyperry.com